Gh

continued . . .

"A great, fast-paced, addicting read."

—Enchanting Reviews

"A great story."

—MyShelf.com

"Laurie's new sleuth, M. J. Holliday, is a winner.... Laurie makes everything that her characters do ring true, which can be a feat in a paranormal story. This highly entertaining book has humor and wit to spare."

—*Romantic Times*

Praise for the
Abby Cooper, Psychic Eye Mysteries

"Victoria Laurie has crafted a fantastic tale in this latest Psychic Eye Mystery. There are few things in life that upset Abby Cooper, but ghosts and her parents feature high on her list ... giving the reader a few real frights and a lot of laughs."

—Fresh Fiction

"Fabulous.... Fans will highly praise this fine ghostly murder mystery."

—The Best Reviews

"A great new series ... plenty of action."

—*Midwest Book Review*

"An invigorating entry into the cozy mystery realm.... I cannot wait for the next book."

—Roundtable Reviews

"A fresh, exciting addition to the amateur sleuth genre."

—J. A. Konrath, author of *Cherry Bomb*

"Worth reading over and over again."

—BookReview.com

The Ghost Hunter Mystery Series

The Psychic Eye Mystery Series

GHOULS, GHOULS, GHOULS

A GHOST HUNTER MYSTERY

Victoria Laurie

AN OBSIDIAN MYSTERY

OBSIDIAN
Published by New American Library, a division of
Penguin Group (USA) Inc., 375 Hudson Street,
New York, New York 10014, USA
Penguin Group (Canada), 90 Eglinton Avenue East, Suite 700, Toronto,
Ontario M4P 2Y3, Canada (a division of Pearson Penguin Canada Inc.)
Penguin Books Ltd., 80 Strand, London WC2R 0RL, England
Penguin Ireland, 25 St. Stephen's Green, Dublin 2,
Ireland (a division of Penguin Books Ltd.)
Penguin Group (Australia), 250 Camberwell Road, Camberwell, Victoria 3124,
Australia (a division of Pearson Australia Group Pty. Ltd.)
Penguin Books India Pvt. Ltd., 11 Community Centre, Panchsheel Park,
New Delhi - 110 017, India
Penguin Group (NZ), 67 Apollo Drive, Rosedale, North Shore 0632,
New Zealand (a division of Pearson New Zealand Ltd.)
Penguin Books (South Africa) (Pty.) Ltd., 24 Sturdee Avenue,
Rosebank, Johannesburg 2196, South Africa

Penguin Books Ltd., Registered Offices:
80 Strand, London WC2R 0RL, England

First published by Obsidian, an imprint of New American Library,
a division of Penguin Group (USA) Inc.

First Printing, January 2011
10 9 8 7 6 5 4 3 2 1

Copyright © Victoria Laurie, 2011
All rights reserved

OBSIDIAN and logo are trademarks of Penguin Group (USA) Inc.

Printed in the United States of America

Acknowledgments

I'm gonna get right to the important part this time, which is to thank the many people who make up Team Laurie and in general make me look good—far better than I'd appear on my own, that's for sure!

First, to my editor, the amazing, astounding, awesome, wonderful, (Shall I go on? Maybe just one more . . .) *glorious* Ms. Sandra Harding, who is simply fabulous to work with! Sandy, your enthusiasm, your engaging attitude, and the encouragement and free rein you've given me to explore ideas and just run with what feels good to me are so very much appreciated. It takes a lot of courage to simply trust that I'll come up with something decent when all I've given you at the start is the tiny seed of an idea, and for that trust, I genuinely, genuinely thank you.

Next, to my glorious agent, Jim McCarthy, who seven years ago reached into the agency slush pile and pulled *my* query letter out of the trash. . . . How do you thank someone for giving you a second chance when no one else would? For literally being *the* person responsible for making one of your closest-held dreams come true? For believing that you'd get there and congratulating you when you did? For simply being the best agent and most amazing friend in the whole freaking world? You can't, because there aren't words to describe the gratitude I feel and how blessed I am to have you in my corner, honey. So, Jim, you'll just have to settle for another "thank you" but know that the feeling of profound gratitude from me is much, much more.

Also, huge thanks go to the rest of my NAL team, including, (but not limited to) Michele Alpern, who has once again delivered an outstanding copyedit! Claire Zion for her unending faith in both Abby and M. J., and my publicists Megan Swartz and Kaitlyn Kennedy, who do amazing things for me behind the scenes.

A set of very special thanks to my .com team: Katie Coppedge, who has been utterly invaluable to me of late and who keeps my clients organized, me on track, and the Web site looking all faaaaabulous! Heart you fierce, pretty lady! Also to my sistah from another mistah, Hilary Laurie, who is my very own Dear Abby and one of my very favorite people on the planet. Thank you for always being there and providing that voice of reason and good sense. Oh, and thanks for the laughs too. Methinks I like that part best!

Finally, I would like to thank my friends and family who have continuously stepped up to the plate to offer support, love, and unending encouragement. A few special mentions here and they are: Mary Jane Humphreys; Nora, Bob, and Mike Brosseau; Leanne Tierney; Karen Ditmars; Neil and Kim Mahoney; Dr. Jennifer Casey; Betty and Pippa Stocking; Shannon Dorn; Silas Hudson; Juan Tamayo; Thomas Robinson; Susan Parsons; Molly Boyle; and Martha Bushko. You guys rule!

Chapter 1

For the record, I am not a morning person. Especially not this morning, because, technically, I believe it was so early, it still might have qualified as being the middle of the night. Still, the hour did nothing to dampen my producer's enthusiasm while discussing the next shooting location for our cable TV show, *Ghoul Getters*. "I know you guys don't want to hear too much about the history of the place we're investigating," Peter Gophner—aka Gopher—was saying as the entire cast and crew were seated around a table at a small café in the airport, "but in this case, I really think it's necessary."

I felt something heavy hit my shoulder, and when I turned, I saw my best friend's head resting on my shoulder.

"Gil," I whispered, nudging him with my elbow.

"ZZZZZZZZZ . . . ," he snored.

My fellow ghostbuster, Heath, laughed quietly. "He's out cold," he said. "He looked pretty wiped out when we left the hotel."

"ZZZZZZZ...," Gilley agreed.

I sighed, yawned, and tried to focus on the map Gopher was laying out on the table. "As you know from your tickets, we're heading to Ireland. From the airport we'll travel by car to the village of Dunlee and check in at our lodgings. Once we get a little rest, we'll head here."

Blearily I followed Gopher's finger, which had zipped over the map to rest on a small *X* that seemed to be just off the coastline of the channel that ran between Scotland and Ireland. "Are we going scuba diving?" I asked.

Gopher smiled and for the first time he seemed to detect the rather cranky mood from those of us still awake at the table. "Ha," he said, flashing a toothy grin. "No. This is actually a very small island just off the northern coast. The island is primarily made up of a small rocky shore surrounding a huge block of rock that juts up about a hundred feet. The top of the rock is quite flat and is about five hundred meters wide and eight hundred meters long."

"That's a big chunk of rock," I said.

"It is, and four centuries ago, in fifteen eighty-four, someone decided it was the perfect place to build a castle."

"How do you get up to it?" John, our sound tech, asked.

"Well, on the island itself, there is a set of stone stairs carved into the rock that lead right up to the top," Gopher said smartly. "But the tricky part is actually getting to the island at all."

"You'd have to go in by boat, right?"

But Gopher shook his head. "Nope. Boats are too dangerous because of the currents, shallow water, and submerged rock formations. Only the coast guard is allowed in that part of the channel."

"So how does one get to the rock?" I asked.

"There's a man-made causeway that, during low tide, extends a little over one and a half kilometers from the Irish coastline directly to the shores of the rock."

"During low tide?" Heath interrupted. "What's it like during high tide?"

"It's underwater," Gopher said with a chuckle of appreciation. "I'm tellin' you, the guy who built this castle was a friggin' master of defense."

"So we can only travel to and from the castle twice a day?"

"Twice a day for about four hours each turn. Plenty of time for us to get in to do a little investigation and take some footage, then call it a day and scoot back across the causeway before the tide rolls in again."

I looked at him skeptically. "How'd you hear about this place?"

"I got a tip from one of the local historians," he said. "But wait. I haven't got to the best parts yet."

Heath and I exchanged a less than enthused look. With a sigh I said, "Proceed."

"So, as I was saying, on this rock is this amazing fortress called Castle Dunlow. It was built in the late sixteenth century and was occupied right up until the early twentieth century. The place is a historical landmark and

I had to get special permission from the town council to investigate it, because normally it's completely off-limits to tourists."

Gopher looked around at us with an expression that suggested we should be impressed. The only one who said anything was Gilley. "ZZZZZZZZ . . ."

"Gil thinks that's great!" I said, hiding a smile. Next to me Heath ducked his chin and snorted.

Gopher scowled. "*Any*way," he continued, "Dunlow Castle comes with a pretty rich history and is reported to be chock-full of ghosts."

"Hopefully it's not quite as haunted as Queen's Close," I muttered, referring to the rather dicey ghost-bust we'd just come off.

Our producer ignored me and laid out an aerial photo of the castle. "Legend has it that in the late fifteen hundreds, before the castle was even fully completed, several ships in the Spanish Armada were sent to attack England, but were pretty soundly defeated, and when they turned back, a storm caused about two dozen ships in the fleet to crash all along the northern and western Irish coastline. One of those ships actually crashed on the rocks right next to Dunlow Castle. The lord of the manor, a guy named Ranald Dunnyvale, sent his men to capture the ship's crew and held them at the castle until the war with Spain was over.

"It turns out that the ship that crashed was carrying some heavy hitters in the Spanish Armada, and Dunnyvale was eventually able to ransom these guys back to Spain for a hefty sum."

I yawned. So far, I wasn't that impressed, but I knew that Gopher wouldn't be this excited about something unless he was working a specific angle, so I waited him out.

After taking a sip of coffee, he continued. "Now, Dunnyvale wasn't the only guy to take prisoners—a lot of ships sank during that storm and several hundred Spaniards found their way to shore and Irish dungeons—but the difference with Dunnyvale's conquest was that the ship that crashed on his rock remained very much intact and he was able to take all the spoils from it, including what many believed was the payroll for the entire fleet in the form of gold bullion."

I sighed. This was getting complicated, and I was getting hungry. "Anyone want a muffin?" I asked, ready to gently transfer Gilley's head onto Heath's shoulder.

"Hold on, M. J.!" Gopher snapped. "I haven't gotten to the best part yet."

"Oh, sorry," I said, hoping he'd get there really, *really* soon.

"Legend has it that Ranald kept the bullion a secret so that he wouldn't have to pay taxes on it, and he sneaked it off the Spanish ship and hid it somewhere in his castle." Again, Gopher looked around at us eagerly, but we all just stared blankly back at him. "Don't you get it?" he asked us.

"Clearly we don't," said Kim, one of our assistant producers.

Gopher tugged impatiently on the brim of his ball cap. "The ghost of Ranald is one of the spooks said to haunt the castle!"

Again, we all just stared at him blankly. "Soooooo?" I finally said.

"Wow, you guys really are slow on the uptake in the mornings," he grumbled. Then he spoke slowly as if we were children struggling with the concept of two plus two. "If M. J. and Heath can find Ranald and talk to him, maybe he'll tell you guys where he's hidden the gold."

That got my attention. "Hold on," I said. "You mean to tell me this bust isn't so much about documenting spooks as it's about sending us on a treasure hunt?"

Gopher beamed at me. "Yes!"

"ZZZZZ . . . ," said Gilley.

I eyed Heath over the top of Gilley's head and saw that he was looking at me to gauge my reaction. Something unspoken passed between us, and he and I both smiled at each other. I then turned back to Gopher and said, "We're in!"

Gopher let out a relieved sigh. "Really? You guys think this is a good idea?"

"Dude, if we find a lost treasure of gold bullion, then it's a genius idea!" I told him.

Heath was equally enthused. "This could open up a whole new line of business for us," he said. "Instead of ghostbusters, we could be psychic treasure hunters!"

"Or we could just cash in the gold and retire early," I suggested.

"There's just one catch," Gopher added softly.

I snapped my attention back to him. "What'd you say?"

Gopher smiled nervously. "It shouldn't be any big deal. . . ."

"A time to worry," Heath groaned.

I folded my arms and eyed Gopher critically. "I'm thinking we're finally going to learn the reason the castle's normally off-limits. Okay, Gopher, what's the catch?"

Gopher sighed. "Supposedly the castle's also haunted by a powerful phantom."

My eyebrows rose in surprise, and I honestly laughed. "A *phantom*?"

Gopher nodded. "Some supernatural shadow that's reportedly eight feet tall and super scary is supposed to haunt the ruins looking for trespassers. I hear the thing is so creepy that none of the locals will go near the place."

"What's he done to make everyone so freaked-out?" I asked. "I mean, other than being eight feet tall and all."

Gopher swallowed and wouldn't meet my eyes.

"ZZZZZZ . . . ," said Gilley.

"Come on, dude, out with it," Heath insisted.

Gopher took a deep breath before he finally answered. "According to the research I have, the phantom has actually thrown a few people off the top of the cliffs."

"What?" Heath and I said together.

"But it hasn't attacked anyone in a few years now," Gopher added quickly. "The last victim was thrown to his death well over four years ago."

I sighed and rolled my eyes. "Oh, well gee golly, Gopher, if it was over four years ago, then I'm sure *we* don't have to worry about it!"

"Who was it?" Kim wanted to know.

Gopher swirled his finger over the papers on the table-top. "A guy heading a small group of treasure hunters. The official report suggests the phantom threw him right over the side."

"WHAT?!" Heath and I exclaimed again.

Gilley woke up at this point, probably because of all the yelling. "What'd I miss?"

"Gopher's trying to kill us," I snapped.

Gilley rubbed his eyes and looked around blearily. "So, nothing new, huh?"

"Seriously, guys," Gopher said calmly. "This phantom isn't anything you two can't handle! I mean, you're great at busting the worst demons and spooks the underworld has to throw at you. I've seen that firsthand."

I eyed our producer skeptically. "Someone's got gold bullion on the brain."

"Want to pull out?" Heath asked me.

I sighed, thinking about the pros and cons for a minute. Finally I looked at him and said, "I'm in if you are."

Heath's smile returned. "Then we're both willing to go for it."

"Awesome!" Gopher exclaimed. "Guys, that is awesome!"

At that moment the call to board our plane was announced, and we all got up and shuffled toward the gate. In the back of my mind I couldn't help but wonder if by agreeing to this bust, I'd just made the biggest mistake of my life.

We landed in Londonderry heavy with fatigue and all of us ready for a nap. Gopher splurged on two vans for the seven of us, and we loaded our luggage and gear and prepared to drive north. I found a spot in the lead van, sitting right behind Heath, who was helping navigate our driver—Gopher—along the winding roads. From the sound of it, the navigating wasn't going so well. "Wait!" I heard Heath exclaim. "You missed the turn!"

"What turn?"

"The one you just passed."

"I didn't see any turn!"

"It was behind that herd of sheep."

Muttered expletives followed while Gopher looked for a place to turn around. A bit later when Heath had apparently directed our van to a dead end, both men's tempers boiled over and Heath tossed the map at Gopher before opening his door to go sit with Gilley in the other van.

For a moment, no one spoke, and Meg—one of the production assistants—shot me a concerned look. "Hey, Goph?" I said cautiously.

"What?" he snapped, eyeing the map with frustration and obviously still irritated.

"Want me to copilot?"

Gopher sighed and ran a hand through his hair. "Yeah," he said, tossing me the map and motioning to the front seat. "You can't be any worse than your boy-friend."

My cheeks reddened. For the record, Heath is not my boyfriend. At the moment, I'm decidedly boyfriend*less*, after having dumped my previous S.O. in Scotland when we both realized that distance wasn't making our hearts grow fonder.

And, strangely, now that I wasn't Dr. Steven Sable's girl—I missed him much more than I had when we were merely separated by an ocean.

It served me right, though, because Heath and I had been crossing the line with each other well before I'd had a chance to talk to Steven, and since then, the guilt of my flirtations with my fellow ghostbuster had chilled things down for us and we'd both agreed to focus on the job at hand rather than getting handsy with each other.

So Gopher's remark cut into me, but I couldn't let it show; otherwise he was the type to continue to push my buttons. Instead I gave him a tight smile, got out of the backseat, and hopped into the front, picking up the map and studying it for a minute before I instructed him to turn us around.

It took a few minutes to get our bearings and find the main road again, but I soon had us back on track, and as we traveled along, I got to once again enjoy the gorgeous scenery. There was a lovely stretch of highway that took us right along the coast, and then we traveled into the countryside, slowly making our way northeast.

Everywhere we looked, the hilly green terrain was dotted with fluffy white sheep. Here and there we saw smoke coming up and out of tall, weathered chimneys attached to quaint little houses with thatched or clay roofs.

Pedestrian traffic was light, and those locals we did spot could be seen getting around on bicycle or horse. "I feel like we've gone back in time," said Meg from the backseat.

I nodded. "But I like it."

We finally arrived in Dunlee near noon and by that time my lids were feeling like sandpaper against my eyes. I was so tired I felt woozy.

Still, I felt a bit better once we found the small bed-and-breakfast Gopher had booked for us and I could stretch my legs and breathe the fresh, crisp air.

"I've reserved the whole thing," Gopher said, waving his hand grandly at the rather small-looking structure.

"How many bedrooms?" I asked, knowing Gopher could be cheap.

"Four."

I frowned. There were seven of us. "So we'll have to double up."

Gopher regarded me in that way that suggested he hadn't expected me to complain. "What's the big deal? John can bunk with Gilley. Meg and Kim can room to-gether. You and Heath can do your own thing."

My eyes narrowed. Not only was Gopher assuming *way* too much here, but he'd purposely avoided men-tioning that the last room would obviously go to him. "Oh, I don't think so," I said as the others gathered round.

"I want my own room!" Gilley pouted. "I have a very strict prebedtime moisturizing routine, and if someone else is hogging the bathroom, my skin's supple texture could be compromised."

My eyes swiveled to Gil. "Jesus, Gilley, could you *be* more of a girl?"

"Well, one of us should be!" he snapped back.

It was obvious that the lack of sleep, long drive, and unfamiliar surroundings were setting everyone on edge. That was when Heath took charge, and not a moment too soon. "Meg and Kim, you don't mind sharing a room, do you?"

They both shook their heads. "We're good," Kim said agreeably.

Next, Heath turned to John. "You okay bunking with me?"

"I am," he said.

"Awesome. Gopher, why do you think you deserve a room to yourself?"

"Uh," Gopher said, "because I sign your paychecks?"

Heath nodded. "That's a pretty good reason." Turning to me, he asked, "Would you and Gil mind rooming together so that we can continue to get paid?"

I smiled. "Yeah, okay."

Gilley's pout deepened. "I get first dibs on the bathroom," he grumbled.

We made our way inside, and I was struck by the cramped feeling of the space. All the rooms were small, and so was the furniture. When I thought about it, however, I realized that I was perhaps being a bit too "American" in my thinking. We're used to big rooms that allow for large overstuffed furniture, giant plasma screens, and lots of legroom. But here, everything was more utilitarian, and if I gave it half a chance, I might actually like it.

The owner of the B&B was a lovely middle-aged woman named Anya, whose hands and lips were all aflutter. "Oh, you've come!" she said with a small hop and a clap as we hustled our luggage through the short hallway into the sitting room. "I've been fretting that you might've missed the torn down the wee road at the train station."

"The torn?" Heath whispered in my ear.

"Turn," I whispered back.

"Ah," he said with a nod. "I think it's harder to decipher the brogues when you're tired."

Anya and Gopher exchanged pleasantries, and Heath and I smiled politely as the rest of the crew was introduced. "I expect you're all a bit knackered, then?" she asked.

Six heads looked at one another, unsure what she meant. "Tired," I whispered to my confused companions. "She means tired."

Six heads swiveled back to Anya and nodded vigorously. I stifled a grin.

Anya clapped her hands merrily. "Well, then! Let's show you to your rooms so you can lighten the sandman's load for a wee spell."

While we followed behind Anya, Gilley leaned in and said, "I have no idea what she just said."

I chuckled and told him only to follow along. Anya explained that her quarters were in the small guesthouse at the back of the property, so we'd have the whole bed-and-breakfast mostly to ourselves and we could come and go as we pleased without fear of disturbing her.

Gilley and I took the last room at the end of a hall-way on the second floor. There were two twin beds and I claimed the one by the window—suffering through Gilley's disapproving look—and lay down on the bed. "I may never get up again," I sighed, closing my eyes.

A knock at the door forced me to reluctantly open them again, and I turned to see Gopher in our doorway. "You two get a few hours' sleep and meet me downstairs at three thirty. I want to have a look at the castle while it's still light out."

"What about food?" Gilley whined, and my own stomach grumbled. We'd had only a muffin for breakfast and we'd skipped lunch altogether.

Gopher's face softened. "You're right," he agreed. "Let's meet downstairs at three. I'll tell Anya that we're eating out so she doesn't have to worry about cooking for us, and we'll grab something quick on the road before we head to the coast."

"Awesome," I mumbled, laying my head back and closing my eyes again. I think I was asleep before Gopher closed the door.

When I woke up, it was very dark in the room, and I had one of those moments of total disorientation and panic where I didn't know where I was and couldn't remember how I had come to be in this unfamiliar setting. The adrenaline pumping through my veins quickly brought it all back, however, and then I realized the room was far too dim to be midafternoon. Fumbling around in the dark, I managed to find the small clock on the bedside table. It read four forty-five p.m.

Great. We'd slept right through our three o'clock meeting.

"Gil," I said hoarsely.

My best friend replied with a rather loud snore.

I got up and found the light switch. Flicking it on, I squinted into the harsh light and Gilley rolled over onto his stomach to hide his face in the pillow. "Off! Light off!" his muffled voice complained.

"It's almost five o'clock," I told him.

Gilley pressed his face deeper into his pillow, and waved one hand in a downward motion. *"Off!"*

With a sigh I turned the light back off, and for a moment I couldn't see a thing. After my eyes had adjusted, I felt my way into the bathroom and took a delightfully hot shower.

Emerging twenty minutes later, I found Gil fast asleep on his back again, and decided to let him slumber. Exiting my room, I crept along the hallway only to bump right into Heath. "I overslept!" he whispered.

"Yeah, me too."

The door next to Heath's flew open and out rushed Gopher. "Shit!" he said when he saw us. "Why didn't you guys wake me?"

I eyed Heath sideways, and he gave me a mischievous smile. "We tried, dude," he told our producer seriously. "I mean, we knocked on your door for at least . . . what?"

"Ten minutes," I said, playing along.

"Yeah. Ten whole minutes. You never woke up."

Gopher's face fell. *"Shit!"*

"Well, we might as well get some dinner," I suggested, grateful that our first night in Ireland would be blissfully uneventful and allow us to catch up on some much needed rest.

Gopher, however, thought different. Looking at his watch, he said, "We can grab a quick bite, then check out the castle."

"In the dark?" Heath and I said together. I hated walking into any deserted location at night—you never knew what unseen obstacles, rotting wooden stairs, or unstable foundation awaited you.

"You plan on busting these ghosts in the daylight?" he asked in return.

"Gopher, that's way too dangerous," I reminded him. "I'm not setting foot in an old abandoned castle without making sure it's safe first and mapping out a baseline, and I can only do that in the daylight."

Gopher scowled. "We're already behind schedule, M. J."

"Too bad," I snapped. I was sick of being rushed into things and forgoing my usual safety precautions. Plus, I was really worn-out, and my bones needed a good rest.

"Can we at least head to the island tonight and check it out from the shore?"

I sighed heavily and looked to Heath; I'd let it be his call. He appeared reluctant too. "You want to try and what, swim there?"

Gopher smiled smartly. "Low tide's at six. The causeway rises above sea level two hours before low tide and stays that way for another two hours. If we eat fast, we'll have just enough time to walk there and back."

"Perfect," I grumbled. The last thing I wanted to do tonight was pick my way across a slippery causeway to a deserted island with a haunted castle that I wasn't even going to investigate until the next day. But I knew that look on my producer's face, and he wasn't about to let us off the hook.

"Please, guys?" he begged.

"Oh, all right," I said with a sigh. "But I want real food at a sit-down restaurant for dinner."

We collected John and Kim (Meg begged off, and there was no rousing Gilley), and found a nice little restaurant in town called the Green Rose by six thirty. There was a lot of lamb on the menu, and my dish, at least, was delicious.

We were on our way again by seven; John was playing navigator this time while Gopher drove. We picked our way along the shore, going slowly down to beach level. There was no one out and about on the roads, and very little in the way of light, which made the night spooky.

To make it all the more eerie, a fog began to roll in from offshore, and Gopher had to slow the van down because he could barely see ten yards ahead. "How are we supposed to find our way across the causeway with this fog?" I asked, when the obvious hadn't occurred to him and he showed no sign of turning around.

"Let's just get down to the beach and see what we see, okay, M. J.?"

I frowned and looked at Heath, who was shaking his head. Gopher could really be a pain in the ass sometimes.

Locating the causeway proved extremely difficult. We discovered that we'd actually passed it at least ten times as we cruised up and down the beach. The darkness and the fog all but obscured it. I was beginning to hope that Gopher would soon give up the search, as by now it was seven forty and we'd have only about twenty minutes left to get across and back, but he rigidly stuck to his plan. "There!" yelled John, finally pointing to our left. "That's it!"

Gopher stomped on the brakes and backed up. "About time," he muttered, and swung the van around to park it off the road, pointing the lights directly at the slick stone path. We all got out of the van and stared at the ten yards of causeway that we could just make out moving away from the pebbly beach.

I shivered in the misty air, and Heath wrapped an arm around my shoulders. "It's cold, huh?" he said.

I felt a rush of heat flow through me and warmed up fast. This was the first time we'd touched in the few days since I'd ended things with Steven. "It is chilly," I said, even as a thread of guilt made its way into my thoughts. I wondered when I would stop bouncing back and forth between my attraction to Heath and the regret I had over letting Steven go.

Meanwhile Gopher was rummaging around in the back of the van and came up with several flashlights. These he passed to John and Heath, keeping one for himself. "Shall we?" he asked. Without waiting for our reply, our fearless leader edged out onto the causeway.

I scowled and moved with Heath after him, while Kim and John brought up the rear. Before long we were completely engulfed in fog and our progress was reduced to a slow and careful shuffle. "Gopher, this is ridiculous!" I finally said, stopping and refusing to go another step.

Our producer turned to look at me with irritation. "It's just ahead!"

"How do you *know*?" I countered. "I mean, with the fog, there's no way to tell where we are along this stupid thing, and have you noticed that the tide is coming back in?"

Gopher inhaled and exhaled loudly. He then looked over his shoulder and pointed his flashlight behind while all around us water began to leak in over the sides of the stone walkway.

"Fine," he relented. "Let's call it a day, but we're coming back first thing in the morning."

I smiled at Heath, who winked at me, and we started to turn around, but at that exact moment we heard a male voice shout, *"Alex!"*

All five of us stopped abruptly. "Whoa," whispered Heath, and he pointed his flashlight back to the section of the causeway leading to the castle. "What the freak?"

"Alex!" cried the voice again, and this time there was more than a little desperation in his voice.

I grabbed Heath's arm and tugged. "Come on! We've got to go help him!"

Heath nodded and we surged forward, running and slipping as we went, and all the while, ahead of us the voice cried the name Alex over and over. "Hello!" I shouted at some point when we'd gone at least a hundred yards and still there was no sign of the owner of the voice.

A sob drifted out of the cool night air. "Alex! Oh, Alex!"

"Hello!" I shouted as loudly as I could. "Sir! Where are you?" My heart was thundering in my chest as I thought about who this man was and wondered if perhaps he was looking for his son, Alex.

But then my feet began to splash, and squinting into the darkness and fog, I could see that the tide was really coming up now, and at the pace Heath and I were racing along, we were sure to slip if we continued. Grabbing his arm again, I pulled us to a stop. We both stood still for a minute, the silence broken only by our winded breathing. "Hello?" Heath called after several seconds passed, and we heard no more from the desperate man lost somewhere out in the fog.

"Where'd he go?"

Heath shook his head. "I don't know, but we need to really consider turning back, because we're about to be in serious trouble." For emphasis he pointed his flashlight down. My toes were now almost completely submerged.

"Damn!" I swore. "This tide comes in quick!"

"M. J.!" we heard behind us. "Heath!"

"We're here!" I called to Gopher's shouts.

"We've got to get off the causeway!"

With one last look to the north, I said to Heath, "Let's go. We can alert the authorities back onshore, and they can send someone out to help him."

Heath nodded and we picked our way quickly through the deepening water. We found Gopher just a bit later and he seemed frantic. "Where're Kim and John?" I demanded.

"I sent them back. And we've got to hurry before we lose sight of the causeway and get swept into the channel. I've read that the currents here are deadly."

"Not to mention that the water's freezing," I added, shivering again with cold as the frigid water now encased my feet from the ankle down.

"Come on," Heath urged. "Let's move."

Hurrying along as quickly as we could, we finally slogged our way back to the beach, and it was without a moment to spare, as by the time we reached terra firma again, the water had moved all the way up to my calves and we could barely keep our footing or make out the causeway under our feet.

John and Kim were shivering on the beach and waved at us when we finally emerged from the fog. "We were about to send for help," said Kim.

"Wish you had," I told her. "We need to send someone to see about that man looking for Alex."

"Why would anyone be out on the causeway this late and given these weather conditions?" Gopher asked.

The four of us looked at him pointedly.

"Besides us," he said. "I mean, at least we have a legitimate reason."

I turned away from Gopher with a bit of disgust and waved everyone to the van. "Come on, guys. We've got to send help."

With the aid of a local man out walking his dog, we finally found a coast guard station, and alerted the authorities, who took down every detail we had to offer before sending out a skiff. More than once they'd asked us what we were thinking by going for a late-night stroll along a dangerous path during midtide. "Everyone knows you don't go walkin' round the causeway after dark," said the coast guard officer taking our report.

This elicited several more pointed looks in Gopher's direction, but he ignored us and focused on getting help for the stranger.

Once we were sure help was on the way, there was nothing left for us to do but head back to the B&B.

This was a good thing because it was late and I was shivering so hard my teeth were rattling. My pants, shoes, and socks were all soaked and I couldn't wait to get out of them.

No one said much on the ride back. Once we were there, we all mumbled our good-nights and turned in. When I entered the room I shared with Gilley, I was a little surprised to find him awake and munching on a late-night cheeseburger and fries. "Hey!" he said when he saw me. "Your pants are wet."

I looked down in mock surprise. "They *are*?"

He gave me a smart smile and popped another fry into his mouth. "What'd I miss?"

Before answering him, I walked over to my suitcase and unzipped the lid. After fishing around for my pj's, I held up a finger and headed for the bathroom. Once I'd changed and draped my jeans and socks over the shower curtain, I came back out and filled Gilley in. "Whoa," he said when I'd finished. "Who'd be crazy enough to go out on the causeway in the dark and dense fog?"

"You mean other than us?"

"Yes. Other than you fools."

I chuckled, and reached over to pick at some fries. "I've no idea, but he wasn't a local."

"Well, duh," Gil said. "I doubt anyone who lives around here would do something that dumb."

"No," I told him, "you're not getting it. What I mean is that the guy sounded Australian or South African."

"Ah," Gil said. "You knew by the accent."

"Yep. We should ask Anya in the morning if she knows of any other foreigners staying in town. In a village this small, I've gotta believe that the locals keep track of outsiders."

"Do you think they'll find the guy on the causeway?"

"God, Gil, I really hope so. You should've heard him crying out for Alex. It was heartbreaking."

"I wonder who Alex was to him."

"Might be his son."

"Might be his lover," said Gil, and when I looked at him in surprise, he added, "Hey, you mention one guy looking for another and I immediately think gay."

I rolled my eyes at him and he gave me a winning smile. "By the way," he added, "Teeko sent you an e-mail."

Gilley routinely went through my e-mail, even though I routinely changed the password. "Did she get Wendell off the plane okay?"

On our last bust I'd adopted a homeless black pug. As most of our ghost investigations tend to be in locations that aren't exactly pet friendly, I'd thought it best to send him home and place him in the care of my best girlfriend. "She got him all right, and he's safe and sound and already making doggy friends in Teeko's neighborhood."

I felt my shoulders relax. I'd been worried about such a long journey for a little puppy. "Any word on Doc?" I also had a parrot back home, being looked after by another dear friend of mine.

"You mean the other e-mail you got from Mama Dell?"

I couldn't help smiling. Gilley really didn't understand the meaning of the word "privacy." "Yep," I told him. "How's my little guy doing?"

"According to Mama Dell, he's swearing like a sailor at all her customers, chewing on all her wood furniture, and throwing beakfuls of food around his cage."

My eyebrows rose. "He's in good spirits, then."

Gilley nodded. "I really miss him, M. J."

I sighed heavily. "I know, buddy. Me too."

Turning to climb into bed, I fluffed my pillow and lay back to watch television without commenting. But for the few hours before I fell asleep, I was acutely aware of how much I missed my pets, and my home. The only other thing my thoughts could focus on was the man from the causeway, and for a long time that evening, the sound of his desperate voice haunted me.

Chapter 2

The next morning was cold, wet, and drizzly and perfectly matched the mood of the team. "Ireland sucks," said Gilley.

"You've been here for less than a day, Mr. Judgmental," I replied.

"Fine," he told me. "Today, Ireland sucks. Tomorrow might be different."

"At least it's good ghost-hunting weather," Heath reminded him.

Gilley shivered. "Yippee," he said woodenly. I should mention here that Gilley's mood often shifts with the weather, choice of menu, day of the week, and even—I'm convinced—time of the month.

"Well, let's not stand around in the rain," I suggested while we huddled under the three umbrellas we were sharing between the seven of us. "Let's go ask about that man on the causeway, then find some grub."

Anya had offered to serve us breakfast, but as we'd

gotten such an early start, we'd told her that we'd grab some coffee and a roll on the road. She'd looked decidedly disappointed, and we understood that tomorrow we'd make sure to eat at her table.

I realized when we'd all piled into one van (Gopher wanted us to save on gas) that I'd forgotten to ask if she knew of any other foreigners who might have been staying in town.

Once we were under way, we made our way back to the coast guard station and waited while Heath and John went in to ask about the lost man on the causeway. They came back grim-faced. "There was no sign of either the man on the causeway or the mysterious Alex," said Heath, shaking off the rain and scooting in next to me.

My heart sank. "Those poor people."

"Maybe they both made it to the island," Gopher suggested, putting the van in gear and backing out of the parking slot.

I said nothing, feeling such a sense of guilt over leaving the stranger and his companion on the causeway while Heath and I sloshed our way to safety. I could only hope that we'd be able to find both of them safe and sound on the island whenever we managed to get to it.

"When does the tide roll out?" I asked Gopher.

"Gil?" he said in turn, and I watched as Gilley retrieved his iPhone from his backpack, to flip through his apps.

"Low tide is at six twenty-four a.m., or in about an

hour and fifteen minutes, so we'll have a little over three hours before it comes in again deep enough to cover over the causeway."

I glanced at my watch. "Damn. No time for a decent breakfast, then."

"We'll have to grab something to go," Gopher said, already pointing to a small café.

We each got coffee and a muffin and arrived at the mouth of the causeway shortly after as the first hints of dawn began to emerge. Still, it was pretty dark out and the drizzle made it really depressing.

"At least we'll be able to see our way across the causeway," Heath said when we had piled out of the van and were standing at the mouth of the cobblestones in front of us.

I followed the path with my eyes and marveled that the stones hadn't eroded too much over the last four hundred or so years.

"Shall we?" Heath asked, offering his arm and a place for me under his umbrella.

I couldn't resist a smile and lifted the strap of my messenger bag over my head before taking his arm and moving forward with him onto the causeway.

We walked for a way in silence, and pretty soon out of the dim light and drizzle we could begin to see the mammoth hunk of granite that Castle Dunlow sat upon. I felt mesmerized by the massive scale of it, and as we neared the shore, a wave of something unpleasant rustled along my energy.

"That rock gives me the creeps," Heath whispered.

I shivered again, but this time not with cold. "Something *bad* lives there," I confirmed.

Heath nodded. "You brought the grenades with you, right?"

"Yep."

"Good, I have a feeling we're going to need them."

Part of the equipment we were sure to never go without these days was the ten-inch-long metallic spikes we purposely magnetized and kept in lead-lined rubber-capped tubes. We called these canisters grenades, because when we popped open the cap and tipped out the spike, it could have a rather explosive effect on any angry spook trying to get too close for comfort.

The magnetism of the exposed spikes alters the electromagnetic energy of ghosts, making it extremely difficult for them to stay within a ten-foot radius of anyone holding an open grenade. Spooks hate the effect. What's more, the spikes themselves can come in particularly handy when driven directly into the portals. Some of the more powerful spirits create and use portals like a doorway to come and go from our plane to the lower realms, where *nothing* good lives.

If we manage to get a spike directly into one of these portals, it will keep the ghost either locked in or locked out—depending on which side of it the spook is on. Either scenario works for us, as the lower planes are typically a source of power for these nastier poltergeists, and once they're cut off from that power source, they're far less aggressive and more manageable.

For the most part, the spikes work great—but I've

learned to respect the sheer power of some of the unnatural forces out there, because I've encountered spooks who could cut right through our magnetic force field and cause me physical harm twice before. As we moved ever closer to Dunlow Castle, I could only hope we weren't in for a charming third.

"Wow," Heath muttered next to me as we stared at what lay ahead. I knew what he was reacting to. The massive rock the castle was perched upon was far higher than I'd expected. "It's got to be a hundred feet tall."

I squinted into the gray morning light. "At least."

"How do we get up to the top again?"

I pointed to a crude set of stairs carved into the side of the rock face. "We hoof it."

Heath shifted his backpack. "We need to keep track of how long it'll take us to climb those stairs. We'll have to figure that into the time it'll take us to get down and get back across the causeway. The last thing I want to do is get stuck here until tonight when the tide rolls back out again."

"I'm with ya."

"M. J.?" Gilley asked from behind me.

I glanced over my shoulder. "Yeah?"

"What's that?"

I saw that Gil was pointing up and over to my left. I turned to look and noticed movement along the top of the cliff. It was still a bit too dim to see clearly, but I swore I saw a tall dark shape moving along the outer edge. "I have no idea. But whatever it is, I think it could be trouble."

There was a squeak behind me and the sound of a zipper. I looked again over my shoulder and saw Gil rummaging through his backpack until he located his magic sweatshirt.

Several months earlier—before Gil and I had begun working on the TV show—I'd realized that Gilley was one of those rather unlucky people who is super attractive to spooks. For whatever reason, they love to haunt him and invariably, as he's actually terrified of spooks, they end up torturing him. To keep him safe, I'd glued about a dozen refrigerator magnets to the inside of one of his old sweatshirts, and as long as he wore it, he would be far less appealing to mischievous or malevolent spirits.

That first sweatshirt had had a few different versions since then, and the one he was currently shrugging into had triple the number of magnets, thus tripling its power and range of protection. Gilley, by nature, was never too careful when protecting what he treasured most in this world . . . himself.

"Need some help?" I asked him when I saw how he was struggling to take off his jacket, hold his backpack, and put on the sweatshirt all at the same time.

"I got it," he insisted, just as he dropped his backpack. Something crunched when it struck the cobblestones, and all three of us stopped to stare at the pack.

"Uh-oh," Heath said.

"What was in there?" I asked as Gilley stared at his backpack in horror.

"The meters," he said weakly.

I reached down and picked up the pack carefully. Glass tinkled inside. After unzipping it and moving aside a few items, I said, "Aww, Gil! You broke all three of them!"

"It was an accident!"

"Well, of course it was an accident," I snapped. "But did you *have* to put the meters at the bottom of the pack where they were the most vulnerable?"

Our electrostatic meters, which we use to isolate ghostly hot spots at all our haunted locales, were pretty fragile gadgets and we often lost one or two due to wear and tear on our investigations, but we hadn't even made it to the island yet and a major piece of our ghost-hunting equipment wasn't just gone; it was likely irreplaceable for the rest of the hunt.

"I can get us some new ones," Gil vowed.

I scowled at him. "From where? The local hardware store?"

"I can buy one or two online and have it shipped to us."

I sighed and handed him the pack, thoroughly irritated that he'd been so careless and stubborn when all he'd had to do was accept my offer to help. Still, as I looked into his guilty face, I softened. "Okay, buddy. We'll work without them for now."

We got moving again and I was really relieved when the thin drizzle stopped and the clouds began to clear. At least we'd soon be dry. Not long after that, we were standing at the base of the cliff on the rocky shore of the island. I tilted my chin up while Heath, Gilley, and I waited for the rest of the crew to catch up to us. Heath shrugged uncomfortably. "You sensing that?"

I nodded. "Feels thick as molasses."

"What feels thick as molasses?" Gopher asked, stepping up next to us.

"The air," I said. "It's thick with spooks."

"Should make for some great footage, then," Gopher said happily. Leave it to Gopher to always think about the ratings. Our show, *Ghoul Getters*, hadn't even aired its first episode yet, but Gopher wasn't about to pull back on the throttle. He wanted footage of majorly creepy stuff. Period.

When John, Meg, and Kim joined us, I pointed to the stairs. "Better get on with it," I said.

We climbed the steep rock staircase for maybe ten minutes and had gone only about halfway to the top when I heard a call coming from somewhere above us. Grabbing Heath's shoulder in front of me to stop him, I asked, "Did you hear that?"

"What?"

Something faint reached my ears again and I turned my head in the direction, which was up and over to my left. *"That."*

Heath cocked his head. "All I can hear is Gilley."

I looked over my shoulder as Gil clutched the old iron railing while he hacked and wheezed like he was running a marathon. "I'll . . . never . . . make . . . it . . . ," he gasped.

I frowned and felt myself getting frustrated again. I'd been trying to get Gil on some kind of exercise regimen for ages, and he staunchly refused to work out anything but his fingers as they flicked across the keyboard of his computer. "You'll make it," I told him flatly. Just then, I distinctly heard a male voice call out, "Alex!"

"Whoa," said Heath, whipping his head in the direction of the mysterious voice. "Now, *that* I heard."

Gilley lifted his head to glare at me, oblivious to anything but his own suffering. "This is the last ghostbust I'll ever agree to that involves this many stairs!"

"Shhh!" I told him, while I listened again.

"Alex!"

"Who is *that*?" Gil asked, turning his head to look in the same direction Heath and I were squinting in.

"I think it's that same guy from last night!" I said.

Heath appeared puzzled. "Why hasn't he recruited some help to find this Alex person he's searching for? I mean, if he's been looking all night, you'd think that the moment the causeway opened up again, he'd head back to the mainland to alert the coast guard."

Gilley was fishing around in his backpack again, and after a moment he came up with a pair of binoculars. "I thought we might need these on this shoot," he said, putting them to his eyes and scanning along the top of the cliff where the voice was coming from.

I watched him anxiously, a terrible sense of foreboding forming in the pit of my stomach. "Something's not right," I whispered.

At that moment Gilley sucked in a breath of surprise. "What?" I asked.

Gilley thrust the binoculars at me. "He's in trouble!"

he said, and pointed to the top of the cliff. I squinted but couldn't see anything, so I put the binoculars up to my eyes and played with the focus while searching along the cliff—and that was when I nearly dropped the glasses. *"Ohmigod!"*

"What?" Heath asked.

I pulled the binoculars away and grabbed his hand, running past him up the stairs. "Come on!"

"What's the matter?"

"Just follow me!" I yelled, pumping my legs as fast as I could to get to the top in time.

Dutifully Heath followed behind. In short order we reached the top of the rock, my legs screaming with the effort, and I tore across the unusually flat terrain, passing the large stone castle as we ran. I barely noticed it because I was so focused on getting to the far end in time.

As we raced forward, we both distinctly heard someone calling for help, and I used every ounce of my reserve strength to run as fast as I could. Heath came abreast of me quickly, and as the cries for help became more urgent, he picked up his speed and zoomed past me in three strides.

By the time he reached the edge of the cliff, he was a good twenty yards ahead of me. I watched him drop to his knees and reach down; then he appeared to jerk forward and I cried out, afraid he was being pulled off the edge. With two more long strides I reached him and flung myself across the back of his legs to keep him from falling.

"Nooooooooooooooo!" I heard him cry, and I gripped his legs even more fiercely.

With a sickening dread I heard someone dropping away from us scream, *"Alllllllex!"*

Using my weight to anchor Heath, I peered over the side and gasped when I saw the same man I'd seen through the binoculars falling, his arms pitifully still reaching up and flailing as his hands grabbed at thin air, all the while falling down, and down and down.

I screamed—the scene was so horrible I could barely stand it. The man's face was so panic-stricken and frightened and there was nothing anyone could do to help him.

And then his form disappeared in what remained of the fog at the base of the rock, and an instant later Heath and I both heard a faint sickening crunch.

I rolled away from Heath and lay on my back, covering my eyes with both hands. A moment later—I burst into tears.

"Stop staring at me," I ordered.

"Sorry!" Gilley apologized. "It's just, you almost never cry, M. J., and this flood's been going for almost thirty minutes now."

I wiped my tearstained cheeks and stared out at the waves crashing onto shore. "Yeah, well, I almost never see someone die right in front of my eyes either, Gil."

"John should be back soon. And Heath and Gopher should also be showing up any minute."

I shuddered. John had gone back to shore to alert

the authorities, while Heath and Gopher were conducting a search at the base of the rocks where the man had likely landed. I knew the distance he'd fallen and the hard surface he'd landed on certainly meant that there was no hope, but I still wanted to cling to it anyway.

"You look cold," Meg said from behind me. "Do you want my coat?"

I worked to control the shivering sending tremors through my body. The wind was cold, but I was probably in a little bit of shock from the scene I'd witnessed earlier. "No," I told her. "Thanks, though. I'll be okay."

Gilley looked guilt-ridden, probably because he hadn't offered to help me warm up. "Here," he said, shrugging out of his sweatshirt and handing it to me. "It's warm at least."

"What're you going to wear?"

Gilley reached for his backpack and pulled out his own coat. "This."

I held out my hand for his coat instead of the sweatshirt, knowing how nervous Gil got when he wasn't wearing it. "Thanks, honey."

"How's she doing?" I heard someone ask.

Turning to look, I saw Gopher and Heath walking toward us.

"She'll be okay," Gilley said.

I blushed because I'd been an emotional wreck all the way back down the staircase. "Did you find him?" I asked softly.

Both men shook their heads. "No," Gopher said. "We looked all the way along the rocks underneath the cliff, and there's no sign of him."

I blinked. "Was he swept offshore?"

Gopher and Heath exchanged an uncomfortable look. "We don't think so."

"So, where'd he go?"

Heath sat down next to me and wrapped a muscled arm across my shoulders. "I don't think he was ever really there."

I cocked my head at him and Gilley said, "Huh?"

Heath eyed the top of the cliff for a moment before he explained. "I know you didn't see it, M. J., but when I got to the edge of the cliff, I dropped down and reached for the guy hanging there. He wasn't far away, maybe a foot or two, and as he grabbed for my hand, I swear, it passed right through mine."

My jaw fell open. "He was a *spook*?!"

Heath nodded. "I think so."

No one said anything for the longest time; we were all too stunned by the possibility that we'd been so easily duped. "He looked so real," I whispered, knowing that I had been so panic-stricken to get to him that I hadn't even considered using my sixth sense to feel out the energy around the man.

"He did look real," Heath agreed. "And we were running on pure adrenaline up there. It never even occurred to me when we saw him hanging over the edge like that that he might be a ghost, which was why I automatically thought his hand passing through mine had to have been a trick of the light. But then Gopher and I couldn't find any trace of him anywhere near the base of the cliffs, and at that end of the beach, the tide is still low enough that there's no way his body could have been carried out to sea. There are at least fifty yards of dry rocky shore between the edge of the water and the cliffs."

I inhaled deeply, my tattered emotions already mending themselves back together. "He fell straight down," I said. "So he should have landed within about ten to twenty feet of the rock face."

"Yep," Heath agreed.

I switched my attention to Gilley. "Can you do some research for us when we get back to the B&B? I want to know if there is anything in cyberspace about this ghost."

"On it," Gil said.

"And don't go back too far in history," Heath told him. "The guy was wearing a down vest, jeans, and a really nice watch. I think it might even have been a Rolex."

"You got a lot of detail in those few seconds," I told him.

"I don't know that I'll ever get that image out of my head," Heath replied, looking pained.

I moved closer to him and squeezed my arm around his waist. "I know exactly how you feel."

"So what do we do now?" Kim asked. She'd gotten very quiet after hearing about the man who'd fallen off the cliff.

"Wait for John," Gilley said. "He'll probably bring the cavalry with him and we'll have some explaining to do."

"Maybe whoever he brings with him will know about our spook," I suggested.

And it turned out that I hadn't been far off the mark. John returned about ten minutes later with one winded-looking constable. "Now, what's this about a man falling to his death from the top o' the cliff?" he asked us.

Gopher extended his hand and introduced himself, explaining that our group was here to film an episode for an American ghost-hunting show, and that we had witnessed a man dropping to his death from the top of the cliffs, but were unable to locate his body.

"Are you the same Americans that alerted the coast guard to this missing Alex person and his companion?" the constable asked.

"Yes, sir," said Gopher.

The constable appeared irritated, and he took his handkerchief out of his trouser pocket to wipe at his brow. "Well, then, you've found your first ghost, haven't you?"

"We already suspected as much," I said. "We're so sorry to have raised a false alarm."

The constable softened. "Don't mind it, miss. Happens at least three or four times a year whenever one of the tourists ignores the signs about not venturing onto the causeway."

"We have permission to be here," Gopher said quickly, and he dug into his coat pocket for the papers to prove it.

The constable took the paper and inspected it, finally nodding. "Everything looks in order," he said. "Although I hardly think choosing Dunlow Castle was a wise move given its history."

"You mean the phantom?" Gilley asked.

"Aye," he said. "This is a dangerous place, mates. And you should know that if you get into trouble here on this rock, there'll be precious little me or the coast guard will be able to do for you." The constable then pointed to the right-of-access document he was still holding and said, "As it says in your paper here, Mr. Gophner, you're assuming all risks while you're here at Castle Dunlow, and the village of Dunlee will not be held liable for any deaths that may occur nor be required to participate in any rescue of you or your party should something dreadful happen at the top of the rock."

Heath and I exchanged a look, and I knew we were both thinking the same thing: That was a really odd thing to put into a legal access permit.

"I almost didn't come along to investigate, in fact," the constable continued. "But the one time I don't is going to be the one time when someone really does need my help."

"Can you tell us anything about this man?" I asked. "The one who fell to his death? And maybe even who Alex might be?"

"I can't say as I know who this Alex was, but I do know that the ghost you might have seen was likely Jordan Kincaid."

For a moment I wondered where I'd heard that name and then it hit me. "You mean *the* Jordan Kincaid? The heir to the Kincaid Mining family?" I'd read about his death several years previously. The story told of the dashing young playboy whose family had made a fortune mining for precious minerals all over the world. He had been the only son and heir of the prominent family, and since his death, I'd heard that his grief-stricken father had taken his own life and his mother had become a recluse.

"The very one," said the constable. "Such a tragedy. Came here on his own treasure hunt with a piece of paper just like yours some four years ago. He fell to his death on the third or fourth day he was explorin' the castle. Such a pity," he added, shaking his head. "From all accounts he was a rather nice lad."

I swallowed hard. "Yeah, well, he died an awful death."

The constable eyed me critically. "Well, then, let it serve as a fair warning to you all," he said, folding the paper and handing it back to Gopher. "If I were you, I'd leave this island and never return."

Gopher appeared uncomfortable. "Our network is expecting some footage later today," he told the constable. "And we're already pushing a deadline, so we'll promise to be careful, but we really do have to stick it out here."

"What do you know about the phantom?" I asked the constable.

The middle-aged man looked to the top of the cliffs and shuddered. It was a moment before he then looked back to consider me gravely. "I know enough not to go to the top of those cliffs even for all the pound notes in Ireland, miss."

"That bad?" Heath said.

"Aye."

No one spoke for a moment and the tension in our group moved up a notch. "We've heard the phantom likes to throw people off the cliffs," Gopher said after a bit.

"Oh, he likes to do more than that. If he isn't tossin' you over the side, he's scaring you into a state of mental collapse."

"Mental collapse?" I repeated.

"Aye. Two years ago a couple on their honeymoon ignored the warnings, and they made their way to the castle. When they came back across the causeway, the poor wife was in a terrible state. Her husband claimed she'd been attacked by the phantom and been driven mad."

"Was she hurt physically?" Gilley asked, his complexion pale.

"No. But she was so stricken with fear that she didn't know who or where she was. In fact, the poor lass could do nothing more than shake from head to toe. The last I heard about it, she'd been given a padded cell."

An involuntary shiver ran down my own spine. I'm not one for tall tales, and I couldn't be sure that this constable wasn't simply trying to scare us away from here because if any one of us got hurt, assumption of risk or not, he'd likely have a boatload of paperwork to fill out.

Gopher must have suspected this too, because he extended his hand and said, "We thank you so much for coming, Constable. We're sorry to have inconvenienced you and we promise to be very careful from here on out."

The constable frowned. As he turned back to the causeway, he remarked, "Don't say I didn't warn you."

After he'd gone, I looked around at our group. "I think we need a new game plan."

Chapter 3

We sat around on the rocky beach for nearly ten minutes, arguing about the best course of action. Heath and I didn't want to proceed until we'd had a chance to do some more research on the mysterious and apparently deadly phantom that lurked above our heads.

Gilley—being the scaredy-cat in the group—was all for abandoning the entire ghost hunt and instead hunting for the nearest pub.

John, Kim, and Meg seemed willing to support us, but in the end we were outvoted by Gopher, who insisted that we at least give the top of the rock a cursory look while we still had an hour and a half, which, he reasoned, was plenty of time to get to the castle, check out a few rooms, then head back down and hurry across the causeway.

What can I say? Gopher was our producer and boss, and money trumps nerves, scary phantoms, and good sense every time.

Reluctantly, Heath, John, and I all worked our way

up the stairs with an enthused Gopher bringing up the rear.

Gilley, Meg, and Kim remained on the beach, as Gil flat out refused to go with us and I didn't want to leave him alone, so I asked the other two most vulnerable people in our group to babysit him.

When we reached the top, I paused to catch my breath. My thighs were burning from all the stairs, and I was grateful to have reached the top without wimping out halfway up.

"Man, that's a long climb," Heath remarked, coming over to stand next to me.

I motioned to the castle with a small groan. "Bet there're more stairs inside."

"Aw, crap," he said. "I didn't think of that."

John appeared at our side looking winded. "Jesus," he wheezed. "How many stairs did we just climb?"

"Eleventy," I told him, using the word Gilley had coined to describe anything greater than a whole bunch.

I moved over to the stairs and looked down. Gopher was still trudging up, and by the look of his pace and the number of stairs he had left to climb, he'd be a while.

"How far away is he?" Heath asked.

"Far enough that we can check things out up here for a bit."

John agreed to wait by the stairs for Gopher while Heath and I moved to the castle, which was located in the center of the massive piece of rock.

"Pretty genius to build your fortress on this thing, don't you think?"

I nodded. "I can't imagine anyone who'd be stupid enough to try and attack it. You couldn't come in from the sea, given the currents and the treacherously shallow water. There's no way you could navigate your way through with a large force.

"The only way to attack it would be from the shore, so first you'd have to attack and conquer the Irish forces on land. Then you'd have to bring your troops to the rock using the causeway, and since you'd only have four hours at low tide to move your troops, you'd be limited in the number you could get across at any given time."

"Still, you probably could get a sizable army across in four hours," Heath reasoned.

"Agreed, but you'd still only be able to move two men up at a time on those stairs. It would only take a small force to defend them, and there's no other way up as far as I can tell. In the sixteenth century, this place would have been impenetrable."

"It does make for one spooky shoot," said Heath as he eyed Dunlow Castle. I stopped walking long enough to look it over too.

The place was impressive; I'll give it that. The fortress was three stories tall, with huge stone walls topped by high narrow windows and parapets running all along the sides. Four high towers with turrets spiraled above each of the four corners, perfect for archers to take aim at any enemy who might breach those stairs.

The views from those four towers also would have alerted the inner keep to anyone approaching the fortress from any direction. Unless one attempted an attack at night, there was no way to sneak up on the occupants of Dunlow.

And I'm not sure if that thought caused the feeling of being watched to creep up my spine, but I distinctly wondered if perhaps we weren't being monitored by someone—or some*thing*—inside the keep.

"You get the feeling we're being watched?" Heath asked me, as if reading my mind.

"I do."

"I have a bad feeling about this, M. J."

I inhaled and exhaled slowly. "Me too, buddy."

I turned to look back where John was still sitting, waiting for Gopher, when I noticed something ominous on the horizon. "Are you *kidding* me?" I asked as I moved my hand up to shield the sun from my eyes so that I could squint at a large thundercloud moving toward us from way offshore.

"What?" Heath asked, and after I pointed to the thundercloud, he added, "Didn't Gilley check the weather?"

On every ghost hunt we did, Gilley always downloaded the local weather report, as rain and foul weather are typically great conditions for ghost hunting, but this particular tempest certainly wasn't welcomed at this point in the hunt, especially since we were all so exposed.

I pulled my headset out of my bag and clicked the radio transmitter on. All I got was static. "Damn!" I swore, yanking the headset off. "We forgot to do a check of the radios before we came up here." I then retrieved my cell from my back pocket and dialed Gilley.

"Yo!" he said, as if he didn't have a care in the world. "Did you check the weather this morning?"

"Uh . . ."

I sighed heavily into the phone. "I take it that means no?"

"I woke up late," Gil said by way of explanation. "Besides, what's the big deal? There's plenty of sunshine and it's not even that cold."

At that exact moment there was a rumble of thunder from the approaching storm and I could just imagine Gilley turning around to look offshore. "Uh-oh," I heard him say.

Fully irritated, I hung up the phone. "We've got to go back down."

Heath was peering at the approaching storm, and his posture suggested he was quite alarmed. "It'll be here before we even make it to the causeway," he said.

More thunder sounded in the distance and we could both see sharp bolts of lightning crackle through the dark cloud. "That storm's looking really mean," I said.

By this time, John had taken notice and he came trotting over to us. "We'll never make it back down and across the causeway in time," he said. "And I don't know that I want to be caught on that slippery bridge in *that*."

As if Gilley were already privy to our conversation, my phone rang, and after I answered it, Gil said, "The causeway's already got water across it from the storm surge. We won't be able to get back across."

I looked skyward for a moment, wondering what I'd done wrong in another life to deserve this particular batch of bad luck. "You and the girls will have to come up," I told him.

"Say what, now?"

"Gilley, there's no other choice. You can't stay down there unprotected from the storm, and the castle is the only shelter on this hunk of rock."

"But—"

"No buts!" I yelled at him, worried that he'd panic and refuse to come up the stairs. "And we don't have time to argue about it. That storm is coming in fast and furious, buddy, so get your fanny up here or I'll come down and throw you over my shoulder!"

There was a pause, then, "Can I be thrown over Heath's shoulder? He's prettier."

"Right now, Gilley Morehouse Gillespie," I said, my voice low and threatening. "And I'm not kidding." I hung up the phone for the second time and cast a worried glance at Heath. "If he's not up here in twenty minutes, we'll have to go down and get him."

"I can go down to help them," John offered. "After all, I've only made the trek up once today. You guys have both come up twice."

In that moment I could have hugged John, but then I remembered that Kim was his girlfriend and he was probably worried about her more than anything. "Go," I told him, even as he turned away and bolted for the stairs. "And make sure they hustle, John. We've probably only got fifteen to twenty minutes before that storm hits!"

As John dashed down the stairs, Gopher finally appeared. He looked sweaty and winded but happy to have reached the summit. "Where's he going?" he asked as he turned back to look at John's departing figure.

In answer, both Heath and I pointed to the thundercloud. "Aw, shit!" Gopher said when he saw it. "Didn't Gilley check the weather?"

The storm moved faster than expected, striking our little island just ten minutes later. Gilley, John, Meg, and Kim were caught by it halfway up the stairs, and tired as I was, Heath and I still had to jog down to take their packs and hurry them along.

It was an awful climb up the rest of the way. We were pelted by water, whipped by wind, and hammered by the reverberating thunder. Lightning seemed to strike all around us, and Gilley was shivering so hard next to me that I thought for certain he'd faint. "Just keep putting one foot in front of the other!" I told him, as I held his free hand and pulled him urgently up the stairs.

"How much farther?" he cried, wheezing and struggling to continue climbing.

I looked up. There was still a long way to go. "We're nearly there, honey! Just a few more steps!" Gilley began to lift his chin to look and I quickly added, "Watch your step! It's slippery on these stairs!"

We moved like that for twenty more minutes and the journey up took twice as long as it would have in calmer conditions, but finally we crested the ledge, all of us gasping for breath, but wanting to get out of the wind and rain. "Let's get to the castle!" Heath called, and he and Meg began to jog tiredly in that direction.

John and Kim followed behind too, and I looked at Gilley, who was doubled over, his hands on his knees. "You go," he said with a small wave. "Save yourself!"

Even though I was exhausted, wet, cold, and miserable, I still smiled. "Oh, Gil," I chuckled. "How could I leave my little drama queen behind?"

Gilley simply shook his head, and continued to try and pump air into his lungs. I gave him another few seconds until a bolt of lightning struck the water just offshore and the resulting thunder was loud enough to sink both of us to our knees. "We *have* to get inside, Gil!" I shouted.

Gilley trembled but nodded all the same and took my hand. I tugged him after me toward the large black abandoned structure, and hoped to God that we weren't about to go from the frying pan into the fire.

We made it through the giant wooden door of the keep, and were finally out of the rain. It was very dark inside, but periodically we were lit up by the lightning still crackling all around the castle. "Which pack are the flashlights in?" Heath asked Gilley, who'd collapsed just inside the doorway.

Gilley motioned weakly to the one John was holding. Just a minute later we each held a flashlight and were pointing them around the spacious room just inside the entrance. "This place gives me the creeps," said Kim.

"Me too," said Meg.

"Me three," said John.

Everyone else chimed in with a number, even Gilley. "Me six," he said, pushing himself off the ground to sit up and look around.

And that was when it hit me: There were seven of us in the group. "Where's Gopher?"

Heath looked at me and blinked. "Isn't he here?"

"No." I pointed the flashlight all around the hall, looking for our producer, and finally called out to him, "Gopher!" My voice echoed through the large hall, down into distant corridors, but no reply came back to us.

"Isn't that his pack?" Meg asked, pointing to his signature silver backpack.

I hurried over to it, and discovered it was indeed his, and next to it was his camera. I looked back to Heath as an unsettling foreboding sank deep into my bones. "He'd never leave his backpack," I said.

"Maybe he's off taking a whiz," said John.

"Gopher!" I shouted. Again, my voice echoed out of the room down into the corridors, but no sign or sound of our producer could be seen or heard.

"Where could he have gone?" Gilley whimpered, looking especially frightened.

"We need to find him," I said, getting up and wiping the wet hair out of my eyes.

"We also need to see about drying out our clothes and maybe starting a fire to get warm," Heath advised.

It was then that I noticed both Meg and Kim standing with their arms wrapped tightly about themselves, shivering with cold.

"Right," I agreed, rummaging around in my messenger bag for the lighter and the small notebook I never went without. Tossing both to John, I said, "You stay here with Gilley, Meg, and Kim. See if you can find some wood for a fire, and use the notebook paper for kindling. I think you should try and get one started by the door, 'cause I don't trust that hearth's chimney."

We left the main group and Heath and I worked our way deeper into the castle. The storm was still raging outside, and the walls reverberated with the sound of thunder, but no flashes of lightning made their way inside. The only illumination was our flashlights. "Gopher!" I called as we moved into the first main corridor off the front hall.

Somewhere in the distance a loud creaking sound made Heath and me both pause to listen. "Where'd that come from?" Heath whispered.

"I think from that hallway down there," I whispered back, motioning to a separate corridor that opened up all the way at the end of the one we were in.

"Gopher?" Heath shouted.

His voice echoed along the walls.

And then . . .

. . . *something* growled back.

"What was *that?"* I whispered. The sound we'd heard was deep and guttural and not at all human.

Heath didn't answer me. Instead, he pulled out a magnetic grenade and popped open the cap. "Whatever it was," he said, bending low to my ear, "I don't think it's friendly."

I pulled a grenade out too and uncorked the top. Tipping out the spike, I held it high, like a knife, ready to stab it into anyone—or any*thing*—that approached. After a moment I asked Heath, "Should we continue down that way?"

"Do we have much of a choice?"

Mentally I cursed Gopher for wandering off. "Okay. Let's keep going but quietly. No calling out to Gopher until we know what we're dealing with."

Heath and I proceeded cautiously down the corridor. I could still hear the storm, and the dripping of water and some sort of scuttling noise I attributed to something like a mouse or a rat, but nothing else disturbed the darkness.

As we walked forward, I began to get a terrible feeling. It was like I was thirteen again, watching a scary movie well past my bedtime. I couldn't seem to shake the creepy shiver seeping along my spine. I leaned over and in Heath's ear whispered, "I *really* don't like this!"

He paused.

I paused.

And for several heartbeats neither of us moved even to breathe. The longer we stood there, waiting, the more unsettled I became. I was about to tell Heath that maybe we should double back—and quick—when a wave of something terrifying wafted through the ether and washed over me with tremendous power. I sank to my knees and closed my eyes as every nightmarish monster I'd ever seen on TV or conjured up in my worst dreams flooded through my mind and wiped away all reason.

It was as if a force that knew everything that had ever frightened me as a child or an adult had kept a record of it, and was filling my mind with all those images at once, while clearing away any ability I might have to form a rational thought. It was an onslaught of horror, and I was powerless to stop it.

The effect crippled me both mentally and physically, and I couldn't seem to form a thought of my own. I was aware only of danger, terror, and panic until I felt something crash into my shoulder, and it knocked me to the ground. That just increased my terror and I screamed, and screamed, and screamed.

I wanted desperately to get away, and so I scuttled and crawled along the floor, trembling from head to toe and barely able to hold on to my flashlight. I must have left the spike behind because very slowly I became aware of things other than the parade of terrifying images surging through my mind—like my empty right hand.

And then, with unexpected abruptness, the onslaught vanished, and I was left gasping and shaking all over but once again in my right mind. "M. J.!" someone whispered urgently to me. "Sugar, please, look at me!"

With effort I lifted my chin and realized Gilley was squatting down in front of me, attempting to get me to my feet.

His sweatshirt sagged on him, and I could see in the dim light how the dozens of magnets he'd secured to the inside of the shirt were bulging right through the fabric. "Gilley!" I croaked, clutching his arms and getting up shakily.

"What happened to you?" he asked, his face filled with concern. "And where's Heath?"

I blinked and for the first time I was able to take in my surroundings. John, Meg, and Kim were hovering close, each of them holding several spikes and eyeing the hallway nervously. "I—I don't know," I said, trying to spot Heath's face among those gathered around me. "He was next to me, and then . . ." My voice trailed off as I tried to remember what had actually happened.

"And then what, honey?" Gilley asked.

I focused on his face again, still struggling to form linear thoughts. "Something attacked us." And then, my lower lip began to tremble, and the shivering increased, and a tear or two leaked out of my eyes.

Gilley and John exchanged a look and John said, "Let's get her back to the front hall. I can get that fire started, and I've got some water and a protein bar in my pack. Maybe that'll help calm her."

I realized I was still trembling and my hands were shaking so hard that the light from my flashlight was bouncing all over the floor. I took a deep breath and attempted to steady the ray, and that was when I saw two spikes illuminated several yards down the corridor.

I pointed to the spikes, and Gilley and John both looked to the spot. "Those yours?" Gilley asked.

I shook my head. "Only one. The other was Heath's."

"Heath!" John shouted.

We all waited breathlessly, but no reply came.

Tears were now streaming steadily down my cheeks as I began to consider that whatever terrifying force had produced such a crippling and mind-altering effect on me had likely done the same to Heath, and without his spike, he was completely at its mercy.

The five of us waited another few heartbeats, shining our beams down the long hallway, waiting for Heath to appear or call out, but nothing disturbed the steady rays of our lights or the eerie silence in the hallway.

"Come on," Gilley said reluctantly. "Let's get back and take care of M. J. Then we'll talk about what to do next."

The guys helped me to our makeshift camp in the large hall. John was able to get a good fire going from several pieces of wood he'd pulled from a nearby door, and we all huddled eagerly around it as much for the warmth as for the small comfort it brought to this awful place.

"So what happened?" Gilley asked me again when I'd calmed down a bit.

I shook my head, closing my eyes against the flood of memories. "I don't even know how to describe it," I whispered.

"Try," he urged. I opened my eyes again and saw him staring at me with concern. I knew that I'd better get it together and explain what I could in order to help us find Heath and Gopher.

Taking a deep breath, I told them all about what had happened, and the last moment I could remember seeing Heath next to me before being attacked by that terrible force.

"So you think something actually *physically* attacked you?" Kim asked.

"Yes. Yes, I do. I think some insanely powerful spook was able to call up my worst nightmares and parade them through my mind as if they were reality. The magnitude of that onslaught was like *nothing* I've ever experienced. Not even the demon we encountered in San Francisco or the Witch of Queen's Close could even touch the power of this . . . this . . . *thing*."

"It must be the phantom everyone's been talking about," Gil said, his eyes large and afraid.

"Is that what knocked you over?" John asked.

I thought back. "No. I think that might have been Heath."

Gilley leaned toward me. "So he was next to you right up until then?"

I nodded. "Yeah, Gil. I think he was."

"Can you remember anything else after that?" he pressed.

I sighed, feeling suddenly exhausted. "Not much, buddy. I mean, I remember falling to my knees, then being knocked over by Heath, then crawling away down the hall where you guys found me, and that's when reality clicked in again."

"What do you think made the attack stop?" Meg asked.

My eyes moved to Gilley's sweatshirt. "That," I said, pointing to his chest.

Gil looked down. "Me?"

"Your sweatshirt."

"But why didn't your spikes work?" John said. "I mean, if Gilley's sweatshirt was able to stop the phantom from attacking you, then why didn't your spikes stop it in the first place?"

I leaned over and felt Gil's shirt. It was packed with magnets. "Have you seen inside his shirt? He's probably got two dozen magnets glued to the inside."

"Three dozen," Gilley corrected.

I sat back and regarded the group. "I think there might have been just enough magnetic energy radiating off Gilley to thwart even the phantom."

I could see the small bit of relief in Gilley's eyes. I knew he was terrified of being in the castle with a powerful phantom on the loose, especially since he'd seen the state I'd been in just twenty minutes before. But knowing he was wearing enough magnetic power to keep the phantom away probably lent him a bit of comfort.

"So what do we do now?" Kim asked softly.

I sighed again, because a tiny idea had come into my mind that was incredibly risky, but perhaps the only choice we had. The problem was that I was so tired, both physically and mentally, that I wasn't sure I could pull it off, and I certainly knew I'd have to make myself a target again in order to try it.

Gilley seemed to notice I had a plan in mind, because he said, "M. J.? What're you thinking?"

I didn't look at him when I spoke, because I didn't want to see the fear in his eyes. "I think I need to try and find a ghost within this castle to communicate with.

I might be able to find a spirit who knows where Heath and Gopher are and maybe even to help me figure out what this phantom thing is and how to deal with it. And to do that, I need to be well away from all of you, because while I'm gone, you've got to keep your spikes out in the open and huddle around Gilley."

We argued for at least ten minutes about my idea. No one in the group thought it smart, wise, or something I should even consider. In the end, we settled on a compromise: I would head into one of the corridors off the main hall and attempt to find a ghost to communicate with, and John would accompany me carrying a fistful of capped grenades. At the first sign of trouble, he'd uncork them and let the magnets rip. The part about John accompanying me was nonnegotiable, or so he and Gilley both told me. I argued that he could become a liability if the phantom found us, and I worried that he wouldn't have time to uncap the spikes. "I'll get to them," he assured me, his face hard and stubbornly set.

In that moment I gained a new level of respect for him, because I knew that deep down he didn't want to go anywhere but off that stinking rock. "Fine," I relented. "But don't uncap anything unless either I give the signal or I go down."

"Got it."

Before we left the group again, Gilley pulled me aside out of earshot of the others. "What happens if you don't come back?"

I looked out the door at the storm. Much of the worst

of it was over, but it continued to rain very hard outside. "Give us an hour, Gil, then get Meg and Kim out of this castle, and back down those stairs. Try to find shelter anywhere you can along the shore until the storm blows itself out and you guys can cross the causeway again."

Gilley eyed his watch. "We missed our window for crossing."

"You'll have another shot later tonight."

"Not if the storm surge keeps up."

"Then use your cell to call for help."

Gilley pulled out his cell phone and showed me the display. "It's been drained," he said. "All of our phones are dead, in fact."

My heart started to hammer as I anxiously pulled my cell out and tried in vain to switch it on. Was *nothing* going to turn out right on this hunt? With a sigh I put it away and focused on Gilley again. "Do your best to stay safe, buddy. We'll be back as soon as we can."

I turned to go then, but he caught my arm and whispered, "Please come back, okay?"

I gave him a brief hug, promised to do my level best, then motioned for John to follow me.

Chapter 4

As Heath and I had traveled the central corridor off from the main hall, I thought it might be wise for John and me to try to avoid the phantom by taking one of the lesser pathways all the way to the right, where I guessed the kitchen or cooking hall might have been. Luck finally gave us a break, because after only going a short way, we came out into a large open room with an enormous hearth and black tar stains against the brick. "What kind of a room was this?" John asked.

"It served as the castle's kitchen," I told him, relieved to have found it.

"Should we try another corridor?"

I shook my head. "Nope. This is exactly where I want to try to connect with a spook." When he looked at me curiously, I explained, "Lots of large old castles like this are home to the ghost of a kitchen maid or cook. I'm hoping to find a nice, gentle female spirit to communicate with. Someone who would have looked after the castle and its occupants."

"Why?"

"Because if they're in ghost form, they're likely still keeping track of the castle's comings and goings, and they might know what happened to Heath and Gopher."

John opened his mouth to say something more, but I shook my head and put a finger to my lips. I needed to concentrate and find my spook because all I could think about was what might be happening to Heath and Gopher at that very minute.

Turning away from John, I flipped my internal sixth sense on, and waited for a particular sensation to let me know we'd hit pay dirt. After a bit, I felt a very light tug on my solar plexus and I moved to the far corner where another opening led us out of the kitchen and into a smaller room.

"What's in here?" John whispered.

"The servants' sleeping quarters," I told him. In the corner of the room I felt a surge of energy. "Hello, there," I said, moving slowly toward it. "My name is M. J."

The energy shifted a bit nervously and I stopped walking toward it. I waited a beat or two and mentally asked for a name. After a few beats I was rewarded with a name that sounded a bit like Eneey. I asked her to repeat it and closed my eyes to concentrate on the very subtle nuance of the name. She obliged me by saying it twice more, and I was able to hear it fully. Something that sounded like Eanin.

A small bird flew about in my mind's eye, and I understood that this particular ghost was telling me her name meant "little bird." "That's a beautiful name, friend," I said to her. "Do you work here at the castle?"

I felt the ghost reply yes. She was a scullery maid.

I nodded. "It's lovely to meet you," I told her, doing my best to send her some warm feelings across the ether. Her energy approached me, and I could feel such a lovely connection to this sweet little sparrow.

"I was wondering if you could help me, Eanin," I said. "I've lost track of two of my friends, and I was wondering, might you be able to tell me where they are?"

In my mind's eye I saw a small fire, and I knew she was referring to the group still gathered in the front hall around the fire near the door. I also had a sense that Eanin didn't care for the fact that we had started the fire on the stone floor instead of using the hearth.

"I'm so sorry we didn't use the fireplace," I said. "We were worried the chimney might be clogged and we didn't want to cause a problem."

Eanin flooded me with warmth, making me feel like she understood fully.

"My friends by the fire are not the ones I'm looking for, Eanin. I'm looking for two gentlemen. They've gone missing."

Eanin's energy was quiet for a long moment and through the ether I could feel her wavering. Then, I felt a sentence waft through my mind. *It's got one of them.*

My heart raced anxiously. I thought I knew what she was referring to, but I wanted to make certain. "Do you mean the phantom?"

There was a hissing sound, as if someone had just said, *"Shhhhhhh!"*

John gasped and looked in the direction from where the sound had come, and I realized that I'd been so focused on Eanin that I hadn't noticed the other energy in the opposite corner of the room. In my mind I could sense that Eanin became alarmed and sent me the equivalent of a curtsy before darting out of the room. I called after her, but it was too late—she'd gone.

Turning to the approaching spook, I sent out a formal welcome, but this particular energy wasn't at all pleased and I could sense a hostility wafting through the ether. "John," I said, quickly moving back to stand near him.

"Yeah?"

"Uncap a grenade, but don't take it out unless I tell you."

There was a pop and a thunk as John uncorked the grenade and let the cap drop to the floor. The spook approaching us halted abruptly and stood about six feet away, just waiting and watching.

"We are very sorry to have disturbed you," I told him formally, and at this moment I was quite certain I was speaking to a "him."

Who are you? he demanded, his voice harsh in my mind.

"My name is M. J. and this is my friend John. Might I know who you are?"

I could almost feel the ghost puff out his chest and say, *I am Caron, and I demand to know what you are doing in my keep!*

"We're looking for two more of our friends who've become lost within the castle."

"Leave!" a disembodied voice demanded.

John flinched slightly and he tilted the tube with the spike, ready to drop it out of the canister. I placed my hand on his wrist and turned my attention back to the ghost. "We will," I promised. "The moment you tell us where we can find our friends."

"Leave now!"

Next to me, I could hear John's breathing become labored. He was starting to get freaked-out by the ghost's verbal command, and I really needed him to pull it together. "Dude!" I whispered, squeezing his wrist. "You have to remain calm!"

In the dim light, I saw John swallow hard and give a reluctant nod.

Turning back to the spook, I said, "We're not leaving without our friends, sir. So please tell us where we might find them, and we'll be on our way."

The angry ghost standing in front of us was growing increasingly impatient, I could tell, and I figured it was only a matter of time before something bad happened.

I was right, as just a few heartbeats later a wave of fear wafted in through the door behind us.

"Shit!" I swore, and turned John's wrist myself, tipping out the spike. I yelled, "Release all the spikes!"

Within seconds we each held several metallic spikes in our hands and I was by now trembling in fear. From outside something approached. I couldn't hear it as much as sense it, and beside me John gasped and looped his arm through mine. "What's happening?" he asked, his voice quavering slightly.

I closed my eyes and whispered a protection prayer as waves of fear wafted in through the doorway and all about the room. With dread, I waited for the intensity of the terror to increase and take over my mind, but it never went past the level that had already affected us. "Stand perfectly still," I ordered.

My flashlight was tucked under my arm and clenched firmly to my side. It pointed directly at the doorway across the room, illuminating a small section of the kitchen.

The beam was suddenly interrupted by a *very* large shadow that darted across the doorway almost too quickly for me to catch ... until the shadow returned and remained in my beam for several long seconds. John stiffened next to me, and like me, he was too frightened to breathe.

The shadow was at least eight feet tall. It looked a bit like a giant man standing in a cloak with the hood pulled up.

Who am I kidding? It looked like Death. All it needed to complete the ensemble was a scythe.

"Je-Je-*Jesus*!" John stuttered. I could feel his panic mounting, and I was terribly worried he'd drop his spikes and run.

"Stay still!" I commanded, feeling a bit of anger creep through my own fear. "John! Pull it together!"

But he was trembling and shaking so hard that I wasn't sure he'd heard me.

I got even madder then. I unloosed my arm from his and took one very bold step toward the phantom. "Get back!" I shouted, waving the spikes about. "Get away from us *now*!"

A laugh so horrible and so evil that it chilled me to the bone reverberated through the hall and into our room. I felt as if I'd been physically punched by it. In my mind's eye I then saw the image of Heath, running along the side of the castle, dodging the rain. He kept looking over his shoulder—as if he was running away from something—and all the while he got closer and closer to the edge of the cliff without slowing down.

A thousand warning bells went off in my head just as the phantom twirled in a tight circle, and with a whoosh, it was gone.

Moving all my spikes to one hand, I reached back for John and shouted, "Let's go!"

Running as fast as I could, I bolted through the old kitchen, down the corridor, and back to Gilley, Meg, and Kim. Without stopping to explain what had happened, I put a hand on John's chest, ordered him to stay with Meg and Kim, then hauled a very startled Gilley up off the floor where he'd been sitting by the fire. "Come with me!" I demanded.

Gilley opened his mouth to say something, but I was in far too much of a panic to let him utter a single word. "Don't speak!" I yelled, grabbing his hand and bolting out the door.

Thankfully, Gilley cooperated and ran stride for stride right next to me. Gil had been a sprinter on the track team when we were in high school—and he'd also been crowned state champ in his day.

I needed Gilley's speed if I had any hope of saving Heath. "Where're we going?" Gil shouted after we'd been running through the rain alongside the castle for a bit.

Instead of answering him, I gasped, nearly tripping when I finally saw what I'd been looking for up ahead. I pointed to the figure of Heath, running through the rain, covering his ears with his hands and blind with fright. He darted right, then left, dashing away in short zigzags. At intervals he also stopped and turned in a circle, as if he were blind and deaf to anything else but the nightmare playing out in his head. To add to the horror, just behind him lurked the phantom. It towered over Heath by at least three feet, a black menacing shadow, stalking our friend, herding him ever closer to the edge of the cliff.

Gilley squealed at the sight and abruptly stopped.

I had to stop myself and wheel around to come back to him. "*What are you doing? We have to get to Heath before he runs off the cliff!*"

Gilley was white with fright. His wet hair hung in his eyes, and his sweatshirt sagged against his frame. "But the phantom!"

"You're wearing the sweatshirt, Gil! It'll protect both you and Heath! But you've got to make it to him, and you're the only one who can sprint to him in time!"

Desperately I looked back over my shoulder, and gasped when I saw that Heath was now just a few yards from the edge of the cliff. Grabbing Gilley again by the hand, I hauled him forward and shouted, "*Heath! Stop! We're coming!*"

Gilley ran with me without fighting. I poured on the speed and Gilley matched me with every step, courage coming to him with every new stride. "Go, Gilley! Get to Heath!" I yelled as he began passing me.

I saw the firm set to Gilley's jaw as he moved on by, his feet moving faster and faster and his arms pumping for all he was worth. Heath continued to stumble and hold his head, and now I could hear his agonized voice. *"Make it stop!"*

"Heath!" I shouted again, desperate to get his attention before he moved too close to the cliff.

Gilley charged right for Heath, who was now only feet from the cliff's edge. The phantom stopped then and it had the appearance of turning to face me. There was no substance really to its form, just a giant black shadow watching Gilley running straight for Heath.

I hoped that Gilley's sweatshirt was enough to make it back off, and my heart pounded in my chest as much with exertion as with anxiety. *"Go, Gilley!"* I shouted again.

Gilley's stride came quicker still and he dug in with everything he was worth. I could hear him groan as he stretched those final yards, whizzing right past the phantom, who whirled away from him and darted to the side.

Heath meanwhile teetered on the very edge of the cliff, and I could tell that Gil would not make it in time, no matter how fast he was running. *"Please!"* I cried, and honestly, to this day I don't know whom I was calling out to, but at that moment a white light appeared between Heath and the edge of the cliff, causing him to twirl and fall back away from the edge, right onto his rear. The light appeared only for an instant, but the image of Samuel Whitefeather—Heath's grandfather—flashed through my mind.

Two more strides and Gilley launched himself, landing right on top of Heath and hugging him fiercely as he pulled our friend away from the deadly drop.

I was a good two dozen yards back and I came to a stop, winded and emotionally exhausted. I bent double and sucked in air until a cold chill prickled my spine. I stood up tall again and eyed the phantom, now planted firmly between me and the boys. "Oh, shit!" I said, realizing the demon was now thinking of me as the target. Whirling around and running back the way I'd come, I bolted away as fast as I could. By now my legs felt like rubber and I began to trip and stumble. I was also trying to get the two spikes I still had in the belt I wore around my waist, but my mind was quickly filling with awful images. I tried to focus on the ground ahead of me, but my vision became compromised as the pictures in my mind turned uglier and more intense.

My heart was racing with panic and fear and I couldn't seem to suck in enough oxygen. My hands were also shaking so hard that I had to abandon the effort to get the grenades loose. A terrible terror was welling up inside of me and I couldn't seem to get away. Somewhere, in the very back of my mind, I knew that I wasn't far from the front door to the castle, and the safety of John and the spikes, but I didn't think I'd make it in time. What was more, I felt something cold and cruel creeping up along my left side. I darted right out of instinct, but it kept coming.

A rational thought seeped through a crevice in the wall of terror filling my mind. It said that moving right would take me away from the center of the rock and move me out to the edge. Warning bells rang, but I felt helpless to stop the panicked dash away from that cold horror still creeping along my left.

I started to cry and shake, blinded by the nightmare images flashing across my mind and the terrible presence of the phantom. "Go away!" I shouted. "Get away from me!"

But the phantom kept coming, pushing me ever farther from safety. I cried out and for a split second I thought again of the white light that had saved Heath and of Samuel Whitefeather. *"Sam!"* I screamed. *"Help me!"*

A buzzing sound rang in my ears. I stumbled and fell to the ground. Closing my eyes, I covered my head with my arms and began to pray. The buzzing sound intensified and white light pushed away the awful nightmares, but I could still feel that cold menacing presence behind me. Still, in my mind I sensed Sam was doing his best to help protect me.

"Sam!" I shouted again, trying to cling to him for all I was worth.

Focus, M. J.! Sam's voice said in my head. *Think brave thoughts. Gather your courage. Do not give in to the phantom!*

I squeezed my eyes as tightly closed as I could and

attempted to call up every ounce of courage I could muster. "It's not real," I whispered desperately. "It's not real!"

Slowly I could feel the menacing presence ebbing away from me, and that bolstered my resolve. "It's not real!" I said a bit louder. "It's all a mirage!"

And with that, another whoosh sounded nearby along with the bright light shining in my mind, and I became conscious of the rain again, and the cold wind, and Gilley shouting at me from somewhere behind.

Lifting my chin, I watched as he and Heath approached. Heath looked terribly shaken and somewhat confused, but otherwise unharmed. Gilley had a death grip on Heath's arm while he tugged him forward as quickly as he could.

When they got to me, both boys were quite out of breath.

"Are . . . you . . . okay?" Heath asked, sinking to his knees to look me over and wipe the hair out of my eyes.

I nodded dully. "Yeah," I said, my voice cracking. "I'm okay."

"Jesus, honey!" Gil said, dropping to his knees as well to lean in and hug me fiercely. "When I saw that thing turn to chase you, I nearly had a heart attack!"

I laid my cheek against his damp hair and took several deep breaths, soaking up Gilley's body heat and the fact that I wasn't reliving my worst nightmares. When Gil pulled away, I looked back at Heath. "How you doin'?"

He forced a smile and I took in the haunted look in

his eyes. "It wouldn't stop," he whispered. "I mean, it chased me through the castle, and then it left me alone for a little while, but when I went back to try and find you guys, it came after me again. I couldn't get away from it, M. J. In the back of my mind I *knew* it was pushing me toward the cliffs, but after fighting with it again and again, I just didn't care anymore. I wanted it to end."

I knew exactly what he meant. "Let's get out of this rain and back to the others," I suggested. Gilley helped me to my feet, which was good because my limbs still felt rubbery and weak; I'd pushed myself well beyond my usual limits that day. Gilley then hooked his arm through mine and the other through Heath's and we started to walk.

After going only a few steps, Gilley looked at me curiously and said, "M. J., what's that?"

He was pointing to my hair. "What's what?" I asked, reaching my free hand up and running it along the back of my wet head. I connected with something tangled there and pulled it out, gasping when I realized what it was.

Gilley gave me a half smile. "How'd you get a white feather stuck in your hair out here?"

Heath's eyes locked with mine. "My grandfather," he said. "Our last name is Whitefeather."

"Looks like Sam saved both our lives today," I said, tucking the feather inside my coat. "Sam," I said, lifting my chin, "wherever you are, we owe you huge for that."

*   *   *

We found the rest of our group safely gathered around the fire back at the castle. Well, everyone except for Gopher, that is. Heath and I collapsed next to each other by the fire, both of us spent and exhausted.

No one spoke for a very long time while we waited for our clothes to dry and periodically fed the fire with wood we found scattered around the great hall. Outside, the storm picked up again and the steady rain gave way to another round of thunder and lightning. Everyone was so on edge that we all jumped with every loud boom.

Finally, John broke the silence. "We've got to get off this rock. It'll be dark in a few hours and there's no way I'm staying here all night."

Gilley frowned and gave John a disapproving look. "We can't leave without Gopher."

But John had had all afternoon to work himself into a foul mood. "I say we leave him here," he groused. "The guy goes wandering off. Let him find his own way back."

"We can't leave him," Gilley snapped. "You saw what happened to Heath! What if the phantom tries to push Gopher over the cliffs too?"

John got up and went to look out the door at the raging storm. Turning back to face us, he said, "Well, we can't stay here, Gilley. I don't care how many magnets we have—that thing is way too freaky for us to handle. We can't search the castle in the state we're in. Look at M. J. and Heath! They're exhausted! And we've been waiting for Gopher all afternoon and there's no sign of him. We can't just sit and wait for the phantom to come back and pick us off one by one. We've *got* to get outta here!"

"You think we'll be any safer at the base of the rock?" I asked. He looked at me like I'd insulted him, so I was quick to add, "The storm surge is probably still covering the causeway. We can hope that by six thirty, when the tide is at its lowest point, we'll have another window to cross, but if not, we could be stuck here all night. And I'm not sure the shore is any safer than here, but I do know that at least we'll be dry and somewhat warm inside the castle."

"That's true," said Heath. "But at least down on the shore the phantom can't push us off the edge of a cliff. I'm with John, M. J. I don't know how much longer I can stay here. Can't you *feel* that thing?"

I could. Even with every magnetic spike we owned out and exposed, I could still feel the phantom, lurking somewhere close, just waiting for one of us to become vulnerable again.

And I knew I was too exhausted to go looking for Gopher. He hadn't shown up and it'd been hours.

"Maybe we can find an overhang to camp out under on the shore, M. J.," Gilley reasoned, suddenly switching sides. "Or a cave or something. We could take a bunch of wood down with us and get a fire going. I'd rather take a chance at getting out of here tonight than stay in this place another minute."

"Are we really prepared to leave Gopher here?" I asked the group.

John came back to squat down next to me. "We'll send a search party for him the moment we get back to dry land, but for now we've got to get off this rock and find someplace else warm and dry."

I looked to Heath, but he only shrugged. "I don't have it in me to go looking for him, M. J. I can't take another encounter with that phantom tonight. I'm sorry, but I just can't."

I then looked to the faces around the dwindling fire. They were all really scared, and worried, and guilt-ridden, and I knew that we had to go. With a sigh I finally agreed. "Fine. Let's make our way down the steps as soon as the lightning and thunder pass, and bring along a bunch of the wood. We'll make camp until four thirty and try the causeway then."

Going down those steps in the dwindling light, pelted by rain and wind, was almost as bad as going up them had been. Especially since I was so physically wiped out.

This time the roles had all been reversed; Meg and Kim were helping each other, John was helping Heath, and Gilley was helping me—and, might I add, complaining all the way. "Have you put on weight?" he asked, adjusting my arm around his shoulder for the tenth time.

I tugged on my arm and pulled slightly away from him. "I can make it on my own!" I snapped. "You just stick close to me with your magic sweatshirt, okay?"

Gilley's brow furrowed with disapproval. "Fine, do it yourself, but don't trip."

With a tired sigh I leaned heavily on the railing and focused on the task at hand, lifting one foot up to set it down on the stair below. By my estimation it was still a very long way down, and I wondered if this day would ever end.

Farther on, Heath and John looked to be making good progress, and Kim and Meg were doing great too. They hadn't said much since we'd arrived on this rock, and I felt bad for taking them to such a scary and treacherous place.

After a few more steps I leaned a little to my left and looked over the railing. I could see the high waves rolling and crashing onto the rocky shore below. Turning my head, I said, "I don't think we'll be able to get across the causeway until well after low tide, Gil."

He nodded grimly. "I know. I've seen those waves too. The best we can hope for is that they die down by eight o'clock."

I shivered in the cold. "Hopefully, you're right and we can find a cave or an overhang or something for a little shelter."

"I think I saw a cave when Heath and Gopher went to look for that dead guy who turned out to be a ghost."

"Where?"

"On the other side of the stairs. It looked big enough for all of us to fit inside."

I brightened a bit. A cave would provide some good shelter and we could build a nice fire until seven or seven thirty, when we would have to check on the conditions for crossing the causeway again.

That thought gave me just the little bit of energy I needed to help me down the next group of stairs. And

I was doing fairly well until I heard an anguished voice cry out, *"Alex!"*

Gilley and I both whipped our heads around and stared at the top of the steps. Instead of seeing our familiar ghost, we saw a huge black shadow at the top of the landing. Gilley shrieked and grabbed onto me. "The phantom!"

My blood ran cold as I stared at it, the edges of its shadow whipping to and fro as if the phantom was wearing a long cloak and it was being blown by the wind. "He's not coming after us," I whispered, and took a tentative step onto the next stair.

Gilley hopped down with me. "Let's keep going!" he squeaked.

With that, we hurried as best we could, both of us periodically looking over our shoulders at the phantom still watching us from the top of the steps.

We reached the others, panting and trembling. Meg and Kim seemed startled by the fact that we were suddenly right on top of them. "What's happening?" Meg asked.

"Don't talk," I advised, leaning heavily on Gil again. "Just move!"

The girls did as they were told without question and the six of us reached the bottom shortly thereafter. Gilley continued to stare up at the steps leading down, as if waiting for that ominous shape to appear.

"The causeway's completely covered," called John from the small platform that marked its beginning.

"Gilley said he saw a cave over that way," I said, pointing to the right of the stairs.

"Can you take us there?" Heath asked.

Gil nodded, still looking very afraid as he hurried along the rocks in the direction of the cave he'd seen.

We shuffled after him and to my surprise and relief discovered he'd really spotted a good one after all.

Because the cave sat just to the right of the stairs, which butted out away from the rock, it was sheltered from the worst of the wind, and if not exactly warm, it was at least dry inside.

Gil, John, Meg, and Kim all pulled out as much wood as their backpacks had allowed them to carry, plus there was quite a bit of driftwood within the cave's entrance, and before long we had a terrific little bonfire going.

We all huddled around it eagerly, and Gilley generously handed out several extra muffins he'd bought at the café. They were squished from being in his pack all day, but no one cared because it was food and beggars weren't about to be choosers.

Heath and I finished our snacks quickly and leaned against each other sleepily. I was still very worried about Gopher, but I was physically and mentally exhausted. Taking a quick peek at my watch, I saw that we still had a few hours before the causeway was clear again, so I thought there couldn't be much harm in closing my eyes and getting just a little sleep.

Judging by the slow regular breathing coming from Heath, he'd decided the same thing. So I closed my eyes and drifted off. . . .

"Hello, miss," said a male voice.

I was aware that I was leaning against the bark of a

massive oak tree under a sunlit sky with the sound of the ocean all around. As I looked farther, I could see that the oak was sitting in the center of a mammoth piece of flat rock, and to one side was the vast openness of the sea, to the other, the bluffs of the Irish coastline and just to my left was the unmistakable shape of Dunlow Castle.

"Who's there?" I asked.

A man in period attire of black leather leggings, knee-high boots, and a brilliant blue tunic stepped out from behind the tree. He was tall and incredibly handsome, with jet-black hair and ice blue eyes. He smiled roguishly at me, and I felt my pulse quicken. "It's only me," he said, his voice a bit hoarse and quite sexy.

I inhaled deeply. My God, the man even smelled good: a mixture of spice and musk. "And *who* might you be, exactly?"

The man bowed formally. "Lord Ranald Dunnyvale, at your service."

I mentally scratched my head. Where had I heard that name before? "Nice to meet you," I said with a nod. "Have we met before?"

Ranald tilted his head back and gave a small laugh. "No, my lady, not formally. But I have seen you dashing about my castle the past several hours."

I gasped. "*Your* castle?"

"Aye."

I blinked at him. "Wait a minute," I said, holding up a hand to stop him from commenting further. I felt like I just needed a second or two to catch up. And then I had it. "You're the man who hid the gold!"

Again, Ranald tipped his head back and gave a hearty chuckle. "Well-done, miss," he said formally with another bow.

I felt my insides go all warm and gooey, and I could have spent the entire rest of the day sitting under that lovely tree and trying to make that gorgeous man laugh again. And then of course, I realized I was speaking to a ghost. Nothing kills the mood of a little flirt-flirt like realizing you're talking to a dead guy. "I'm sorry if we trespassed on your property," I told him.

He winked at me. "It's not the trespassing I mind so much as the hunting for me gold."

I gulped. "Yeah, well, you don't have to worry about that anymore. At least not from us. That phantom's guarding it *really* well."

"Ah, yes, the phantom," he said, walking over to sit down next to me under the tree. "About that . . ."

"Yes?"

"I'd like you to rid my castle of the phantom."

I stared at him incredulously. "And I'd like to see a pig fly, but it doesn't look like either of us will get our wish anytime soon."

Again Ranald laughed merrily. "Ah, but you're a brash lass, now, aren't you?"

"I have my moments."

"How might I convince you to take on the phantom?"

My brow furrowed, and I squinted at Ranald. "Why is

it so important to get rid of it? I mean, isn't it guarding your gold after all?"

"It's scaring the others," he said to me. "All those wonderful souls who stayed behind to look after my keep can hardly function with that dreadful creature lurking about."

"But wasn't it you who brought it here in the first place?"

Ranald appeared taken aback. "Oh, why, no, lass!" he said. "It wasn't me a'tall."

"Who was it, then?"

"I've no idea, but in order to find your friend, you must deal with the phantom."

I shook my head. "Wait . . . what?"

"Your tall friend with the funny cap," he explained.

"You mean Gopher?"

"Oh, I don't know his name, my lady, but I do know that all your efforts to recover him lie along the path of getting rid of that dreadful phantom."

I felt alarm bells go off in my head. "Do you know where our friend is?" I asked carefully.

"I do."

"But you're not going to tell me unless I agree to help you with the phantom, right?"

"Correct. In part at least; I shall tell you where your friend is if you rid my castle of the phantom."

I sighed in exasperation. "Lord Dunnyvale, did you not *see* how clearly our asses got kicked by that thing? Do you not *realize* how deadly it can be? One of my friends almost *died* up there! Hell, *I* almost died up there!"

But Ranald was unfazed. "Ah, but *you* didn't die, miss! In fact, I watched you fight back. No one has ever been able to hold their own against the phantom . . . until you."

I shook my head again. What was this guy even talking about? "Are you insane?!" I yelled at him. "I didn't fight back! I barely managed to stay on the rock without falling over the edge!"

But Lord Dunnyvale wasn't buying it. "You did fight back, lass. I saw it. You reached out to the spirits beyond, and someone very powerful answered. I've waited some time for someone with powers like yours to come here and help me with the phantom, and at last, you're here."

"You don't understand!" I cried. "I can't take that thing on! It's way too powerful! And all the time we're sitting here arguing about it, my friend is at the mercy of that thing. He's probably going completely insane right now!"

"He'll not go insane," Ranald assured me. "Well, no more than he already was. The man's a bit daft, don't you agree?"

I inhaled and exhaled slowly. There was no way to argue with a ghost. They're impossibly stubborn sometimes. "You want me to defeat this thing, Lord Dunnyvale, and I'm telling you that I don't even know where to begin!"

"Ah," he said with a knowing grin. "That may be

something I can assist you with. Begin with the mystery of Alex. You'll learn so much by starting there."

I squinted at him again. "What?" I asked. "What does that even *mean*?"

Instead of answering, Ranald got to his feet and tipped his head to me. Then he turned without a word and strolled away.

"Hey!" I called after him. "Wait! I don't understand! Come back here and talk to me some more!"

"M. J.!" I heard from somewhere off to my right.

Distracted, I turned my head, but no one was there.

"M. J.!" I heard again.

Then I was being roughly shaken by unseen hands, and I felt myself startle awake and I was staring into Heath's intensely brown eyes. "What's going on?" I muttered, realizing I'd only been asleep and having a very vivid dream.

"It's Gilley!" he said urgently.

"What about him?"

"He's gone!"

Chapter 5

I jumped to my feet and stared around the cave, searching for Gilley. Heath, Meg, Kim, and John were staring back at me, but Gilley was nowhere in sight. "Where'd he go?" I demanded.

Meg and Kim shrugged and John explained, "We were all asleep. I woke up about ten minutes ago, and realized the fire was getting low, so I went to get some driftwood and when I came back, I saw that Gilley wasn't in the cave. I checked around, and he's nowhere."

A thought occurred to me. "What time is it?"

"A little after seven."

"Did you check the causeway?"

John shook his head. "No."

I grabbed one of the flashlights and dashed out of the cave. Hurrying past the stairs, I barely resisted the urge to look up because I could almost feel the presence of the phantom staring down at us from high above. Running over to the causeway, I stopped at the platform and saw that the storm surge had subsided a bit, but it was still gusting and waves were still washing up over the worn cobblestones.

"Gilley!" I shouted across the water.

When no one replied, I called again . . . and again . . . and again. By the end I was practically screeching.

"Where could he have gone?" Heath said, moving up next to me.

My heart was racing and panic coursed through my veins. "I don't know," I told him as tears welled up into my eyes for the third time that day. "But we have to find him!"

Heath looked uncertainly up the stairs. "He wouldn't have gone back up, would he?"

Deep in my gut I felt strongly that Gil wouldn't have willingly gone there, and I was quite certain that if the phantom had come down the stairs and entered our cave, we would have known it. The demon was just too powerful.

"He wouldn't have gone back up," I said firmly, "and why he moved away from our group I have no idea. I mean, Gil's practically attached at my hip even when we're not in some haunted location—so I can't imagine why he'd leave us without saying anything."

It then occurred to me that Heath and I were the only ones out there. "Where're the others?"

"Back at the cave."

I took his hand. "Come on, we have to make sure we stay together and don't lose one more person. We'll look for Gilley as a group."

Heath and I hurried back to the cave and saw that

Kim and Meg hadn't moved, but John was nosing around near the back of the cave.

"Did you find him?" Meg asked.

I shook my head. "John!" I called. "We have to stay together."

"I found a set of footprints," he said in reply while waving us over. Heath and I darted over to join him. "What size shoe does Gilley wear?"

I stared down at the footprints. They were about Gilley's size. "He went this way!" I said, and darted forward to follow the prints.

Heath caught me by the shoulder. "Remember, we go everywhere as a group."

I nodded distractedly and waited for him to call to Kim and Meg, and then, when everyone was huddled together, we moved forward, pointing our flashlights down at the ground to track the footprints.

They led to the very back of the cave and a somewhat narrow tunnel, where the sand stopped and stone became part of the floor. "He must have gone in there," I reasoned.

"How can you tell?" asked Meg.

"Because there are no footprints coming out." Without waiting around to discuss it, I boldly entered the tunnel and began hurrying along. Shuffling noises behind me told me the others had followed.

The tunnel was wide enough for two people to walk abreast, and Heath quickened his pace to come up next to me. In his hand, I noticed, he firmly held on to two spikes. "That's a good idea," I said, handing over my flashlight long enough to pull out my own two spikes. Over my shoulder I held them up and told the others, "Make sure you're armed, people."

With a bit of satisfaction I heard the plastic caps on the canisters being removed and the sliding metal of spikes as our crew followed orders.

The tunnel curved slightly ahead, and I could see a beam of light coming from it. Heath placed an arm across my middle, stopping me, and John, Meg, and Kim came up to huddle right behind us. "We don't know if Gilley's in there, so let me go first," he whispered cautiously.

I shook my head. "No. We're stronger as a group. We go in together."

Three other heads nodded vigorously. "Okay," Heath relented, removing his arm from in front of me. I stepped forward, and the tunnel opened up to a good-sized cavern, in the center of which sat my best friend, cross-legged on the floor with his back to us, thumbing through a weathered old journal.

"Gilley!" I cried when I saw him.

"Ahhhhhhhhhhhhhhhhhhhh!" he screamed, jumping to his feet and reeling backward.

"Shhhhhhh!" Heath commanded.

"Ahhhhhhhhhhhhhhhhhhhhh!" Gil repeated.

"Stop it!" I ordered.

"Hee, hee, hee!" Gil wheezed, grabbing his chest with one hand like Redd Foxx while his eyes bulged out to stare at us.

I moved quickly into the cavern and up to him. "Honey," I said, gripping him by the arms. "It's us."

"You scared me!" he shouted.

"Gil," Heath warned, putting a finger to his lips. "Keep it down, buddy."

Gilley took a few more deep breaths and continued to stare at us with his wide eyes. "Why does it matter how loud I am?" he finally asked.

"We don't know what's in here," I said to him. "This cavern could be haunted too."

Gilley's wide eyes got even bigger. "It could?"

"You didn't think of that before you came in here?"

"No!" he shouted, looking around wildly.

Heath gave him a dirty look but didn't reprimand him again, which was wise, because when Gil gets really worked up, it's hard to rein him in. "What were you doing in here by yourself, honey?" I asked in a nice soothing tone.

Gil blinked and took a minute to answer me. "We were low on firewood. Everyone else was asleep, so I went to look for more, and I found the tunnel at the back of the cave, and I was just curious to see where it led—you know, in case the gold was hidden back here—and I came to this room and found all that."

Gilley pointed his flashlight to where he'd been squatting and it was then that I noticed the makeshift camp.

There were a dust-covered lantern, two sleeping bags, a kerosene heater, and a couple of backpacks. And something else caught my eye and made me gasp.

"What?" asked Heath as I moved away from Gilley to the object on the ground.

"Look!" I said, squatting down to pick it up.

Heath's face registered complete surprise when I held it up. "No way!" he said, hurrying over to me to inspect the metal spike I'd just picked up. "Is it magnetized?"

I stood up and moved to one of the packs. When I held the spike near one of the buckles, we all heard a clink as the metals connected. I inspected the spike closely. "Magnetized spikes are standard equipment for most serious paranormal investigators," I said.

"Whoa!" said John. "Ghostbusters were in this cave?"

"That's not all," Gilley added smartly, and he moved away from the wall to the journal, which he'd dropped when we called his name. "Guess whose journal this is!" he said.

No one said anything.

"Go on! Guess!"

Again, we all just waited him out and said nothing.

"Wrong!" he crowed, completely ignoring the fact that we weren't playing along. "It belonged to Jordan Kincaid."

My jaw dropped. "The guy who fell off the cliffs?"

Gilley smiled like a Cheshire cat and held out the journal to me. I took it and inspected the cover. The leather-bound book had the initials *JCK* embossed in the lower right-hand corner, and I opened it and studied the contents.

Kincaid had very symmetrical writing; he didn't use cursive, but wrote in a block style. His sentence structure was short and to the point, and I wondered if his conversations with people went that way too.

"Did you read this?" I asked Gil, already knowing the answer.

"Of course I read it! And you won't *believe* what I found in there!"

"What?" Heath asked.

"Kincaid was gay!"

I did a mental head scratch. Thinking back to an interview I'd seen of Jordan Kincaid on *60 Minutes*, I'd never have guessed he played on Gilley's team.

"He was gay?" Heath said. "Man, I saw him in an interview a few years ago and I didn't get that vibe from him at all."

"Me either," I said. "Are you sure, Gil?"

Gilley looked insulted. "Of course I'm sure!" he insisted. "My gaydar is never off."

One of my eyebrows rose skeptically. "Your gaydar is *always* off, Gil."

"Nuh-uh!" he snapped.

I waved an impatient hand at him. "You think everyone in the world is gay."

"That's because everyone in the world *is* gay—they just haven't admitted it yet." With that, Gilley bounced his eyebrows at Heath, who cleared his throat uncomfortably and moved a little closer to me.

I sighed. We didn't have time for Gilley's games. "What is it about this particular journal that tells you Kincaid may have preferred men?"

Gilley held his hand out for the journal and I gave it back to him. Turning to the middle section, he pulled out a folded letter, which he then handed to me.

I looked at it for a moment before unfolding it and held it so that Heath could read it over my shoulder. It read:

Dear Alex:

If you're reading this, I'm probably dead, and if that's the case, then I'm really sorry that I insisted we come here. I know I haven't always been honest with you, and I also know it's been tough keeping you in the shadows so that no one found out about us, but I want you to know that I love you.

Loved you.

And, wherever I am right now, I'm probably still head over heels for you and only you. Those groupie girls never mattered to me; they were only to keep up appearances and I hope you know that. I knew you were the one the very first time we met, and I've never doubted it. I'm so sorry I left without telling you to your face. I hope you understand that once this job was over, I planned on telling the whole world about us. I meant what I said last week. I wanted to marry you and I don't give a damn what my parents think. And if we had come back with the gold, well, we could have lived an amazing life together, away from prying eyes and judgment.

Anyway, the one thing you have to do for me if I don't come back is get off this stinking rock and never, EVER come back. I've figured out where Dunnyvale hid his gold, and it's not anywhere we thought. It's in a place that's kind of impossible to get to, and I can't risk taking you with me because if anything happened to you, I couldn't handle it. I'm going in alone, and I really hope I come back to you. If I don't make it past the phantom tonight, then you have to leave, because you will have been right—this job was too much for us.

The note ended cryptically there with just Jordan's signature, and I felt my heart go out to the man I'd assumed was just another shallow rich playboy, living off his trust fund. I also had to agree with Gilley—the letter really did point to Kincaid's preference for men . . . or Alex at least.

I sighed and folded the letter carefully back up. Tucking it into my back pocket to review later, I said, "So what happened to Alex?"

Gil shrugged. "Dunno. The last journal entry was written to Alex as well." Gilley flipped through the pages of the journal and handed this to me again. I read the entry out loud so that everyone could hear.

"'Dear Alex. I know you waited until I was asleep to sneak off to the crypts, and I know you think they're safe from the phantom, but I woke up to tell you that the answer came to me in my sleep. We've been looking in all the wrong places, and I now realize exactly where both the disk and the gold are. I see you've only left me a few spikes, but I'm going for it. If I don't make it back, this letter is for you.'"

"Crypts?" Heath asked. "The castle's got crypts?"

"Disk?" Kim said. "What disk is he talking about, and where did he think the gold was?"

I turned to look at Gilley, hoping that he might have a clue, but he only shrugged and shook his head. "Got me," he said. "I haven't had a chance to look through the whole journal yet. I just got finished reading that letter when you guys all sneaked up on me."

I remembered the ghost of Lord Dunnyvale, and his instruction to start with Alex. But I couldn't commit my team to such a dangerous undertaking as ridding the castle of the phantom right now.

"We need a plan to deal with this phantom and get Gopher back," I said to the group when I realized they were all looking at me expectantly. "But first we need to get off this freaking pile of rubble. Let's see if we can get back across the causeway." I then turned and led my team out of the cave, pausing only briefly to say, "Gilley, bring that journal."

We made our way out of the cavern, back through the tunnel, and finally out of the cave to the shore. With some relief, I realized it had stopped raining. I held my flashlight up, and although the causeway was slick, and there was the occasional small wave that crested over the edge, it looked passable. "We'll need to hustle," Heath advised, looking at his watch. "We've only got about twenty minutes left to get across it."

Without speaking, I stepped onto the causeway and started to jog. Gilley must have decided that he needed to be the first one to reach the beach at the other end, because he flew by me. "Be careful!" I called. "It's slippery."

And no sooner had I said that than Gilley tripped and went down. "Uh-oh," Heath grunted, moving past me to hurry to Gilley's side.

My best friend was holding his knee pathetically and whining. "Ow, ow, ow!"

I hustled over to him and crouched down. "You okay?"

"NO!" he yelled, right in my ear.

"Dude," I growled, standing up, really irritated with him and this whole stupid adventure.

"Sorry," he groused. "But that hurt."

I inhaled and extended my hand. Gil took it and I helped him up. He limped for a step or two, but then seemed all right.

"What's that?" Meg said from behind me.

A chill ran down my spine, and I looked behind me back toward the rock, but then I noticed that Meg was looking down about six feet out into the water where the journal was just starting to sink below the waves.

I pointed my flashlight where I saw her looking and gasped. *"Gilley!"* I yelled, sinking to my own knees and trying to reach out to it. "You dropped the journal!"

Heath's hand landed firmly on my waistband and he pulled me back from the edge. "Careful!" he said. "The water's deeper than it looks here and the currents are likely to pull you under if you fall in."

I got back to my feet and sent an exasperated look at Gilley. He looked mournfully up at me. "I'm sorry!"

I was so angry that I simply turned and stomped off.

Heath came with me and slipped his hand into mine. "It was an accident, M. J.," he said after a bit.

"It was careless," I said through gritted teeth.

"We can figure this all out without it," he insisted reasonably. "And at least you still have the letter."

I stopped and blinked up at him. "I do?" And then I felt all my pockets discovering that I'd tucked the letter into my back pocket. With a relieved sigh I started walking again. "A load of good that'll do us," I said after a bit, my foul mood returning. "The important parts were all in the journal."

When we finally reached the shore, our feet and pants up to our shins were all soaking and I couldn't have been more cold, tired, and miserable. All I wanted to do was crawl into the van and point it back to the B&B.

We found the van right where we'd left it, but only then realized that Gopher had taken the keys. "Look in his backpack," I told John, who'd been shouldering it all the way from the top of the rock.

John sifted through the contents while Heath shone his flashlight into the interior. No keys.

"I think I saw him put them in his pocket after we got out of the van this morning," Kim said quietly.

"*Why* did we only take one van this morning?" Gilley wailed.

I remembered that it had been Gopher's idea. He'd wanted to save on gas.

Bone-weary and in a now truly terrible mood, I stared up the road and began to walk. "Looks like we're hoofin' it," muttered John from behind me.

I sighed again. This night just continued to offer up crap sandwiches. Heath held out his hand to me as we got to the steep part of the climb up the road. "Come on," he said. "It can't be that far."

Unfortunately, it was close to five miles. It took us well over an hour to reach the B&B. When we arrived, there was a note on the door from Anya saying that she was sorry we'd missed dinner, but that she'd have a hearty breakfast waiting for us in the morning.

Once we'd tiptoed inside, Meg asked, "Should we use the other van to go alert the authorities about Gopher?"

I was beyond exhausted by then, and every muscle in my body ached, but thoughts of Gopher's welfare made me say, "Yeah. We need to see if they'd be willing to send a search party to the castle."

But Heath reminded me about the permissive-access paper Gopher had shown the constable. "They'll never go for it. We assumed all risks when we went to the rock. You heard what that constable said, that the village wouldn't help us if anything happened. Plus, if they do go, that phantom's likely to make mincemeat out of them."

"We can't just leave Gopher there alone," I argued. "Seriously, Heath, we've got to do *something*."

"I can go," said John. "You two did more running around than me. Plus, the keys to the van are in my room. I can go file a report at least."

Heath sighed wearily. "Yeah, okay, John. Thanks."

John moved quickly and quietly up the stairs, and everyone else worked their way up at a much slower speed. "I'm so tired I don't even think I'll change. I just want to do a face-plant into my pillow," said Meg.

"Me too," said Kim.

"Me three," said Gil.

Heath and I did not play along this time, but I was thinking, *Me four . . . big-time.*

I don't remember my head hitting the pillow. I don't even remember the final steps to my room. I do remember falling immediately into a deep and blissful slumber, and somewhere near daybreak Lord Dunnyvale visited me again. "Hello, good lady Holliday," he said cordially.

"Lord Dunnyvale," I replied, with a dip of my chin.

"Have you considered my offer?"

"I have," I told him. "And I don't think I like the terms."

Dunnyvale appeared taken aback. "Why, I thought they were quite agreeable," he said to me. "Don't you want to see your friend again?"

"Of course I do. But it hardly seems fair that the longer you hide his whereabouts from me, the more likely it is that he's in mortal danger."

"Ah," said Dunnyvale. "Yes, that's a good point. Shall I sweeten the deal with a little bullion?"

I blinked at him. "A little what?"

"Gold, dear. A little gold."

Was he for real?

"I don't want your gold, Lord Dunnyvale. I want my friend."

But Ranald eyed me with a look that suggested he didn't believe me. "Everyone wants the gold, lass."

I glared at Dunnyvale. "I *said* I didn't want it, Lord Dunnyvale. I just want my friend."

"Yes, well, start with Alex, then follow the trail to the gold, and there you shall find the clues that will lead you to your friend. You can't have one without the other, I'm afraid, and you can't do the last without dealing with the phantom."

I rolled my eyes. "You talk in riddles, my lord."

Dunnyvale gave me a look of mock surprise. "Do I?" he said coyly. "Why, I believe I've spoken quite plainly."

And with that, I woke up to the thin pink light of dawn seeping in through the blinds, and Gilley's soft snores in the next bed.

"Gil," I whispered.

"ZZZZZZZ . . . ," he said.

I frowned. He looked really deep in sleep, and he was a bear to wake at times like that, but I really wanted to talk this whole visitation from the lord of Dunlow Castle over with someone.

"Gilley!" I said, right into his ear.

"ZZZZZZ . . . *snort* . . . ZZZZZZ," he replied.

"Fine," I told him. "Have it your way."

With that, I moved off to the shower and soaked up all the hot water.

A bit later, showered, in clean clothes, and feeling quite refreshed, I tiptoed out of the room in search of food. As I closed the door softly behind me, I found myself staring right into a manly bare chest. "Morning," said Heath, his voice husky with fatigue.

I felt a blush hit my cheeks. "Hey, there. You're up early."

The corners of Heath's mouth lifted. "Thought I'd grab a quick shower before everyone else took the hot water, but I couldn't get the temp above lukewarm for some reason."

The heat in my cheeks intensified. "That may have been my fault."

Heath's grin widened. "I thought I heard you in there. Maybe next time we could share."

Sweat broke out onto my forehead, and my eyes darted to the floor. I opened my mouth to say something clever—and absolutely nothing came out.

I thought of making an excuse and darting away, but Heath wound his strong muscled arms around me and pulled me close. "I've missed you," he whispered into my hair.

Jesus, he smelled good. I wrapped my own arms around him. His skin was soft and smooth under my touch, and holding on to him, I felt safe and good.

He rocked us gently back and forth, and for the longest time that was all we did, just held each other and swayed a little. I wanted to kiss him—hell, I wanted to throw him down and mount him—but as I tilted my chin up, my stomach gave a loud rumble.

The romantic moment evaporated and Heath chuckled. "Hungry?"

Another blush hit my cheeks. "Yeah, you?"

Heath's eyes smoldered into mine. "Oh, I'm famished, M. J. But enough flirting. Let's get you something to eat."

Heath turned away, still holding my hand, and I boldly stood firm, pulling him back. He looked curiously at me, and I took a chance, leaned in, and touched my lips to his.

He inhaled sharply and there was a sizzle of energy that crackled between us. He then kissed me long and passionately and I wondered why it'd taken us so long to do something that felt so amazing.

We probably could've gone on like that for a while, but someone cleared his throat loudly behind us and we both jumped back. "Morning," John said, his eyes looking anywhere but at us.

I fiddled nervously with my hair and Heath looked slightly chagrined. "We were just . . . uh . . . ," Heath said, his voice trailing off as he looked at me for help.

"Heading down to breakfast."

John cleared his throat again. "Thought you two would want an update on the search for Gopher."

I bit my lower lip. Damn. I'd briefly forgotten all about our producer, and I felt awful for indulging in a little tongue hockey instead of focusing on finding him.

"Did the authorities find him?" Heath asked.

John shook his head. "No. I smell pancakes and I think Anya's making us some breakfast. I'll fill you in downstairs."

We trooped quietly after John to the first floor and made our way to the rather cramped dining room.

"Well, there you all are!" Anya said happily. "I've been watchin' for you, but I didn't want to disturb your sleep when you likely got in so late. Am I right?"

I sat down next to Heath and under the table he squeezed my hand. "This looks amazing," he told her, nodding at the spread on the table.

I had to agree. There was an enormous plate of pancakes in the center, flanked by both sausage and bacon, a huge bowl of sliced fruit, juice, tea, coffee, muffins—enough food for an entire platoon of soldiers . . .

"Are those *pancakes* I smell?"

. . . or one Gilley.

My best friend bounded into the dining room with a flourish and immediately took his seat and began piling hotcakes onto his plate. "I'll just have a little," he said to those of us staring at his lack of decorum. "I don't want to go overboard on the carbs, you know."

I counted five pancakes on his plate.

Patting his stomach, he added, "I've got to watch my figure and all." Gilley's attention then snapped to a large basket in the center of the table. "Oooh! You made muffins too?"

"They're blueberry," said Anya, her face flush with pride as she watched Gilley sweep aside the towel keeping them warm.

He then picked the largest muffin, which was nearly bursting with blueberries, and plopped it onto his plate. "Has anyone seen the butter?"

I rolled my eyes and handed him the small dish with what looked like freshly whipped butter. Gil snatched it greedily and began slathering it onto his muffin. "I'll just have a nibble," he vowed, before taking a *huge* bite.

Tearing my eyes away from Gilley, I turned to John again and asked, "How'd it go with the authorities last night?"

John took two pancakes from the plate in the center. "It didn't go well."

"Mmuff mwpned?" said Gilley, still chewing on the half of the muffin he'd stuffed into his piehole.

"What'd he say?" John asked me.

"He said, 'What happened?'" I speak fluent Gilley, no matter what language he's talking.

John eyed Gil, now thirstily gulping down a large glass of juice. "Uh ... they said that, given the storm surge and currents around the rock, that they couldn't get a boat out to check out the island until this morning, and they also said that the most they'd be able to do is to search the base of the rock. They flat out told me they would *not* be going up the stairs to the castle."

I stopped spreading butter on my own muffin and looked at John. "Damn. I was afraid of that. They really won't help us search the castle?"

John shook his head. "Nope. They were definitely firm on that point. They pretty much repeated what it said on Gopher's permissive-access papers. That anyone who goes up those stairs is assuming the risk of great bodily harm or death, and they can't be responsible for someone who gets lost up there or doesn't come back from Dunlow Castle."

"Myrf gddig!" said Gilley, crumbs dribbling onto his sweatshirt.

"No, he's not kidding," I told Gil, before focusing back on John. "So the most they'll do is, what? Walk around the base of the cliffs looking for Gopher's dead body?"

John sighed heavily and leaned back in his chair. "They won't even do that, M. J. They said that they would only be willing to send a boat, take a few circles around the rock at high tide, and see if they spotted anything. If they saw a dead body, then they'd consider landing onshore. Otherwise, we're on our own."

"That is unbelievable!" I nearly shouted. "I mean, I know Gopher agreed to the no-rescue terms, but *how* can they justify not helping us?"

"They've lost a member of their own crew, miss," said Anya.

I realized suddenly that she was still in the room, and listening to our conversation. "I'm sorry," I said to her. "What did you say?"

Anya came over to the table and pulled out a chair. Sitting down, she looked at us gravely for a moment before speaking. "Am I to understand you've left one of your group back at Dunlow Castle?"

I nodded. "Our producer, Peter Gophner, became separated from the rest of us and we were unable to locate him."

Anya's face twitched and there was a haunted look in her eyes. Lowering her voice, she asked, "Did you see the phantom?"

Heath and I exchanged a look, and I knew he was wondering how much to tell her.

"Mwf," said Gilley, with a vigorous nod and crumbs dotting his chin.

"Oh, my," said Anya, crossing herself before continuing. "That curse has been a bane on this village for some time now. If I'd have known you were off to explore Dunlow, I would have warned you like I did the others who came through here."

Anya had my full attention. "Others?" I asked. "What others?"

Anya shifted uncomfortably. "Many a guest here has asked me about Castle Dunlow and I always warn them not to go there. A few years back there was an incident at the rock, you see. A young man fell to his death, and the coast guard was called to investigate. One of their new recruits made his way to the top of the rock, and was immediately set upon by the phantom. Within moments, he too was tossed over the side to his death." Anya then made the sign of the cross, clearly disturbed by the local story. "As we've lost one of our own, my American friends, I'm afraid our good lads at the coast guard'll not be so willing to venture up those stairs ever again, even for the sake of your friend. They believe it's simply too dangerous."

"So what do we do?" Heath asked her.

Anya exhaled, made another sign of the cross, and refused to meet Heath's eyes. "At this point, you can only pray, lad. Just pray."

Chapter 6

Anya left us alone after that and no one spoke for several minutes. Finally, Heath broke the silence and he said exactly what I was thinking. "We can't just leave him there."

"We have to go back and search for him," I agreed.

"But how do we get around the phantom?" asked John. "Guys, I'm all for rescuing Gopher, but that spook is *seriously* dangerous, and I'm not interested in getting myself killed in the process."

"Mwfnts!" said Gilley, halfway through his pancakes. The rest of us had stopped eating, but Gil still managed to soldier on.

John and Heath looked at me. "What'd he say?" asked Heath.

"Magnets."

"Ahhhh," they said together with a nod.

"You know, that's a good idea. We could all get sweatshirts like Gil's, and that phantom wouldn't be able to touch us," Heath added.

But I was worried about the time it would take to get us all oversized sweatshirts, find enough magnets to then glue onto the insides, allow the adhesive to dry—it would take most of the day just to create them. "What if we all just went with our spikes out and exposed?" I suggested, telling the boys also about my concerns with the time.

"I'm worried we won't have enough spikes," said Heath. "I mean, you saw that thing, M. J. We had our spikes out the first time we went looking for Gopher and it pretty much ran right over us. I think sweatshirts are the way to go."

"Okay," I relented. "But I think we should leave the girls behind. It's dangerous enough with just us, and I don't think it's fair to ask them to go back to the rock."

"Agreed," said Heath and John in unison again.

I glanced at Gilley. He was busy fiddling with his belt buckle, trying to loosen it a few notches. "Will you come with us, Gil?"

He stopped fiddling and focused on me but quick. "Are you serious?"

I knew I was asking a lot, but I had my reasons. "We can't all be wrapped in magnetic sweatshirts, Gil," I explained. "One of us has to be able to communicate with the castle's ghosts to find Gopher."

Heath eyed me sharply. "What are you saying?"

I took a deep breath. "I'm saying that I can't go in there wearing one of the sweatshirts. I've got to try and communicate with the resident spooks and see if any of them know where Gopher is. Otherwise, we'll be stuck there searching that enormous castle while the phantom waits to find a weak spot and attack us again."

"Aren't *you* going to be our weak spot?" said Gil reasonably.

"Yes. But I may be able to keep the phantom at bay long enough for you guys to get to me."

Heath studied me for a long moment. "I should be the one to go in naked."

Briefly, my mind went places it shouldn't have, before I shook my head and focused on the mission again. "I'll need you to keep your radar open, and alert me to the phantom's approach. You three are going to have to stay at least a dozen yards away from me at all times."

"Unless the phantom approaches, in which case we'll have to tackle you all at the same time," said John.

"Why do you need me, again?" Gilley squeaked. "You'll have John and Heath with you."

"You run the fastest, my friend."

Gilley looked like he was ready to cry.

"It's up to you, buddy," I told him gently. "If you can find the courage to come with us, great. I could sure use you on the team. But if you'd rather stay here, then I won't judge."

"I'd rather stay here!"

My hopes fell and my eyes dropped to the table. Intuitively I *knew* I'd need Gilley along, but I also understood what I was asking him to do. Still, it was really disappointing.

"I mean, I'd really, *really* rather stay here . . . but I'll go anyway, M. J.," he added after a moment.

I lifted my chin. "You will?"

Gilley was pouting fiercely at me. "Yeah, yeah," he said. "On one condition."

"Anything."

"We don't stay longer than an hour. My delicate nerves can't take hanging out there longer than that."

For much of that morning we searched for our supplies. We finally found a shop that sold sweatshirts—although none was in a size large enough for Heath or John. "How about T-shirts?" I asked, holding up two XLs.

"We can wear our jackets over the magnets," said Heath, coming over to grab one of the T-shirts. "'Kiss me, I'm Irish,'" he read, and before I knew it, he was shrugging into it. He then stood in front of me and pointed to the lettering expectantly.

I chuckled and pushed him away. "You fool," I teased. "We don't have time for that. We need to get some magnets."

The four of us spent the rest of the morning and early afternoon scouring the Irish coastline for a shop that sold magnets. We came up with two small refrigerator magnets encased in plastic with the Irish flag on them.

"I had a feeling this was going to be harder than it sounded," I grumbled as we purchased those two and moved on.

Heath looked at his watch. "We need to make a decision," he said. "If we really want to go back to the castle before it gets dark, then we'll only have two hours of good daylight and a tide low enough to cross if we leave in the next hour or so."

"And there's no way I'm going back there when it's dark," Gilley said firmly.

I sighed in frustration. "Fine. Let's head to the B&B and get suited up. We'll have to go in using only the spikes and Gilley's sweatshirt, which really should be enough firepower. But keep the spikes fully exposed, guys. Strap them to your tool belts so there's no way you can drop them."

"Done," said Heath.

An hour and a half later we'd gone over our plan, changed and loaded up our tool belts with spikes (I carried some spikes too—but all mine were in their canisters), and we were on our way to the causeway.

John made a quick stop at the coast guard station to check if there had been any progress in the search for Gopher.

He rejoined us after a few minutes to report that no sign of our producer could be seen from the cursory check of the island.

Heath drove us down to the water and I wondered why I didn't see many local fishermen out and about. Certainly they would know the channel well enough to navigate the treacherous waters. "The currents are really strong," said Gil. "And there are lots of rocks that jut up to right below the surface. Small boats are advised to stay clear of Dunlow and the causeway."

"How do you know all that?" I asked him.

"While you guys were buying your T-shirts, I asked about renting a boat to get to Dunlow. I was told that no one rents to anyone going there, because so many boats have been damaged or sunk on the rocks near the island."

"Great," I muttered. "So if we get stuck on that stupid rock again, the only way off is to wait for low tide."

"Yep," said Gil. "Which is why we're only staying one hour. We are *not* getting stuck again."

When we reached the causeway, Heath parked next to our other van and secured the keys to the inside of his coat. "Ready?" he asked me.

I squinted at the ominous rock in the distance, where the castle was barely visible. "Not really. But when did that ever stop me?"

Heath wrapped an arm around my shoulders and pulled me with him as we walked. "You realize that if I have my spikes drawn, I might not sense the phantom until it's nearly on top of you."

I swallowed hard. "I do now."

"But your own intuition should alert you in time."

I nodded. "Yeah. That's something."

"We should have a signal," he advised. "If you feel it before I do, and you need us to get to you, we should have a code word."

I smiled. "How does 'Help!' work for you?"

Heath chuckled. "It works."

"You guys just remember to stay together," I reminded him. "No one gets separated this time, okay?"

Heath saluted. "Aye, aye, Captain."

*   *   *

The causeway was easy going that afternoon. The storm surge had died down and there was no fog to obscure our path. We made it to the island without incident and as one we tilted our heads up to peer at the edge of the cliff.

No lurking shadow peered down at us, which I took as a good sign.

"Oh, man!" Gil whined.

I turned around and considered him. He was shaking a little and definitely pale. "You're fine, honey," I told him gently. "Remember, you're wearing the super sweatshirt. Nothing can hurt you as long as you're wearing that."

My best friend appeared to be ignoring me and his breathing was coming in quick little pants.

"Gil!" I said firmly. "You have to get a grip, okay? I can't have you flaking out up top. I'm depending on you." Gil said nothing. Instead he just continued to stare at the cliffs. "Seriously, honey, this is the only way we can get Gopher back. Please let me know you can do this."

Gilley's large round eyes met mine and he pressed his lips together and pumped his head up and down. "Mmmm, hmmm!" he said.

I patted him on the shoulder. "That's my Gilley."

John made note of the time and we all moved to the stairs. My shoulders sagged a little as I thought about the arduous climb up—my legs were still tired and aching from the day before—but there was no use complaining about it.

We moved steadily up the stairs, huddling close together. On the way both John and Heath unsheathed
their spikes and secured them to their tool belts. I left
my canisters alone, but it was hard to resist the urge to
pull them out and walk up there fully armed.

We reached the top and paused at the landing, waiting and watching for any movement or sense of the
phantom's presence. All was still and quiet except for
the wind and the call of a few seagulls.

Ahead of us, the massive form of the castle loomed,
and its dark exterior appeared to mock us in the bright
light of day. "Shall we?" Heath whispered.

"I think we'd better," I replied.

Heath led us cautiously to the large keep door and
we ducked inside, bypassing the ruins of the fire we'd
burned the night before. Inside the front hall we paused
again and listened.

Nothing moved and no disturbance came to our ears.

Heath motioned us forward again and I could feel
my heart begin to race and goose pimples prickled my
skin. The phantom was somewhere nearby, waiting and
watching.

"Come on," I said. "Let's get this over with."

We moved quickly and quietly down the central corridor to the branch where the phantom had previously
attacked Heath and me. There, I held up my hands to
stop the group. "This is where I move forward, and you
guys keep about twenty to twenty-five feet back."

Heath really looked like he didn't like the idea, but
he held his tongue and gave my shoulder a soft squeeze.

"Please be careful, M. J.," Gil whispered.

"Count on it," I told him. I then turned and walked away from the magnetic protection of the group.

In one hand I held my flashlight; in the other I held a grenade. On the drive to the beach I'd practiced popping off the lid with my fingers so that I wouldn't have to tuck my flashlight under my arm to get at the spike. I hoped that opening the canister and dropping the spike at my feet would give the guys enough time to reach me.

At twenty feet, I knew Gil could reach me in about three seconds. Flat.

"One Mississippi, two Mississippi, three Mississippi . . . ," I counted. It didn't feel like very long.

The problem was that the corridors and hallways weren't always going to be twenty feet long. There would be times on this search when my backup couldn't see me. And that was a real problem, but Gopher needed my help—of that I was certain—and I couldn't leave him to the phantom. Not after experiencing the power of that horrible thing firsthand.

I looked back at my bodyguards one last time before moving forward alone. All my senses were on high alert—including number six. That dial had been turned up to eleventy. I walked cautiously and carefully, feeling the ether, listening for any sound louder than my own heartbeat, and focused on sensing which way to go.

My gut led me straight ahead to a side corridor that was much narrower than the central hallway. I flashed my beam down the hallway. A rat scuttled away from the beam. I flinched, then shivered.

"What's down there?" Gilley asked from a safe distance.

"I'm not sure. But my gut's telling me to check it out."

"Wait for us there," Heath instructed. "I don't want to lose sight of you."

I waited patiently for them to come up next to me. "Okay?" I asked Heath, who was also shining his flashlight down the corridor.

"It's about thirty feet long," he said, squinting in the dim light. "We'll wait for you to check it out right here."

I nodded and moved into the narrow space. Fifteen feet away from the boys I could feel the energy shift, and I knew I'd crossed the threshold of their magnetic field. They would still have an effect on other spooks, but the phantom was strong enough to bother me if it put its mind to it.

And that thought made me extremely nervous. I felt a sinking sensation in my stomach, and considered telling the boys to come in closer. I had the eerie perception that I was being herded, like a sheep to slaughter, and I didn't like it one little bit.

I stopped in front of the open door to a room off the corridor, and before waving for the boys to come forward, I held my flashlight up to inspect it.

The room was empty.

I decided it was best to bring my backup forward to this doorway before continuing alone down the hall. There were more doors and likely more rooms to inspect, and hopefully, Gopher was in one of them. "Gopher?" I called into the stillness.

I heard a low, mournful moan.

It was farther down the hallway, in one of the rooms near the end. Forgetting to signal to the boys, I hurried down the corridor. "Gopher?!" I called anxiously. "Dude, is that you?"

"Help me!" came his muffled reply.

"Oh, sweet Jesus, honey, I'm coming!" I cried, and began to run to the last door on the right. "Goph—"

And that was all I could get out before something large, black, and horrible barreled into me like a freight train.

I was knocked sideways through a doorway and into a room with such force that I hit the wood floor with a loud thud, and smacked the side of my head hard enough to leave me dizzy. I'd managed to hold on to the flashlight, but the metal canister I'd been holding flew out of my hands as I hit the floor, and it took me a moment to catch my breath.

In the distance I heard yelling, and my name being called, and I looked up in time to see the door slam—closing me off from my backup.

I got up fast and stumbled toward the door, but stopped dead when I saw a shadow form against the wood and sinister laughter filled the room.

My fingers flew to my other grenade, which should have been at my belt, but I realized in the tumble I'd taken, the belt had twisted at my waist, and I couldn't find the loop with my other canister.

Pounding erupted on the other side of the door, and the handle was twisted and pulled, but it held firm.

The phantom flew away from the exit to the opposite side of the rather large room, away from the door and the magnetic energy wafting through it. I heard the phantom emit something like a growl and I resumed my plan to get to the door. "Help!" I yelled, but my voice sounded hoarse with fright.

I tugged on the door handle even as my head began to fill with horrible images of monsters, demons, and slithering creatures from my worst nightmares. "G-G-G-G-*Gilley*!" I stuttered.

The pounding on the other side of the door grew frantic, and a wham from the other side let me know someone was throwing his weight against it in an effort to break it down. Meanwhile, the phantom hissed and growled and stepped closer to me.

The air became cold as ice, and I had to abandon the door handle and hold my hands protectively over my head, trying in vain to stop the images taking over my every thought. In the back of my mind I knew I was losing control, and I knew there was something I needed to do to stall the awful onslaught, but I couldn't remember what it was.

And then, another sound reached me. A voice, urgent and commanding, said, "This way, lass!"

I shook my head, scuttling away from the approaching phantom. It hissed again, but as it did so, it must have taken its focus off me, because the images abated just a bit.

I blinked and moved along the wall, away from the black shadowy nightmare in the room. "Here!" the voice insisted. "Lass! Come quickly!"

I blinked again and saw a man in period dress that I swore I recognized, waving at me. He was standing next to a set of wooden panels. I watched as he turned his attention to the phantom and yelled, "Back, you blasted boggart! Get back, I say!"

The phantom hissed and growled and the nightmare in my head abated even more. I stumbled toward the man. When I reached his side, he said, "There's a good lass. Now, push that bit of panel."

With shaking fingers I pressed where he indicated, and an entire section of the wall slid inward to reveal a spiral stone staircase. "Down you go, then," said the man.

A growl from behind me was all the encouragement I needed. I darted through the section of wall to the top stair. I glanced over my shoulder for just a moment and saw the phantom racing toward me. Instinctively I threw my weight against the back side of the panel and slammed it shut; then I bulleted down the stairs as fast as my shaking legs could carry me.

Reaching the bottom, I found myself in a long stone tunnel. Trembling from head to toe, I moved away from the staircase, trying desperately to get some distance between me and the phantom. I was so frightened that I could barely walk, and tears welled in my eyes, blurring my vision.

And then I remembered what had saved me the last time. Heath's grandfather Samuel could help me.

I closed my eyes and called out to him in my mind.

Push aside your fear! I heard him say clearly in my

head. *To fight this demon, you MUST push aside your own fear!*

I took a deep breath and opened my eyes, willing myself to get a grip. "You're fine," I said aloud. "M. J., you're just fine."

I took a few more deep breaths and after a moment or two I didn't feel "fine," but I did feel a bit better.

"That's good, lass," said a voice right next to me.

I jumped a foot and spun around, my hand finally finding the canister with the spike. When I searched the narrow stone corridor, I realized no one was actually in it. "Who's there?" I asked cautiously.

The same man who had saved me from the phantom appeared some way down the hall. "Me," he said simply.

And then I remembered where I'd seen him before. "Lord Dunnyvale," I said. "Thank you for saving me."

He bowed formally to me. "The least I could do," he told me. "You were in a very bad state up there, after all."

I glanced over my shoulder at the stairs and shuddered.

"He can't get to you now," he told me. "Especially while you're standing there."

I turned back to Dunnyvale. He looked as real as any living person, but I knew it was all a facade. And then what Samuel had told me clicked in my head. "Fear acts like a beacon for the phantom, right?"

"It does," said Ranald. "The more afraid you are, the easier it is for the phantom to find and torture you."

I took another steadying breath. "I have to get back to my friends," I told him.

"Yes," he said, and I thought he'd say more, but instead he turned and pointed down the corridor. "This tunnel will lead you where you need to go. But you might wish to pause here and inspect your surroundings for a bit."

I cocked my head at him. "Why's that exactly?"

Instead of answering me, he said, "Remember our bargain, lass. You rid my castle of that wretched creature, and I will tell you where to find your friend."

I looked at him incredulously. "You *seriously* want me to go back for another round with that *thing*?"

"No."

That gave me pause. "No?"

"I want you to find out where the phantom came from. And for that, you'll need Alex."

"Can't you just tell me where it came from?"

"No."

"Why am I not surprised?"

"I've already told you where to start. Find Alex, good lady Holliday. You won't be sorry you did."

With that, Lord Dunnyvale disappeared in the blink of an eye, and I was left alone again to ponder his riddles.

The moment he left, I uncapped my remaining grenade, tipped out the spike, and eyed the corridor warily.

I realized there were small rooms just off the main hallway I was standing in. The rooms were about the size of a walk-in closet and they had no doors on them, just names carved into the stone. I squinted at the nameplates and I realized with some surprise that these were actually crypts.

Stepping cautiously into the vault in front of me, I could see that it was in fact Ranald's tomb.

His sarcophagus was a huge marble creation with a likeness of him carved into the top. It was a very good rendition if the man's ghost truly looked like him when he was alive. As I inspected his coffin, my foot hit something and I looked down to see a medium-sized bundle made out of canvas leaning up against the sarcophagus.

Bending down to inspect it, I was surprised to find a very modern-looking backpack, covered in dust, but otherwise in excellent condition. Wiping away some of the dust, I realized there were initials embroidered into the top of the pack. "*A. M. N.*," I recited.

I wanted to unzip it and dig through the contents, but I knew I needed to get out of this underground corridor and find the boys quick. They had to be out of their minds with worry by now.

So I picked up the pack—which was surprisingly heavy—slung it over my shoulder, and tripped over something that clanked on the ground. Shining my flashlight at it, I realized it was a crowbar, which was really curious. Still, I didn't give it much thought because I was on a mission to find the boys, so I headed out of Ranald's crypt and hustled down the corridor.

I finally came to the end of it a few minutes later and was shocked to see a large metal door hanging open a crack. I pulled on the handle and it creaked and groaned open, to reveal a set of stone stairs and the open air of the outside.

Stepping onto the stairwell, I realized I'd come out at

the stairs that led up to the castle. I looked over the railing, guessing that I was about three-quarters of the way up from the bottom. I was surprised to find that none of us had noticed the door on the several trips we'd made both up and down the stairs.

"M. J.?!" I heard someone gasp.

I looked behind me and there, just a few steps up, were Gilley, Heath, and John, all appearing incredibly shocked at my sudden appearance.

"Hey, guys," I said with a small wave.

"Ohmigod!" Gilley shrieked, and he flew down to hug me fiercely. "You're alive! *You're alive!*"

I squirmed in his arms—he was hugging me supertight. "Of course I'm alive," I said to him. "What'd you expect?"

Gilley stepped back and considered me. "We thought the phantom ate you."

My jaw fell open. "You thought *what*?"

"Only Gilley thought that," Heath said, coming down the stairs looking immensely relieved.

"I actually considered the possibility," said John. We all turned to stare at him. "What?" he asked. "Dude, Gilley had a point."

"What point?" I demanded.

"We finally broke through the door, and that thing hissed and growled at us and then it took off right through the wall!" explained Gil. "So, after it left, we searched the whole room, and there was no sign of you. I mean, it just stood to reason that the phantom had eaten you."

I gaped at him. "Stood to *reason*?"

"Yes," he insisted, sticking by his theory.

Heath and I exchanged a look, and I knew he was thinking what I was thinking. Anyone who could consume a breakfast as big as the one Gilley had might think it quite reasonable that a phantom would want to make a buffet out of me. "Well," I told them, "I haven't been eaten."

"So what did happen to you?" John asked.

I adjusted the backpack and reached for Heath's wrist where his watch was attached. Noting the time, I said, "I'll explain it all to you on the way back to the B&B. I think we should regroup and come up with an alternate plan to find Gopher tomorrow. For now we'll just have to hope that he can hang on, because we need to get the hell off this rock while we can."

No one argued to stay. As one we all hurried down the steps.

Once we reached the van, I explained everything that had happened to me after I'd been pushed into the room by the phantom, and also learned that Gil, John, and Heath had looked through all the adjoining rooms and linking hallways before deciding to go get help—even if that meant making a few calls to the U.S. Embassy.

"There was no way I was just going to leave you," Heath said firmly. "M. J., I would have searched day and night to get you back."

I ran my hand through his dark hair. "I know."

From the backseat Gilley groaned. "You two really need to get a room."

I regarded him with a scowl. He could be so frigging annoying sometimes.

"We still need a new plan to find Gopher," John reminded us. "Because that whole letting you go in unarmed is clearly not the way to go."

I nodded.

Heath pulled into the driveway of the B&B at that moment and I laid a hand on his arm. "Let's check in with the girls and then find a restaurant. I'm famished and I have a bit more to share about Lord Ranald Dunnyvale."

Chapter 7

The girls had left us a note that they were out exploring the village, so we in turn left them a note that we were back from the castle, and off in search of grub.

We found a lovely pub called Sláinte's, and ordered a round of fish-and-chips and a pitcher of beer. While our food was being prepared, I told the group about the two dreams I'd had where I'd been visited by the spirit of Ranald Dunnyvale, and then what he'd told me down in the crypts' tunnel.

"He wants you to personally rid the castle of the phantom?" John asked incredulously.

"Yep."

Heath looked deeply worried. "And he won't tell you where Gopher is?"

"Nope."

"I don't like it," Gilley said.

"You never do," I muttered.

Gilley looked at me crossly. "What'd you say?"

"Nothing," I said quickly. "The point is that I don't

think there's any other way to get Gopher back. We're not finding him on our own, and we've seen how tricky that phantom can be. I think it's way too dangerous to go back there and continue to explore the castle without knowing a little bit more about what we're dealing with. We need to research the phantom, and this Alex person."

"But the longer we take to do that, the more danger Gopher could be in," Heath reasoned.

I knew he was thinking back to the awful time he'd had when he'd been held in the phantom's grip. I understood fully how difficult it was to be patient and do our homework, all the while knowing what kind of torture Gopher was likely experiencing.

"I don't know that we have much of a choice, Heath," I said honestly. "Gopher will just have to hang on while we figure out how to find him."

Our food arrived then and for a little while we ate in silence. Gilley was the first to break it when he said, "Mwt mabt da bkpwk?"

I smirked. "I personally know that your mother taught you better table manners, Gil."

He appeared chagrined. He then chewed thoroughly and swallowed. "What about the backpack?"

I'd left it in the van and I'd almost completely forgotten about it. Excusing myself from the table, I dashed out to retrieve it and hauled it out of the passenger's seat. Bringing it back into the pub, I set it on the table with a thud, and unzipped the top.

I gasped when I inspected the contents.

"What is it?" Heath asked.

I tipped the flap so that they could all see inside to the dozens of spikes bound with cord weighing down the pack.

"Whoa," said Heath and John, while Gilley whistled appreciatively.

"That's why the phantom didn't come after me when I went down those stairs," I said, pulling one of the spikes free and testing it against the metal zipper. The zipper clinked against the magnetic metal. "I wondered why it didn't chase me into the tunnel. And I also remember that Ranald had stayed a good distance away from his crypt when he was talking to me."

"Are those initials?" Gilley asked, squinting at the lettering embroidered on the canvas.

"Yes. They read *A. M. N.*"

"Do you think the *A* stands for 'Alex'?"

I nodded. "I do, Gil."

Gilley reached into his coat pocket and pulled out his cell phone. "Crap," he said.

"What?"

"That stupid phantom must have drained my charge again. The phone was working fine after I recharged it last night."

"Who were you planning to call?"

"No one. I was just going to make a note to research those initials and see what I could come up with."

I glanced back down into the belly of the backpack, spying a small notebook and a pen. I pulled these out and tossed them to Gilley. "You can use these."

He caught them easily and began thumbing through the pages. "Whoa," he said.

"What now?"

He looked at me oddly and turned the page around. I squinted at the writing but couldn't make any sense of it. "What is that?" I asked. "Shorthand?"

Gilley turned the page back to face him. "No," he said. "I think it's a foreign language. Russian, maybe."

That surprised me. "See if you can translate it when we get back to the B&B, okay?"

"On it."

"While Gilley's researching, what do you want us to do?" John asked.

"We need to talk to the locals," I said. "Find out more about what happened at Dunlow four years ago. Kincaid and this Alex guy were obviously doing exactly what we attempted when we first arrived. They were after the gold, but got caught by the phantom. Dunnyvale insists that the phantom was brought to that rock by someone other than him, which means he was likely brought there after Dunnyvale died. Let's find out when the legend of the phantom first appeared around these parts, and see if anyone can link it to a particular person."

Heath polished off the last of his beer and pushed his empty plate aside. "Sounds good."

Plan in hand, we paid the tab and made our way back to the B&B.

Once there we dropped off Gilley and John—who was going to wait for the girls and fill them in and also pick Anya's brain. Heath and I headed to the coast guard station, figuring that was as good a place as any to start.

When we entered the station, which was located right in the middle of Dunlee's port, we saw the constable who had warned us about staying too long on the rock at Dunlow.

I waved to him as we got out of the van, and he shuffled over. "I hear you've lost a member of your party," he said by way of greeting.

"Yes," I told him. "Our producer went missing yesterday afternoon, and we're really worried about him."

"You should be," he said grimly.

Heath and I exchanged a concerned look. "We're here to see if the coast guard has found any further trace of him?" I said, my voice rising to a question for the constable.

The village cop looked over his shoulder at the station. "They haven't."

"Are they at least still looking?"

The constable turned his attention to the left and out to sea. "I doubt it. There's another storm approaching."

I glanced at the sky, which was perfectly clear with only a few white fluffy clouds floating on the horizon. "They come in fast and furious here, don't they?" I remarked.

"Aye," he said. "That they do, miss."

"Constable," Heath began.

"Call me Quinn," he said with a kind smile. "Or Constable O'Grady, whichever you prefer."

Heath seemed to waver as to which name to call the man, and finally settled on the more formal. "Constable O'Grady," he said, "we seem to be in a jam here. We've tried to go back to the castle to search for our producer, but the phantom keeps attacking us. We need to know more about it. Where the villagers think it came from, how long it's been haunting Dunlow Castle, and maybe even a little more about what happened four years ago to those other two ghost hunters."

O'Grady regarded Heath curiously before he lifted his wrist and looked at his watch. "Well, for all of that, brother, you'll need to buy me a pint. I get off me shift in about an hour. Come find me at O'Grady's Pub on Clemens Street, and I'll tell you all I know."

"You own a pub?" I asked.

"Aye," he said. "I've got seven little ones at home. A man's got to have more than one livelihood when he's got so many mouths to feed."

Heath and I agreed to meet Constable O'Grady later, and occupied ourselves in the meantime by talking to the coast guard. We found the two officers on duty monitoring a thick patch of clouds moving in from the northwest. "It's even bigger than the one that came through yesterday," remarked one. "We'll need to alert the wharf of the small-craft warning immediately." Then he noticed us and asked if he could help us.

"We're here to ask about the search for our friend," I said.

"The man missing from Dunlow Castle?"

"Yes."

The officer shook his head. "I'm sorry, miss, but we've found no trace of him. And we can't rightly go out now. There's another big storm a-comin'."

"Will you go out in the morning?" I pressed. I didn't want to give up the pressure on the coast guard to help us find Gopher.

The officer eyed his computer screen, displaying various shades of red, pink, yellow, and green. Just to the south of the wash of color was the outline of the Irish coast. It looked like it was a truly massive storm—something we New Englanders would dub a nor'easter.

"It depends on that storm, miss," he told me honestly. "But I wouldn't count on her blowing herself out by mornin'. She looks like she'll want to stay and have some fun with us for a wee bit."

Heath and I headed out of the station feeling really defeated. "There's no way to get back onto that island during the storm," I said. "No matter what we try and do, it looks like Gopher's stuck there."

Heath dug his hands into his pockets, and it was then that I realized the wind had picked up. "I don't even want to think about what he's going through," he said miserably. "Assuming he's still alive, that is."

And then something occurred to me, and I grabbed Heath by both arms. "Oh, my God!" I said. "Why didn't I think of that before?"

"Think of what?"

"I've been so worried about Gopher, and I think I assumed that there was no way he could withstand more than a few hours with the phantom. In the very back of my mind I wondered if he had already been murdered, but it never occurred to me to reach out to him using my intuition to see if he'd really crossed over!"

Heath's eyebrows lifted in surprise. "I didn't think of it either, M. J. But you're right. We need to see if we can reach Gopher. That way we'll know for sure if this is a rescue mission, or a recovery."

I motioned Heath to the van and we got in and drove at breakneck speed to the causeway. There we got out and I could see that the cobblestones were covered by about two inches of water as both the storm surge and the tide were moving in.

"We'll need to get a little closer to the castle," I said, eyeing Heath to see if he agreed.

Heath, however, was staring at the causeway. "It's dangerous," he said. "You know how slippery those rocks are when they get wet, and the tide's coming in."

"I'm willing to risk it," I told him. "If you want to stay here, you can."

"Right," he said, a hint of irritation in his voice. "Like I'm just going to let you cruise out over the causeway without help."

"Then let's stop talking about it and get going, sugar!"

Heath and I sloshed our way onto the cobblestones and I hurried as fast as I could without taking too many risks. The water was freezing and my feet were soon numb with cold. It took us about fifteen minutes to reach the island, and from there I could just make out the line of thick dark clouds on the horizon.

"We'll have to work fast," I said, noting the fading light and that the water on the causeway was inching up more and more.

Heath closed his eyes and lifted his chin in the direction of the castle. I did the same and in my mind I called out as loudly as I could to Gopher.

There was no response, save for a cold prickle on my forearms. I opened my eyes again and thought I saw the phantom's dark figure swaying in the wind at the top of the rock. In the distance I heard Jordan Kincaid's voice yell, "Alex!" But that was it.

Heath was still deep in concentration, and I wondered if maybe he'd connected to Gopher. My heart sank with that thought, because even though I was prepared for it, I still didn't want anything awful to happen to our producer.

A few seconds later, Heath opened his eyes, a grim look set firmly on his face.

"Anything?"

He took my hand and turned me around to head back across the causeway before speaking. "Nothing," he said. "I tried reaching out to Gopher and kept hitting a brick wall."

"I think he's still alive," I admitted, noting that I'd felt exactly the same thing. "And I also think we'll find him."

Heath stepped onto the watery cobblestones and paused. "When?"

I shrugged and slogged my way forward. "I don't know. But soon."

"I hope it's in time," he told me.

I couldn't have agreed more.

We were late getting to O'Grady's. By the time we made it back to shore, our pants were soaked and I was shivering with cold. Heath drove us back to the B&B, where we changed quickly, told Gilley what we were up to, and left a note for Meg, Kim, and John before hustling to the pub.

We found Quinn sitting comfortably at the bar, a tall pint of dark ale in front of him. "There you are," he said when we came to sit next to him.

"Sorry," Heath and I said together. "We were delayed."

Quinn didn't appear to mind; instead he asked us to pick our poison. Heath ordered a beer while I went with a vodka and cranberry. "Now, if I remember, you want to know all about the phantom."

"Yes, please," I said, just as my drink arrived.

"It's a dark tale," he began dramatically, and motioned for us to follow him to one of the booths. "But one worth the tellin' if you think it will help find your friend," he added as we sat down.

After taking a long sip of ale, he wiped his mouth with the back of his hand and told us what he knew. "The first time I heard of the phantom was about twenty years ago. I was a young lad then, just back from holiday at me cousin's further up the coast, and me mum told me that some poor bloke had died that very mornin' while out explorin' Dunlow Castle.

"The poor chap was a Frenchman who'd come across the legend of the hidden treasure a bit before that, and in his research he'd discovered an old letter written by Ranald Dunnyvale's second wife to her cousin, describing the last words of her husband on his deathbed.

"According to this Frenchman, Dunnyvale's final words gave away the exact location of his treasure. So the Frenchman came here to look for it, only telling us in the village that the gold was hidden in a secret location, and with the aid of the original blueprints to the castle, he was sure he'd find it.

"After searching the castle top to bottom for near a week, he claimed to have discovered the secret location, but he needed to return to France for a spell to tend to some urgent business."

Quinn paused here to take a long pull from his pint, and outside we all heard the first rumble of thunder.

"Storm's comin'," I heard Heath whisper.

"Aye," said Quinn. "And she's likely to be a moody little tempest from the weather reports I've seen."

But I was anxious to hear more about Quinn's story. "You were saying about the Frenchman?"

"Ah, yes," he said, wiping his mouth again with his sleeve. "Where was I? Oh, I remember—he'd returned to France. Well, we weren't sure he'd come back to our village after that, truth be told. We were a wee bit skeptical of his claims, but return he did a bit later. With him was another bloke, who was not from France, as I remember, and they and one other chap they'd hired to carry the heavy equipment set off for Dunlow."

Another loud rumble of thunder reverberated against the walls and tinkled the glass bottles on the shelves. This was immediately followed by the drumming sound of a hard rain on the roof.

Quinn squinted through the windows and signaled

for another pint of ale. "Now, here in the village, we had our doubts about the Frenchy's claim. I mean, we've lived here all our lives, and most of us had been to Dunlow a time or two. Never had we seen any sign of this supposed treasure, but being naturally curious, we waited to see what the Frenchman and his friends would bring back.

"Not in our wildest dreams did we think that the three men would release a demon like the phantom!" Quinn said with a slight shiver.

"What happened on that rock that morning *exactly*, Constable?" I pressed. I wanted to know what the Frenchman had done to call up the phantom.

Quinn shrugged. "I only know what I was told," he said. "And that was that on that terrible day the Frenchman did discover where the gold was hidden, but when he went to take a few handfuls, the phantom was released. It chased him off the cliffs, drove another man quite mad, and left the third a cripple."

"How did the village react?" Heath asked.

Quinn gave his empty glass to a waitress, who replaced it with a full pint. "No one quite believed the story. That is, until a few of us bolder lads went to have a look for ourselves."

I sucked in a breath of surprise. "*You've* seen the phantom?"

"Aye," he said. "It was right after word spread that a terrible demon had been set loose at the castle. Me daddy, in fact, was one of the men who helped retrieve the Frenchman's body from the rocks. He told me that when he set foot on that island, he knew something had changed, and he vowed to never go back there.

"I, of course, was far too curious for me own good back then, and I gathered me courage and decided I'd go to the castle and have a look for myself. I was only about fifteen at the time—you know how impulsive and daft you can be when you're young?"

Heath and I both nodded.

"Aye, I knew you'd understand. So, the very next day I crept across the causeway at low tide and made it up to the top of the rock when out of the castle a monstrous shadow appeared and came racing toward me. I've never been so bloody scared me whole life!" he said, shaking his head at the memory. "And I ran down those steps faster than any Olympic sprinter, I tell you!"

I smiled at the visual. "Oh, I've seen that thing up close and personal. I know how it can put a rocket booster to your feet."

"Aye," he agreed. "And I didn't stop runnin' till I'd reached the shore on this side. And other than a few times when duty has called me back across the causeway, I've not returned to that cursed place. Nor could you convince me to go up those stairs ever again," he said.

I remembered Quinn arriving on the rocky shore when we reported the dead man at the base of the cliffs. He'd kept very close to the causeway, and I remember him eyeing the top of the rock nervously. Something clicked in my head then, and I said, "The phantom never comes down the stairs, does he?"

Quinn gave me a sardonic smile. "No," he said. "We've learned over time that it only haunts the top of the rock."

"But where did it come from?" I asked. "I mean, you can point to its first appearance twenty years ago, but was there any mention of it before then?"

Quinn shook his head. "None a'tall. And no one in the village knows why it suddenly appeared other than it was released when the Frenchman went for Dunnyvale's gold. We all believe Dunnyvale himself set the phantom as a trap should anyone get too close to his treasure."

I remembered Dunnyvale's ghost insisting that he'd had no part in setting the phantom loose.

Meanwhile, Quinn was still recounting how tame Dunlow had been prior to the Frenchman's interference. "Why, I remember playing at Dunlow as a wee lad," he was saying. "Me schoolmates and I used to go there nearly every chance we had. In those days, the castle had a few ghosts roaming the grounds—but most of them were quite tame. None of them ever frightened us or attacked us. Not until the phantom."

I shifted uncomfortably in my seat. I remembered again Ranald telling me the phantom was put there by someone other than himself. But who, and why? "Have you ever heard of anyone making something of an outlandish claim, like they were responsible for bringing the phantom to the castle?" I asked.

Quinn laughed heartily at the suggestion. "Why, no,

miss. There's no legend or story of that sort connected to the phantom."

Another thought occurred to me. "What if the phantom wasn't placed at the castle by Lord Dunnyvale, but by someone more current? Someone who, say, twenty years ago heard that a Frenchman was after Dunnyvale's gold?"

Quinn looked at me as if I'd just said the oddest thing. Shaking his head, he told me, "I've heard some fairly strange boasts in the village and around this pub, I assure you, but no one's ever claimed they were responsible for delivering Dunlow its phantom."

Heath looked at me curiously, but I didn't want to go into what I knew in front of Quinn, so I moved away from the topic to another related one. "What can you tell us about the incident four years ago with Jordan Kincaid?"

Quinn sucked in a breath and blew it out in a heavy sigh. "Ah, now, that's a terrible tale as sad as the first one I've told you."

"We're all ears," I assured him.

"As you know, it happened four years ago. We heard that the famous Jordan Kincaid was determined to come to Dunlow and find Dunnyvale's treasure. When he arrived, we did our best to warn him about the phantom, and he seemed to listen to us and take it all seriously. In fact, he abandoned his first plans to go there alone, and came back a few months later with two companions."

"Was one of them a man named Alex?" I asked carefully.

Quinn scratched his head. "You know, I'm terrible with names, but Kincaid did have one man in his group, and one woman. The gentleman's name might have been Alex, though I'm not certain."

"He had a woman with him?" I asked. For some reason, that surprised me.

"Aye. And she was a beautiful lass, let me tell you. . . ." Quinn's voice drifted off and his eyes held a faraway cast to them. I could tell he'd been very attracted to Kincaid's companion. "She was Russian, I think," he said.

Heath and I looked at each other, the memory of the notepad written in Russian floating between us. "Do you know what her role was?" I asked.

Quinn looked at me curiously. "Role?"

"I'm assuming that everyone Kincaid brought with him had some sort of expertise for the mission."

"Well, that I wouldn't know. I believe I was too busy admiring the lovely lady's figure to pay much attention to what she was there for," he told me with a hearty chuckle.

Heath smiled knowingly and I barely resisted the urge to roll my eyes. "*Any*way," I said, getting us back on track, "you were saying?"

"Oh, right," said Quinn. "So, Kincaid comes to the village with his two traveling companions and they set off for Dunlow loaded down with camping gear and gadgets and all sorts of odd-looking equipment. They planned to stay somewhere on the rock, and take their time explorin' the castle. I thought they were daft for wanting to take on the phantom, but I also thought that if you were determined to fight that demon, the best way to go about it was the way they'd mapped out. As I've said, the phantom doesn't come down those stairs, so if you can study it from relative safety, and find a weak spot, you might be able to defeat it."

"So what went wrong?" Heath asked.

"Well," Quinn said, tugging on his chin. "Everything. The man in Kincaid's party was captured by the phantom and sent insane. Kincaid fell to his death, and the woman barely escaped with her life. It was a terrible tragedy made all the worse by the fact that our coast guard station had been assigned a new recruit from outside our village who wasn't familiar with the legend of the phantom. He went to the rock to help recover Kincaid's body, and curiosity got the best of him. We heard the tale from his partner, who went back to secure the boat and bring along the stretcher, that the new man went up to explore the top of the cliff where Kincaid had fallen, and disappeared.

"His partner couldn't raise him on the radio, so more help was sent for, and I arrived just in time to watch the poor man teeter on the edge of the cliff, covering his head with his hands, before he too fell to his death."

Quinn finished his story with a shuddering breath and a long sip of beer. His eyes appeared haunted by what he'd seen. "Since that day, we've a standing rule in this village: If you're fool enough to go explorin' the rock of Dunlow—you're on your own and there'll be no help for you other than to recover your bones from either the water or the base of those cliffs."

Quinn reminded us again why there was so little effort made to help us find Gopher, as he'd just finished telling us the same tale we'd heard from Anya. "Do you know where we can find the woman who was in Kincaid's party?" I asked.

Quinn shook his head. "She left the day after Kincaid's father came to claim his son's body, and I've no idea where she went after that. You might want to ask him, though."

"Who?"

"Kincaid's father. He and the woman had a terrible row outside the morgue the day after the accident."

"What were they fighting about?"

"I don't know for certain," Quinn admitted. "I just remember hearing from more than a few local blokes that they'd been yelling and blaming each other for the young man's death."

"Well, there's no chance of that," I said to him. When he looked at me curiously, I explained. "Jeffrey Kincaid, Jordan's father, committèd suicide a year and a half after his son's death."

O'Grady looked stricken. "I'd no idea," he said.

"I read about it on the Web," I told him.

"Oh," he replied. "I'm not much for the Internet, I'm afraid. Too many wee ones at home always at the computer. I've not sat down at it since me and the wife bought it three years ago."

Just then a terrible crack of thunder sounded right

outside, and the lights went out. "Oh, bloody hell!" Quinn swore. "Not again!" He then excused himself and moved out of the booth. Heath put some money on the table, and then he and I followed the rest of the patrons, who shuffled through the dark to the outside.

Once there, we dashed through the pouring rain to the van, and after slamming closed the doors, we had a moment to consider the storm. "I think this one's even worse than the one we got caught up in," I said as bright lightning lit up the sky all around us and wind whipped the trees to and fro.

Heath started the engine and put the wipers on their highest setting. "We'd better get back to the others."

We arrived at the B&B only to find it—and all the surrounding houses—completely dark. "Looks like the storm took out the power grid," Heath said.

From inside I saw a small circle of light bobbing up and down the curtains. "At least we've got flashlights," I said, opening the door to hurry into the inn.

We found Anya in the kitchen lighting a few candles. "This tempest's going to be a wee bit of a nuisance, I'm afraid," she said, looking apologetic as she darted about lighting several more candles. "And it might be a touch cold tonight, so I've set out an extra blanket for each of you on your beds."

Heath and I told her not to worry about us and went in search of the others.

We located Gilley and the girls in the sitting room, huddled in front of the fire. "Hey," I said in greeting.

"Hi, guys!" said Meg.

"Hey," said Kim.

"Humph," said Gil.

Great. Gilley was in a mood. How unusual . . . and yes . . . the voice inside my head *is* dripping with sarcasm.

"What's goin' on?" Heath asked.

Gilley looked at him like he was exceptionally slow on the uptake. "There's no electricity!"

"Really?" I mocked, holding up the candle Anya had given me. "Why, Gil, I hadn't even noticed!"

He scowled at me and muttered something I didn't catch under his breath.

"So we have to use candles and our flashlights for a night. What's the big deal?"

"The big deal, M. J., is that without electricity there is no Internet. I can't charge my phone, and I can't use the computer to translate the journal, and if I can't do any of *that*, then I can't help us find Gopher!"

Oh. Okay. He had a point and that was a problem. "Sorry, buddy," I said.

Heath and I sat down and filled the group in on what we'd learned from Quinn.

"That explains why none of the local authorities will help us find Gopher," Kim said.

I stifled a yawn. "Yeah, but we still don't know who this mysterious Alex person is. I mean, all we really know about him is that he's the guy Quinn said was sent insane by the phantom."

"She," said a voice from the hall.

We all turned to see John coming into the room. "Hey, dude!" I said. "Where you been?"

John shrugged out of his wet coat and came to sit next to Kim by the fire. "I asked Anya earlier if she'd had Kincaid and his group here four years ago. She said they hadn't stayed with her, but she thought they'd spent at least one night at the Dunlee Inn. I headed there and spoke with the owner, a Sean somebody."

"What'd he say?" Kim asked.

"He said that Kincaid had stayed with him back then. They'd booked two rooms for one night the evening before they'd gone off to Dunlow. I then asked if he remembered an Alex in their group. He said he didn't know of an Alex, but he knew of an Alexandra."

My eyebrows rose. "You said Kincaid booked two rooms. There were three in the group. Let me guess, Alexandra and Kincaid stayed in the same room."

John pointed a finger gun at me. "Bingo."

I smiled at Gilley. "Guess your gaydar was a little off target, huh, buddy?"

"Whatever," he said with a flip of his wrist, clearly still in a mood.

"Did the innkeeper give you a last name?" I asked hopefully.

"He said he couldn't remember, but he did tell me she was a total knockout. He described her as tall with long red hair, gorgeous face, a good rack, and a great set of legs."

"Gee, if only he could have gotten a better look at her," I said drily.

John smiled. "He also said she was Russian, if that helps."

"Well that makes sense—the notepad was written in Russian. It must have been hers, then. And that means that we know that her first name was Alexandra, and her last name begins with an *N*."

"You know where we might look?" Heath said.

"Where?" I asked.

"The local paper. I'm pretty sure they would have covered the tragedy of Kincaid falling to his death—it made national headlines back in the States, after all."

I brightened at the suggestion. "You're right! And if they covered the story, they likely got everyone's name."

"We can check there in the morning," John said.

"Not if the electricity doesn't get turned back on," Gilley grumbled.

I sighed. He could be such a pill sometimes. "We'll keep our fingers crossed that it comes back on by then."

I should have crossed my toes too, because in the morning the electricity was still out all across town, and steady gusts of fifty- to sixty-knot winds with sheeting rain weren't helping the situation.

"This sucks," said Gilley, still pouting at the breakfast table.

I had to hand it to Anya: She'd managed to make us all breakfast of fruit, leftover rolls, oatmeal with raisins, and hot tea in spite of having no electricity. "I've a kettle that fits right over the fire," she said smartly. "Comes in quite handy during weather like this."

I smiled and thanked her for her efforts, while subtly elbowing Gilley in the ribs. "Be nice," I hissed when Anya wasn't looking.

He scowled and hunched farther into the blanket wrapped round his shoulders, nibbling away at his third breakfast roll like a hungry squirrel with his last nut.

The room was quite chilly, even though I had on long underwear and two sweaters. Heath joined us, rubbing his hands together and blowing on his fingers. "Brrrrr," he said, sitting down and reaching for a cup of steaming tea.

The temperature had dropped significantly, and as I looked out the front window, I wondered if Gopher was suffering from hypothermia. I tried to remember what he'd been wearing. . . .

"You thinking about Gopher?" Heath asked, reading my mind.

"Yeah. I'm worried about him in this weather."

Heath followed my gaze out the window. "That castle was cold."

"And damp."

"Great ghost-hunting conditions, though," Gilley remarked. "If that phantom weren't there, I wonder who we'd be able to make contact with. I mean, you could probably talk to Kincaid or that French guy, no problem."

And just like that, an idea bloomed in my mind. "Gilley," I said admiringly, "I do believe you're a bit of a genius."

He lowered his lids and said, "Well, duh!"

That made me laugh.

"What's the plan?" Heath asked.

I focused on him. "Maybe Dunnyvale had it wrong," I said. "Maybe we don't start with this Alexandra chick. Maybe we start with the first sign of trouble."

Heath nodded. "The Frenchman."

"Exactly."

"You'll never get across the causeway today, though," Gilley remarked. "I checked the weather on John's phone—thank God he had a chance to charge his before the electricity blew. The winds aren't going to die down until tonight, which means the storm surge will be covering the causeway all morning."

That unsettled me, because I felt we might be running out of time. "What time is low tide tonight?"

Gilley bent down to retrieve a notebook from his backpack. "Should be around seven thirty, and you'll have until about nine thirty to get back if the surge isn't high."

Heath and I exchanged glances. "I'm in," he said softly.

Gilley looked sharply at us. "Hold on," he said. "You're not thinking about going back to that castle *in the dark*, are you?"

"What choice do we have?" I asked him.

"To stay here today and go tomorrow morning!"

"Gilley," I said, using my best "Please remain calm" voice. "We can't let an entire day go by without doing something for Gopher. My gut says he's running out of time."

"It's too dangerous!" Gil insisted. "M. J., look at what happened just before dusk the last time we went to the castle! You almost died!"

I inhaled and exhaled slowly. "Honey," I said softly. "I'm not going to go up to the castle. The Frenchman, the coast guard officer, and Kincaid all died at the base of those cliffs. It stands to reason that I might be able to reach at least one of them there on the safety of the shore and talk to them without encountering the phantom."

"You don't know that it won't come down the stairs after you!" Gilley insisted, his eyes wide and frightened. "M. J., be reasonable! Now that we know how deadly that thing is, I'm not up for you going there at all, much less at night. You *know* spooks get stronger at night. And we've already made that *thing* angry. We don't know what it's really capable of. It could come down those stairs, and in the dark you'd never know it until it was on top of you. At least in the daylight you might see it coming."

I turned back to Heath to see if he'd been swayed by Gilley's argument. "I'm still in if you want to go," he said.

Gilley glared furiously at him.

"We're going," I told Gil. "Sorry, buddy, but we have to do this."

Gilley's face turned downright mean, and he shoved his chair back and stomped out of the room. "I'm not going with you!" he called from the stairway. He then stopped abruptly, returned to the table, and grabbed three more rolls before turning away in a huff again.

*   *   *

Heath and I found our way to the local paper, which was located in a rather small building in the center of town. The door was locked tight, and the interior was dark, as were most of the businesses along the narrow street.

I huddled inside my coat, shivering in the chill rain and damp air. "I hope we catch a break from this weather tonight when we cross the causeway," I said.

"It would be the first time we caught a break on this bust," Heath grumbled.

And then I had another idea. "Hey, you know, if Kincaid stayed at the Dunlee Inn, maybe the French guy did too."

"Worth checking out. Did John tell you where it was?"

I saw a small café down the street with lights on and the sound of a generator's motor humming on the otherwise quiet street. "No. But someone in there is bound to know."

After getting directions from the café owner, we made our way to the Dunlee Inn. It was a sweet-looking structure with dark brown shingles and a thatched roof. Moving inside, we inquired about the owner, and a portly gentleman with thick white hair and a ready smile greeted us. "Top oh the mornin' to ya," he sang. "I'm Sean Tierney. How can I help you?"

Heath and I explained who we were, and reminded him that he'd spoken to our colleague the evening before. "Ah, yes," he said. "John from America. Lovely young man. He was inquiring about Mr. Kincaid and his party."

"Yes," I said. "And we're very grateful for the information you gave to him. But today I wanted to come by and ask about the Frenchman who first encountered the phantom."

"You mean Gaston Bouvet?"

My eyebrows shot up. "You remember him?"

The innkeeper smiled wide. "Oh, I remember him all right. He stayed with me those first few weeks he was exploring the castle. O' course, on his return trip he stayed in the Mulholland house, but while he was here, we got to know each other quite well."

"We're interested to learn anything we can about the phantom that haunts Dunlow Castle. We understand that Gaston was the first to encounter it."

Sean's expression turned grave. "Aye, miss, he was the first. But he made no mention of it on his visit with us here at the Dunlee Inn. No, we think he encountered that frightful thing on his return visit when he and his mate went putting their noses where they didn't belong."

"How long was the time between his two visits?"

Sean scratched his head and thought back. "I'd say at least a fortnight. He said he had business to attend to before he came back and continued his search for Dunnyvale's gold."

Heath asked, "Do you really believe Bouvet knew where the gold was hidden?"

"He said he did. In fact, he insisted that he knew exactly where it was hidden. He claimed to have a secret letter telling him precisely where to find the gold—though I never got a peek at it. He carried the letter on his person at all times, and only took it out when he could be sure no one was havin' a look over his shoulder."

I wondered what had happened in the two weeks between Bouvet's first visit to the rock and his second that sparked the appearance of the phantom, and remembered that Dunnyvale had told me the phantom was brought there by someone. I asked Sean, "In the time that Bouvet was back in France, did anyone else report having any strange encounters at Dunlow Castle?"

The innkeeper shook his head. "No, miss, quite the opposite. There were many a local person here in Dunlee who wanted to see if they could find the gold before the Frenchman came back. But no one had any luck at it. There were treasure hunters on that rock right up to Bouvet's return, in fact."

I turned to Heath and shrugged my shoulders. He nodded; then we thanked the kindly innkeeper and headed out. "What was it about Bouvet's return that brought on the phantom?" I asked him after we'd dashed through the rain to the van and buckled ourselves in.

"I have no idea," he admitted. "The only thing I can think of is that Bouvet somehow either brought the phantom with him on his return visit or woke it up when he went in search of the treasure."

"Huh," I said, wondering about what he'd just revealed. "Maybe that's it, Heath."

"Maybe what's it?"

"What if the phantom has really been on that rock all along, guarding Dunnyvale's treasure, and only got woken up when that treasure was disturbed?"

"You mean like the mummy's curse, or something?" Heath said with a chuckle.

But I wasn't joking. "Exactly like that," I told him. "It sort of makes sense given the fact that no one remembers seeing the phantom until Bouvet returned for the treasure. And up until his second visit when he went to retrieve it, the phantom was apparently lying dormant."

"But what about what Lord Dunnyvale told you?"

"You mean the part where he told me that someone else was responsible for the phantom? And that the answers to the phantom's origins lie with this Alexandra person?"

"Yeah."

I shook my head. "I think he was lying." Heath looked skeptical, so I explained my reasoning. "Alexandra and Kincaid didn't show up until sixteen years *after* the first appearance of the phantom. It was haunting that castle all that time, so how could it possibly be connected to her?"

"Good point," Heath admitted.

"And," I continued, "Alexandra's Russian. If I remember correctly, Kincaid was South African—right?"

"Right."

"Sean said that Bouvet went back to France to tend to his business and returned with a friend. Kincaid would have been about ten years old at the time, living in South Africa—so we know the friend wasn't him. And from what John said about this Russian chick, she was probably of a similar age at the time, so how could it have been her? All roads lead back to that rock and

Bouvet's search for the gold. I think that Ranald used the phantom as a guard to keep his treasure out of any prospective thief's hands."

"So the spirit of Lord Dunnyvale lied to you, but for what purpose?"

And that stumped me. For the life of me I couldn't think of a reason why Dunnyvale would save me from the phantom only to send me in circles about its origin. "I haven't figured that part out yet."

Heath leaned back in his seat and sighed tiredly. "Well," he said, "we'd better figure it out soon if we're going to save Gopher."

Chapter 8

Heath and I stood on the first cobblestones of the cause-way, shivering in the cold wind, blowing out of the north. "Jesus," he said, ducking his chin against the elements.

I pulled at the cuffs of my gloves and patted the scarf wound thickly about my neck. "At least it's stopped raining."

"You ready to get this over with?"

I switched on my flashlight. Heath did the same and our beams swept over the cobblestones. An occasional wave slipped over the lip of the causeway, but otherwise, it remained dry. "I'm up for jogging it," I told him, relieved to see it fairly clear of water.

Heath made a sweeping motion with his arm and, adopting an Irish brogue, said, "Lasses first!"

I gave him a sidelong grin and trotted forward. As we broke away from the surrounding rocks and shore, the cold wind bit into us even more. Thank God I'd packed some long underwear.

I increased my speed, wanting to get across the

causeway as quickly as possible. Behind me I could hear Heath's quick steps, telling me he was keeping pace.

We reached the rock without incident, and only my feet and the cuffs of my jeans were wet. Still, that was enough to quickly temper the burst of heat I'd created running across the causeway.

Heath stepped up beside me, breathing hard. "Where should we start looking?"

I pointed to my left. "That's where we saw Kincaid fall."

Heath nodded. "Maybe we'll get lucky and call up both Kincaid and Bouvet."

I frowned. "We haven't had that kind of luck so far."

"So we're due," he said with a grin. "Come on. The sooner we find out if these two are willing to communicate, the sooner we can get back to the B&B and that warm fire."

I hurried along after Heath as he scouted the path to the place right below where we'd watched Kincaid fall. When we stopped, I chanced a glance over my shoulder, nervous to be so close to the phantom.

"Did you see something?" Heath asked, pointing his flashlight in the direction I was looking.

"No," I assured him. "I was just thinking how odd it is that the phantom doesn't seem to come down those stairs."

"It's not that unusual," he replied. "Especially if it wants to stick close to the gold and protect it."

"Maybe," I said, but something about the phantom haunting only the top of the rock bothered me.

I was silent for a few moments and Heath nudged me. "What're you thinking?"

I inhaled deeply and exhaled slowly. "That we might want to find out what its range is."

"That could be dangerous."

I cracked a smile. "And this bust has been such wholesome fun so far?"

Heath appeared to waver at my suggestion. I saw his hand move to one of the canisters tucked into his tool belt. We'd come to the rock somewhat "unarmed." Neither of us was openly wearing magnets, but we'd brought enough canisters to give the phantom pause should we encounter it.

Finally, he said, "Let's tackle Kincaid and Bouvet first, and see how we feel about playing tag with the phantom after, as long as we have time."

"Cool."

I switched off my flashlight and Heath did the same. I then pulled out one of the small handheld cameras with night vision and flipped it on. Looking through the view screen, I considered the dark green landscape. "You want to go first?" I asked Heath.

"Sure," he said, before cupping his hands around his mouth and calling out to Kincaid. "Jordan Kincaid! If you can hear us, please give us a sign!"

We both listened for any unusual sounds, but only the wind and waves reached our ears. "Jordan Kincaid!" Heath called again.

I counted to ten, and focused the lens of the camera

all around the rocks. Nothing moved and there were no unusual shadows lurking about.

"Try Bouvet," I suggested.

"What was his first name again?"

"Gaston."

Heath called out to Gaston, but there was no reply. I closed my eyes and focused on the ether, flipping my intuition on to high. There was a mixture of energy there at the base of the rocks. I could feel the tragedy of the three lives lost, along with other older rifts in the ether. "This rock has seen a lot of death," I said.

Beside me, Heath reached for my hand. "I can feel it too. But none of it wants to communicate."

I tucked the camera into my messenger bag and turned my flashlight back on. "I say we move to the stairs and see how far up we can go before we start triggering the phantom."

Heath held my hand firmly, keeping me next to him. "Tell me why again?"

I was thinking about the crypt where Dunnyvale was interred, and about the journal entry that Kincaid had entered the night he died. He'd talked about those crypts and I just knew there was a reason Alex had gone to explore them. My own intuition was tugging me up those stairs back to that secret door, and I felt compelled to honor the impulse.

"I just want to know what our boundaries are," I told him.

Again Heath appeared to waver.

"You can stay here," I told him. "I'm okay going alone." Man, was I good liar or what?

Heath slanted his lids at me. "You're not going alone."

"Cool," I said, pulling my hand from his. "Then let's get to it."

I hurried ahead of Heath lest he think it a good idea to pick me up and haul me away caveman-style. That was only okay if we were near a bed.

We reached the stairs and I checked myself. We had to proceed slowly and carefully; otherwise, that phantom could be on both of us faster than we could react.

While holding the flashlight in one hand, I lifted out a canister with my other, and held my thumb against the rim to pop the cap quickly should I start to feel the phantom's energy. Looking over my shoulder, I asked Heath if he was ready.

"No," he said, pulling out two canisters himself. "But I'm not letting you go it alone."

I smiled winningly at him before turning back to the stairs. We moved up slow and steady-like, pausing every so often to listen for any sign of any spirits including the phantom.

As I climbed, I'd periodically shone the beam of my flashlight to the left, searching for that hidden door.

"It's up a little further," Heath called from behind me.

He knew me too well.

A few minutes later he tugged on the back of my shirt. "There," he said, pointing out the door in the shadow of my beam.

I stopped on the stair opposite the door. "I have a gut feeling."

"You think Gopher's in there?"

I shrugged. "I'm not sure. But something's tugging me there."

Heath tucked one of the canisters under his arm before closing his hand over my wrist and moving the flashlight up the stairs. We were about three-quarters of the way up, and nerve-rackingly close to the phantom's territory.

No dark shadows presented themselves, and although the edges of my senses were picking up the uncomfortable feeling of being near the phantom, I didn't feel that it was about to attack us.

Of course, I hadn't truly sensed that it was about to attack me the last time either.

"Your call," Heath said, nodding his head toward the door.

I took a deep breath and edged my way to the entrance of the crypts. The door was heavy and difficult to pull open, but with little more than a loud nerve-jarring screech, it allowed us to pass through it.

We stood in the dark entrance for a few beats, waiting, listening, and feeling the ether.

"Someone's here," I whispered, sensing the telltale signs of a spook nearby.

"Yep."

I quickly turned off the flashlight and got my camera back out. Flipping it on, I held it up to eye level before clearing my throat and saying, "Hello?"

"Bonsoir," said a very soft voice, and Heath and I both jumped.

But I saw no one either with my naked eye or through the view screen. "Hello?" I said again.

"Ah-lo?" a male voice replied.

"I think it's Bouvet!" Heath whispered excitedly in my ear.

"Oui," said the voice. *"C'est moi."*

My eyes widened. The voice was disconnected but clear, and I waved the camera around, trying to find a shadow or form to which it might belong.

"Bonsoir, Monsieur Bouvet," Heath said. *"Je m'appelle* Heath."

My eyebrows rose and I turned to him. "You speak French?"

"That's all I know."

There was a chuckle and the hair on my arms prickled. "Ah-lo, Heath," said the voice with a heavy French accent. "Perhaps you will assist me?"

I smiled wide. We definitely had Bouvet!

"Certainly, sir," said Heath. "And maybe you can help us too?"

"But of course! I am looking for *mes amis.* Have you seen zem?"

"No," Heath said. "We just got here a little while ago, Mr. Bouvet. And we haven't seen anyone else but you."

I squinted at the view screen. *And I wish we could actually see you,* I thought.

"Zey are supposed to help me with za lid. It is most

'eavy, you know. Perhaps you might be of some assistance?"

"Sure," Heath offered. "What lid is it that you need help with?"

There was a pause, and I wondered if we'd lost Bouvet. "Ah, zere you are!" he exclaimed suddenly before switching back to French. *"Oh là! Tu m'as apporté un cadeau? Encore un de tes trésors merveilleux de l'Amérique du Sud, il paraît. C'est un vrai honneur que tu me fais là, mon vieux, et je vais l'ouvrir sur-le-champ!"*

"What's he saying?" I whispered.

"I don't have a clue," Heath whispered back.

Bouvet's tone was casual and lighthearted, but I was worried. Something about the energy around us had shifted, and I thought that maybe the spirit of Gaston Bouvet had moved away from conversing with Heath and me to enter the memory of what had happened to him in the moments leading up to his death.

"Oh, but of course, *mon ami*!" he said, switching partially back to English. "But first you must 'elp me with ze lid!" Bouvet chuckled, as if he was still engaged in conversation with someone other than us. *"Qu'est-ce?"* he added, as if someone had just said something he didn't quite hear. After a moment he said, "Oh, very well! *Un, deux, trois!"*

There was a popping noise . . . a bit of a pause . . . then the most terrified scream I'd ever heard. I jumped back against the wall, shocked and scared down to my toes as I also heard frantic footsteps racing along the stone while that scream went on, and on.

In the next instant there was a rush of wind as something whizzed right past me, and footsteps continued to sound out the doorway and up the stairs. *"What the hell?"* I heard Heath gasp.

My fist clutched my grenade, and my shaking fingers poised themselves on the edge of the lid. For a few seconds I considered popping the top and unleashing the spike, but then I realized that although I was scared, I wasn't actually sensing the phantom approach . . . yet.

"Time to go," Heath's ragged voice whispered in the dark. He clicked his flashlight on, and in the dim light I could see that he looked as scared as I felt.

"I'm right behind you," I told him.

We left the tunnel leading to the crypts and hustled down the stairs. From the top of the rock we could still hear snatches of Bouvet's terrified screams. His reliving what I suspected was an encounter with the phantom had elicited other spirits to stir in the night. More than once I heard Kincaid shout out for Alex, and eerily, I also heard a man with a thick Irish brogue shout, *"It's after me! Get away with you! Get away!"*

"That's gotta be the coast guard officer," Heath called over his shoulder as we raced down the stairs.

I mentally agreed but was too busy focusing on the sounds in the night and keeping my footing to reply. What I didn't tell Heath was that I was also listening for Gopher's voice. If he had been killed, I suspected I might hear it mixed in with the other victims of the phantom.

But no sound or sign of him came to my senses. "I

just want off this damn rock!" I swore as we neared the bottom.

Heath cleared the last step, pausing briefly to catch his breath and wait for me. I joined him and he reached for my hand. Together we ran to the causeway.

I took a step onto the cobblestones, feeling a wash of relief to be so close to leaving this cursed place, when an agonized cry descended from high above, followed by a sickening *WHUMP* somewhere behind me near the base of the cliffs. A flurry of shivers shot up my spine.

Heath and I both froze midstep. I swallowed hard and tried to resist the urge to look behind me. "Sweet Jesus!" I gasped. "Please don't tell me that was what I think it was!"

And then, we both heard Kincaid's voice scream, *"Allllllllllllllex!"* followed by another *WHUMP*.

I thought I was going to be physically ill, and I did actually begin to wretch and gag. I staggered forward onto the causeway, dizzy with the horror playing out in the ether, and nearly stumbled right over the side and into the water.

Heath's hand caught my shoulder, keeping me on the cobblestones, but my knees gave out and I started to sink down. I felt his strong arm sweep under my back while his other arm moved under my knees, and before I knew it, he had swept me off my feet and was carrying me quickly over the wet stones.

Only then did I realize I was crying.

I clutched his coat and wept, trying to still the flash of memories of Kincaid falling off the cliff. Hearing the sound of him hitting the rocks was almost more than I could bear.

He and Bouvet were reliving those terrifying moments before their deaths over and over again, and *no* soul deserves such torture. "We ... have ... to ... help them!" I sobbed.

Heath came to an abrupt stop, his breathing labored. He squeezed me tight and lowered his head to my shoulder. "Yes," he whispered. "But not tonight."

I hugged him fiercely and tried to collect myself. "I'm okay," I said after a bit.

He set me down and took my hand again. We didn't waste any more time hustling our butts back across the causeway.

We arrived at the B&B only to find the lights still out. The two of us made our way to the sitting room, which was surprisingly warm and cozy by the fire. Heath sank onto the couch and stared a little forlornly at the fire.

I shrugged out of my coat, kicked off my shoes, and was taken by how handsome his face was in the glow of the fire. I moved to the cushion next to him, and ran a finger along his black silky hair.

He turned to me and our eyes locked, and I wondered why I'd ever thought I could resist the attraction I had to this man.

He didn't try to kiss me; he just waited for me to decide. I hesitated only a second or two, wondering where my true feelings were amid all the chaos of the last few days. And then, I realized I really, really, *really* wanted to kiss him; so I leaned in and touched my lips to his, and it was like opening a release valve. All that fear and adrenaline and awfulness that he and I had so recently witnessed melted away and a wave of passion flooded between us.

It wasn't long before our clothes came off and we moved it upstairs.

The next morning I woke with Heath's naked warmth curled around me. For a few heartbeats I felt content and happy. His body fit so nicely around mine. There was a synchronicity about us—even our breathing was in time together.

I opened my eyes, and a bit of the magic evaporated. He and I had made our way to the only unoccupied room—Gopher's.

Our producer's suitcase was still sitting on a nearby bench, opened and overflowing with his clothes. I sighed and closed my eyes again, pushing away the rush of reality.

"Hey," Heath said softly.

"Hey."

I felt gentle lips on my shoulder. "You okay?"

A smile crept at the corners of my mouth. He was so good at reading me. "Yeah. Just worried about Gopher."

Heath's arms wrapped tightly around me. "We'll find him."

I sighed again. "Finding him means going back to Dunlow."

"Yep."

"I hate that stupid rock."

That won me a small chuckle. And then, "Did you notice the clock is working?"

I opened my eyes and peered at the nightstand. The digital clock was flashing 12:00. "The electricity's back on!"

Heath sat up and looked around, squinting in the morning light. "About time," he muttered with a yawn.

There was a sudden eruption of noise out in the hallway, and Heath and I both jumped out of bed, naked and staring at the door. I knew that shrieking anywhere. "Gilley!"

I ran toward the door and Heath caught my arm. He shoved his flannel shirt at me and reached for his jeans. I threw the shirt over my head and dashed to the door. Pulling it open, I saw Gilley crying and waving his arms around, raising a ruckus, while John, Kim, and Meg all stood by trying to console him.

"They never came back!" he wailed. "The phantom's got them! *It's got them!*"

I heard Heath clear his throat from over my shoulder and four heads swiveled abruptly in our direction.

Followed by four jaws dropping open.

Followed by four pairs of eyes opening wide.

Gilley was the first to recover himself. "Are you two *serious*?"

I winced. He can really reach those higher octaves when he's upset. "We're fine," I said calmly.

Gilley put both hands on his hips and snapped, "Oh, we can all *see* that, M. J.!"

I smiled sheepishly and pushed Heath back inside the room, closing the door quickly behind me.

"We probably should have left them a note or something," Heath whispered.

I sighed yet again. "Yeah, well, hindsight's twenty-twenty."

Heath and I took our time going down to breakfast. I wasn't interested in facing the reproachful glare I knew Gilley would be issuing my way the moment he saw me. I hoped that if I took my time, he'd eat, grow tired of waiting for us, and move on to his computer now that the power was back on.

I hoped wrong.

Heath and I arrived in the dining room to find it still full. All conversation died away the moment we appeared. "Uh, boy," I mumbled.

Heath cleared his throat and laid a gentle hand on my back. "Morning," he said to our group.

"It is for some of us," Gilley snapped.

I felt my shoulders sag, but Heath ignored the sarcasm and took a seat near the end, patting the chair next to him. I took my seat and immediately got busy loading some eggs onto my plate.

I was acutely aware of the palpable silence all around me.

Heath also busied himself, pouring some tea into my cup, before adding some into his.

I thanked him but avoided all eye contact and dived into the eggs. They were stone cold, as was the tea, but I wasn't about to complain or even hint that the meal was anything less than scrump-dilly-icious.

"We're waiting . . . ," Meg said.

My fork stopped halfway to my mouth, and I set it down. Heath and I exchanged a look, and I was irked to see the corners of his mouth lifting. He thought this was funny.

Still, I was going to stick to my guns. "For what?" I asked innocently.

Meg started laughing. Kim and John joined in, as did Heath, but Gilley had folded his arms and was scowling at us. "Details," Heath said. "They want details."

"Uh . . . ," I said. Were they serious? "How about if I tell you that what happens between Heath and me is private?"

This made the group laugh even harder, and even Gilley's scowl turned less frowny. "We don't care about your extracurricular activities," Kim said delicately. "We're waiting to hear what happened at Dunlow."

"Ahhhhh . . . ," I said, relieved down to my toes.

Heath and I then filled them in on everything that had happened, including the detail about the ghosts of Kincaid and Bouvet falling to the rocks.

Gilley now appeared troubled. "Have you ever heard of a ghost reliving their actual moment of death?"

He had a point. Most spooks go right up to that moment where things start to go really bad, but almost never step into their actual death scene. "I've heard about it only rarely," I said. "I've never actually witnessed it."

"What could cause a ghost to want to go through

that?" Meg asked. "I mean, forcing themselves to relive that horrible fall. Why?"

I pushed my plate away. My appetite was gone. "There's only one reason," I said. "And that is that they're so desperate in those moments to get away from the thing chasing them that they see death as an actual escape route."

"So why don't they cross?" Gilley wondered. "I mean, at some point they've got to realize that they're really dead."

I felt goose bumps rise on my arms. "It's the phantom," I said. "I think it might have some sort of captive power over their spirits."

Everyone at the table fell silent for a moment as we thought about those poor men and all the years their spirits were spending reliving their worst nightmares.

Gilley broke the somber silence when he asked, "What about that section in the middle?" I looked at him curiously and he added, "The part about Bouvet talking to someone else."

I rubbed my temples. "I'm not sure, Gil. I don't know who he was talking to or half of what he was saying."

"A lot of it was in French."

"But you had your camera on the whole time, right?"

My eyebrows rose. "Yeah."

"So it should be on the tape."

"As long as the microphone picked it up," I said.

"I'd be interested in looking at that footage," John said. "I mean, from everything you've told us, it seems like that's the exact moment when the phantom was released."

"Yeah, but from where?" I asked. "All we know is that Bouvet lifted a heavy lid, and out it came."

"From one of the crypts?" Meg suggested.

I nodded. That made the most sense. "Gil, can you do a little research on who's buried at Dunlow Castle? See if you can find anything on one of Dunnyvale's successors talking about coming back as a phantom or placing a curse on any trespassers."

"I still have to research this Alexandra chick," he reminded me moodily.

I smiled. "Then you'd better get crackin'."

In the end, Heath, John, and I decided to see if we could at least provide Gilley with the full name of Alex by heading to the newspaper. To our relief the building appeared to be open and functional.

The paper was a typical small-town affair; it was run by a father-and-son team with a circulation of slightly over a thousand people.

As it happened, Jordan Kincaid's appearance in Dunlee and his subsequent death were the biggest stories the paper had ever covered, so they had no trouble providing us with the articles from the days leading up to and including the tragedies. Of course, they also requested that we grant them an interview, which is why it took us two hours to get back to the inn with our intel.

We found Gilley upstairs in his room, tapping away on his laptop, a cord connecting the camera to his computer.

I laid the articles on his bed. "The best we can do is show you a picture of her," I said.

Gilley pulled his eyes reluctantly away from the screen. "Huh?"

"Alex's name was withheld from the article at the request of Kincaid, but the reporter did manage to snag a picture of her right before she, Kincaid, and some other unnamed dude set out for Dunlow."

Gilley squinted at the grainy black-and-white image. "Pretty, though, isn't she?"

"Yeah," said Heath. I cut him a look and he smiled sheepishly.

"Anyway," I said, "now I want more than ever to track her down. There's got to be a reason why Kincaid worked so hard to keep her a secret, and I want to know what that was."

"Can I finish this first?" Gil asked.

I sat down next to him on the bed. "Are you working on the camera feed?"

"Yeppers," he said, focusing back on the frozen green image. "I've been running the sound through a filter trying to pick up what he's saying, but a lot of it is so corrupted or muted that I can't really make a lot of sense out of it."

"Were you able to get anything at all?"

Gilley swiveled the screen toward me. "I can distinctly hear this word," he said before hitting the play button. Through the computer I heard, *"trésor . . ."*

I closed my eyes and thought back to what I'd just heard. "Did he say 'treasure'?"

Gilley nodded. "I think he was talking about finding the treasure in one of the crypts."

But Heath still appeared skeptical. "But why would Dunnyvale tell you the phantom was brought to Dunlow by someone else?"

I turned to him. "Like I said before, he could have been lying."

"But why?" Heath pressed. "I mean, what good would it do to ask you to rid his castle of the very thing that's currently protecting his treasure? And what good does it do to tell you it was put there by someone with some sort of a connection to Alex? I mean, does this whole thing make sense as a wild-goose chase just for his amusement?"

Gilley sighed. "Nothing about this bust makes any sense, Heath."

I was silent for a moment, weighing the possibility that Dunnyvale was lying just to have some fun with us, and I finally had to admit that it didn't sit well with me at all. I finally admitted it to the guys. "My gut is telling me that he wasn't lying."

"Maybe it was one of the other descendants?" Heath suggested, as if he'd just thought of the idea. Gilley and I both turned to him. "What I mean is, maybe one of Dunnyvale's heirs brought the phantom to the castle to protect the family treasure."

"That's possible," Gil conceded.

"And in line with what Dunnyvale claims, that he didn't bring it to Dunlow."

"So where does this Alexandra person fit in?" Heath wondered.

My eye went to the paper on the bed. I picked it up

and squinted at the tall lanky figure. "I've no idea," I admitted. "But she must be involved somehow. Maybe she's a descendant of Dunnyvale's line or something."

Gilley rubbed his eyes. "There's too much conjecture here," he said. "We know little to nothing about who brought the phantom or where it came from or where the treasure is or even where Gopher might be."

"We definitely need more to go on," I agreed when something else occurred to me. "You know who might be able to give us a few more clues?"

"Who?" Gil and Heath both said together.

"The man who was with Bouvet when he opened that crypt."

Heath's eyes widened. "That's right!" he said. "He was with his friend from France when they opened the lid!"

"Didn't you guys say that he went insane, though?" Gil asked.

"Maybe he's better now," I said. "What we really need is a name, which might lead us to a phone number."

"I know where you could kill two birds with one stone," Gil suggested. "The library. I bet someone there can tell you who Bouvet's friend was, and they might also give you all the names of Dunnyvale's descendants."

I got up from the bed and gave him a peck on the cheek. "Thanks, Gil. We'll check it out first thing in the morning, but in the meantime, could you please keep working on that tape?"

"Only if you go out and bring me back some food. I'm in the mood for a nice burger and fries."

"You've been pretty hungry lately," I said. Gilley had been carbo-loading like he was preparing for a marathon.

"You know I eat when I'm stressed!"

"Fine," I agreed. "We'll bring you some dinner. But I'm having them put extra lettuce on your burger."

"Go right ahead," Gilley said sweetly. "I can pick it off later when you're not looking."

Chapter 9

The next morning, Heath and I headed to the village library, which was larger than I expected. There we met with the librarian, a lovely elderly woman named Mary, who was something of an expert on Dunlow Castle, and she graciously agreed to sit with us and answer our questions.

"We know that Dunlow was built by Ranald Dunnyvale in the late sixteenth century," I said after we'd found a nice quiet corner. "But what I'm more interested in is anything you can tell me about his descendants, and this rumor of the Spanish gold hidden somewhere in the castle."

Mary tilted back in her chair and lifted both hands. "Oh, is that *all* you'll be needing to know, then?" she said with a laugh.

I grinned. "I realize it might be a lot to tackle."

"Oh, aye," she said. "Seven generations of Dunnyvales lived in that old keep after Ranald. In fact, there were Dunnyvales living there right up until the turn of the twentieth century, when no more male heirs survived to pass it on."

"What happened to it then?"

"It went to the oldest daughter, Cleona Dunnyvale Mulholland, and then in the late 1930s to her son, Carney Mulholland, who lost it about ten years after the war."

The name Mulholland was swirling around in my head. I knew I'd heard it before, but where? "How did he lose it?" Heath asked.

"Carney Mulholland was as nice an Irish gentleman as you'd ever want to meet," Mary said. "But the poor man had a terrible gambling problem, and lost the entire family fortune. He then sold off his properties one by one to pay his creditors, but he tried to hold on to Dunlow, you know, because he believed the legend of the hidden gold, and just needed time to do a proper search for it—or so he tried to tell the tax man when he came round to collect. The collector gave him a month, but Carney died in a terrible motorcar accident just a few days shy of the deadline. He never did find the treasure—and truthfully I don't believe it ever really existed. The castle fell to the government after that. It was made into a historic landmark shortly thereafter, but a few years ago when the whole world began struggling financially, it came up for sale and has been on the market since two thousand eight. There've been no offers made, though, as no one wants a haunted castle so far away from shore."

"You said there were seven generations of Dunnyvales that lived at the castle," I said. "Do any of them stand out in your mind—either for good or bad?"

Mary tapped a finger to her lower lip as she considered my question. "A few," she said. "There were Ranald's twin sons, born to his second wife not long after his first wife passed. His first son, Malachi, died some years before too. It's said that Ranald was truly a broken man after his first wife died. He'd adored their son, and when Malachi died at the tender age of twelve, and then his beloved wife just a few years later, Ranald had no heart left to share with the next two boys born to him, nor was he much of a husband to his second wife, Josephine, even though by all accounts she loved him dearly. He all but ignored his family, and with no guidance or interest from their father, the twin lads grew up to be quite dreadful. They were said to be simply wretched young men, always drinking and fighting and carrying on.

"In later years, as Ranald's health began to decline, he grew so tired of their behavior that he bequeathed his castle to the winner of a joust between the pair to be held the day of his funeral, which took place in fifteen ninety-nine."

"Who won the joust?"

Mary chuckled. "Neither really. The brothers killed each other on the battlefield, and both had sons, but Carrack died before Keevan, so, technically, Keevan was declared the winner and heir, and the castle fell to his son Aidan."

I remembered then the angry male ghost I'd met in

the kitchen on our first day in the castle and how his name had sounded like Caron to my intuitive ear. I'd have bet dollars to doughnuts that Caron had actually been Carrack.

"When did rumors of the treasure start circulating?" I asked next.

"Oh, those rumors were quietly whispered about well before Ranald died, but no one had the nerve to voice them while the great lord of Dunlow lived. At the joust, however, Carrack publicly announced that he'd learned his father had whispered the location of the gold to Josephine while on his deathbed, and that right after Carrack won the joust, he would make haste to force his mother to reveal it. As you can see from that story," Mary chuckled, "Keevan was obviously his mother's favorite.

"That declaration is what likely led to Carrack's death, as the overt disrespect to their mother inflamed his brother's anger, sending him into a mad rage. Carrack was cut down by his twin, but not before he managed to inflict a mortal wound to Keevan. After both her sons lay dead, and all because of that cursed gold, their mother, Josephine, was so distraught that she returned to France, her birthplace, joined a nunnery, and took a vow of silence. She never again uttered another word to her dying day."

"But she wrote," I said, remembering the letter that Bouvet claimed to find.

"Wrote?" asked Mary.

"She wrote letters, right?"

"Oh," said Mary. "Are you perhaps thinking of the letter said to have been written to Josephine's dear friend? The one that Monsieur Bouvet discovered?"

I nodded.

"Well, I'm sure that she did, Miss Holliday. But that letter is long since lost, I'm afraid."

"What happened to it?" Heath asked.

"No one knows. When Monsieur Bouvet was killed, no one thought to look for it until much later, and by then, it was far too late. He'd been long buried and his personal items sent back to his family in France."

I wondered if anyone realized that Bouvet had been in the tunnel leading to the family crypts when he'd first encountered the phantom, and that was likely where Ranald's treasure was buried. But now that we were talking about Bouvet, I didn't want to miss the opportunity to ask her about his companion. "Do you remember the name of the man that Monsieur Bouvet brought with him from France?"

Mary's forehead creased with wrinkles as she thought back. "I believe his first name was Jeffrey. I remember sitting in a café one day for lunch and watching Monsieur and his friend come in and order at the counter. Bouvet was always the gentleman, and insisted that his friend Jeffrey order first."

"Do you recall a last name?" I asked.

Mary sighed. "I'm afraid I don't," she said, and then something across the library caught her attention. "Oh! Those naughty young lads are at it again!" Getting up quickly, she excused herself and we watched her shuffle across the floor with a determined look on her face as she approached three boys who appeared no older than twelve or thirteen. They each wore the same innocent look on their faces, which was a sure sign that they were up to no good, and Mary stepped right up to them and held out her hand as if she expected them to hand something over. One of the boys shuffled his feet before pulling out a paperback from under his shirt and handing it to her. Mary glared hard at them, and shook her finger at each of them before pointing sternly to the door. All three boys hung their heads and moved quickly out the exit.

When our librarian came back, she set the paperback on the table and I noticed it had a rather steamy-looking cover with a half-naked woman and a shirtless man curled around each other. "Those three are always scuttling in here trying to nick a book out of the adult section," she said angrily. "One more time and I'll turn them over to their mother, and won't they be sorry for it then!"

I pressed my lips together to hold in a laugh, and I noticed that Heath ducked his chin. After he'd had a moment to compose himself, Heath asked, "Did any of the other Dunnyvale heirs ever try and find the location of the gold?"

"Oh, aye," Mary said. "They all did, I believe. Even our very own Mr. Mulholland tried before the accident."

I nodded. She'd mentioned that Carney had searched for the treasure right up to his death. "Do any of the old legends contain stories of the phantom?"

Mary made the sign of the cross and shifted uncomfortably. "No," she whispered. "There was no mention of that wretched creature until Monsieur Bouvet arrived in our village. We'd never even heard that such a thing could exist—except perhaps in our nightmares."

"Have you lived in this village all your life?" I asked, looking at the old woman's creased face and wispy white hair.

"Aye," she said.

"And there was no mention of any kind about a curse being placed on Dunnyvale's gold?"

Mary shook her head. "A curse? Why, no," she insisted. "There's been no such talk of curses, why?"

I scratched my head, and the look on Heath's face made me realize neither of them understood what I was getting at. "If our theory is correct, and the phantom was something Ranald or one of his heirs hid in the castle to watch over the family gold, then the phantom only serves as truly adequate protection if the world knows about its existence. It's a bit like having an alarm on your house without a sign posted outside saying that you have an alarm. It can only act as a deterrent if people know about it beforehand."

"Oh," Mary said with a vigorous nod. "I see what you mean and that makes perfect sense when you put it like that. But I can assure you that no one in our little village knew anything about this phantom until that poor Monsieur Bouvet fell to his death some twenty years ago."

Mary appeared to be very well-informed, and I wondered suddenly if Kincaid had ever approached her about some background on the castle. "Speaking of tragedies at the castle, Mary, did you ever happen to meet Jordan Kincaid?"

Mary's eyes remained sad. "Oh, aye," she said. "And a lovely lad he was."

"Did he maybe come to you for some background on the castle?"

Mary nodded again. "He did. And so did Monsieur Bouvet. I met both of them, and liked each of them very much. Of course, they were both very similar in personality. Both a bit of fearlessness in them, and a thirst for knowledge and history."

I eyed Heath, who was looking as surprised as I felt. "What kinds of questions did they ask?" I wanted to know.

"Much the same sorts of questions you've been asking me," she said. "And they also each asked for a copy of the blueprints to the castle."

Heath leaned forward. "There are blueprints to the castle?"

"Oh, aye," she said. "The original blueprint was designed by Ranald himself for the stonemasons that built his castle. He was a masterful engineer and an architect with great vision. A true Renaissance man."

"We'd like a copy of those blueprints too, please," I said.

Mary frowned. "I'm so sorry, but that artifact and all its copies were stolen from the library, oh, some four years ago. Right after Mr. Kincaid's death, I'm afraid."

Heath's leg nudged me under the table. "The map was stolen?" I repeated.

Mary nodded.

"Who would have stolen an old blueprint?"

"Someone who wanted to try to go for the treasure," said Heath.

"But how could they get past the phantom?"

"Same way we initially did," he reasoned. "With magnets."

"But we didn't get past it—" I started to argue.

"We did until it came after you," he said, cutting me off.

"So if someone used the blueprint, and has already stolen the treasure, what the heck is that thing still guarding?"

"Something else, I'd wager," said Mary.

I thought about that for a bit before I asked, "Do you know what happened to the copy of the blueprint that Kincaid was carrying?"

"Oh, my!" Mary said, leaning back in her seat. "I suspect his fiancée took it with her when she packed up his things."

My eyes got wide. "His *fiancée*?"

"A lovely young lass," she went on. "Alexandra something. She was Russian, you know."

"You met her?"

"Why, yes, of course I did," Mary said. "Although she preferred to be called Alex. She'd been all over the world, which is why, I believe, Jordan adored her. She'd traveled even more extensively than he had."

"What did she do, exactly? Professionally speaking," I asked carefully.

"Oh, she was an expert in ancient artifacts. Jordan told me that he'd gone looking for an expert in ancient relics, and instead, he'd found that and his heart in South America when he interviewed her for his team. Alexandra had been living in Peru for a year before she came with him here."

My heart was thundering in my chest. Finally, we were hitting real clues! "Do you remember her last name or even what it sounded like?"

Mary tucked a loose strand of hair behind her ear. "It began with an *N*. *N-A-R*, I think, were the first few letters. Something like Naratova, I believe. I'm so sorry, dear. I only heard her last name once."

"And how old did you think she was?"

"Oh, my," she said. "Perhaps only twenty-eight or twenty-nine at the time, but very mature for her age. She was a smart young woman. Spoke several languages, as I recall, and beautiful English at that."

Heath had pulled out a notebook and was scribbling furiously. I was so anxious to get back to Gilley with the information that I thanked Mary quickly, and begged her to excuse us.

He and I then dashed back to the B&B, but when we got there, John greeted us at the door, and he didn't look happy.

"What?" I asked when I saw him.

He held up his cell phone. "I just got off the horn with the network brass," he said. "They're furious that we've been here six days and have nothing to show for it."

I scowled. "Oh, screw them," I snapped. "We have bigger fish to fry than worrying about getting their stupid footage, like finding our missing producer."

"That's the point, M. J.," John insisted. "They don't believe that Gopher's really missing. And they aren't buying the whole phantom thing either."

Heath cocked his head. "Wait—what?"

"They think that we're covering for Gopher."

"I'm not following," I said with a sigh.

John collected his thoughts for a minute. "Before we came here, Gopher told me that he and the network brass had an argument about production times, which escalated into an argument over where we'll fit into the weekly TV schedule. We were given Friday night at ten."

I frowned. "Friday night? That's a sucky time slot."

"Exactly," John agreed. "Which is why Gopher threatened to take us to a competing network if they didn't give us either Tuesday or Thursday night at nine."

"What does that have to do with any of this?" I asked.

"Unfortunately for us, it has everything to do with it. They think we're covering for Gopher by inventing the story that he's MIA when he's really gone back to the States to negotiate a new deal with A&E or the Travel Channel."

"Bottom line it for me," I said, feeling a bit of dread in the pit of my stomach.

"They've pulled the plug. Our show's been canceled."

Heath and I just stood there dumbstruck for several

moments while I tried to work through the implications of all that. "Okay," I said with a sigh. "We'll wrap up this bust, find Gopher, and head home."

John shifted on his feet uncomfortably.

"What?" Heath asked him.

"See, that's where we *really* have a problem. I've got student loans, man. And rent. And bills to pay."

I closed my eyes and let my shoulders sag. "You have to go home and look for another job."

"Yeah. And so do Meg and Kim."

I opened my eyes again, and did my best to withhold any judgment that might creep into them as I looked at John. "I understand," I told him, reaching for his arm. "Really."

John's face registered all the guilt I'm sure he felt. "I'd stay if I could."

"We know," Heath said. "It's okay, dude. We got this."

Something occurred to me then and I asked, "Does Gilley know?"

"Nope. He's been upstairs on his computer since you guys left, and I didn't want to interrupt him."

And that was when I had an idea. "Hey!" I brightened. "Maybe we can send the network brass the footage we took the other night. Maybe that'll be enough to convince them that we weren't up to anything sneaky."

But both Heath and John looked skeptically at me. "There are only maybe three minutes of footage, M. J.," Heath said. "By showing them that, you'd risk them thinking we staged it after hearing they'd pulled the plug, or making them even angrier that we've been here six whole days and only have three minutes of footage to show for it."

I felt my spirits sag. "In other words, we're screwed."

"Pretty much," said Heath.

"Totally," John agreed.

Oh, boy.

I found Gil stretched out on his bed, eyes closed, listening to something through his headphones. He looked like he might be sleeping, and I didn't have the heart to wake him with bad news, so I went to the other bed and switched on the television, turning the sound down low, and was soon fast asleep myself.

"Hello, lass," said a familiar voice.

"Lord Dunnyvale," I replied. "Nice to see you again."

There was a chuckle, and then Ranald said, "You haven't seen me yet."

I looked around. I was sitting under the large tree again on the rock, but this time, Dunlow Castle was looking marvelously new and glorious. There was also a lovely cool breeze whistling through the branches of the tree as the sun warmed the air around me, but there was no sign of Dunnyvale. "Good point," I conceded. "Why don't you join me, though, and we can talk?"

Dunnyvale appeared from behind the tree and sat with a flourish. " 'Tis a lovely day, now, don't you agree?"

"I do. Too bad there aren't more days like this at the Dunlow I've visited. It's always raining or windy and cold."

"You must come back in the summer," Ranald told me. "We've beautiful weather then."

"I'll consider it," I told him, right before getting to the heart of the matter. "So to what do I owe the pleasure of your company this time?"

Dunnyvale picked a long blade of grass and nibbled at the ends. "You're a very lovely lass, Miss Holliday, but you're not nearly as clever as I'd hoped."

Even in my dream I was shocked, but I decided to play it cool. "Oh?" I said coyly. "Why's that?"

"Because you should have been much further along in this by now."

"Finding Alex, you mean?"

"Aye."

"Well, *pardon me*, Lord Dunnyvale, but I believe you gave me precious little to go on. After all, we only know Alexandra's first name."

But Dunnyvale was unmoved. "Oh, I expect you know a wee bit more than that."

I tilted my chin toward the breeze. There was the strong smell of brine mixed with a sweeter flower scent. "We know that she's Russian, and her last name begins with an *N*, and that she has red hair. Even in your day, my lord, that was not a lot to go on."

"You've enough to locate her," Dunnyvale insisted. "She holds the secret to the origins of the phantom, as well as being able to help you to rid it from my keep so that you may then find your friend. You must focus your efforts on reaching her quickly, and you must also be aware that you're running out of time. I've been doing my best to reach her, but she hasn't listened to me in years."

That last sentence caught me off guard. "Wait . . . what?"

But Dunnyvale refused to explain more. Instead he got up, looked down at me with a meaningful stare, and said, "Act quickly, now. Before it's too late."

"Hold on!" I said, leaping to my feet, as he began to turn away. "I need for you to tell me something, and this time, I need the truth."

He paused then and turned around, the look on his face clearly insulted. "I've told you nothing but the truth from the start."

I took a breath and tipped my chin. "I apologize," I told him. "I didn't mean to imply that you were a liar."

"What is your question, miss?"

"I need to know if you really did have a treasure hidden away at Dunlow."

Ranald smiled, but it was filled with melancholy. "Aye," he said, as if that was a secret he was weary of. "And you'll find it exactly where I told Jordan to look."

I gasped. "You spoke to Jordan?"

"Aye," he repeated. "I visited both him and Alex in their dreams the same way I'm visiting with you. I made the same request to them as well: to rid my castle of the phantom."

"Where did you tell him to look?"

"I told them what I told my lovely wife, Josephine, on my deathbed," he said. "That the treasure was hidden within another treasure, that of my heart's truest love."

I considered that for a moment. "That's not much of a clue," I said honestly.

"It's a perfect clue, lass," he told me. "And if you find it, you'll also find the key to rid the castle of the phantom. But to use that key, you must first learn about it, and that you can only do if you locate Alex. She's the one living soul who will help you fill in all the rest."

I opened my mouth to say something else, but the most horrendous scream jolted me awake, out of bed, and onto the floor.

The door of the room crashed open and Heath hurtled in, holding a spike and looking like he fully intended to use it.

In the bed opposite me, Gilley sat frightened and pointing at the TV. "What?" I gasped when no one said anything.

Gilley just continued to point at the screen, and I realized there was a children's show on with a talking sheep.

"Oh, Jesus, Gilley!" I snapped as I got up and switched off the television.

Gilley immediately calmed down. "You know how I hate that!" he yelled when I turned to glare at him.

"What's he talking about?" Heath asked me, still holding the spike up defensively.

"He gets freaked-out by talking animals," I said, moving back to the bed in a huff. "You should have seen him when they did the remake of *Charlotte's Web*."

"It's not natural!" Gilley insisted with a shudder.

"Grow up!" I yelled, truly pissed off that he was being such a child and that he'd interrupted my important visit with Dunnyvale.

Gilley gave me a scathing look. "You know," he growled, swinging his legs over the side of the bed, "I don't have to take that from you, M. J.!" He then threw off the covers, but the cord to his headphones was tangled around him, and as he whipped himself away from the mattress, the camera went flying and crashed into the wall, where it broke into several pieces.

"Shit!" I swore, looking at the mess. *"Gil!"*

"Stop yelling at me!" he shouted, and began to cry.

Meanwhile, Meg, Kim, and John all hurried into the room. "What's happened?" asked Meg.

"Gilley's having *a moment*," I said, moving over to the crushed remains of the camera. Now that we'd had our funds cut off, we had only one working camera to help us on our busts.

"So you told him," John said.

I felt my jaw tighten when I saw Gilley turn to him. "Told me what?"

John looked surprised. "You know. That the three of us are on the first plane out tonight to head back to the States."

"What?" he gasped. "Why?"

"Because we got fired," said Meg. "Didn't you know?"

"You guys got fired?" Gilley cried, staring at me as if I'd withheld that news on purpose. "You poor things!" he went on. "I'm so sorry for you!"

Meg squinted at him. "Yeah, Gil. We *all* got fired. Including you."

"WHAT?!"

I stood up with the pieces of the broken camera in my

hand, knowing that I should have been the one to tell him, which helped to immediately dissolve my anger. Walking over to him I laid a hand on his shoulder, and said, "It's okay, buddy. We'll be all right."

Gilley's eyes were the size of saucers, and his breathing was coming in short little pants. *"We got fired?!* Like, for *real*?"

"We'll be fine," I assured him.

Gil's breathing started to quicken even more and he sat down on the bed again, holding a hand over his heart. "But . . . but . . . what about the money? We were being paid *so* much money!"

"There are other gigs," Heath said, coming to sit next to Gil.

"Why me, Lord?!" my partner wailed. *"Why?!"*

It took us half an hour to calm Gilley down. It took us another two hours to convince him to stay with Heath and me and work on finding Gopher. Gil's not so good under pressure. And he's not always good at taking one for the team. Which is likely why, in grade school, he was always the last one picked for dodgeball.

Still, eventually we did calm him down in time to see Meg, Kim, and John off. They each gave me a great big hug, and looked terribly guilty as they loaded their luggage into the taxi. I was really going to miss them—especially on this bust, because we could have used the extra help.

After watching their taxi rumble down the road, Gil, Heath, and I turned back to the B&B.

Anya was waiting for us on the front step, holding a slip of paper and what looked like a letter in her hand. "I'm so sorry to trouble, you," she said to us. "But it's a matter of the bill, you see."

"Let me guess," I told her. "The credit card Gopher had on file has been rejected."

Anya's pleasant expression turned down in a frown. "Aye, I'm afraid so."

"Great," I muttered, irritated that the network had moved so quickly to cut off our funds.

"I even gave them a bell," she said. "Rang the credit card company right up, but they're refusing the charge."

Heath reached into his back pocket and pulled out his wallet. He handed her his Visa with an apologetic smile. "You can put the tab on there."

"Gil and I will each pay a third," I told him.

He smiled gratefully.

Anya took the card and beamed a warm smile. "Thank you for understanding," she said, turning to go back in. I was about to follow her when she seemed to catch herself and swiveled round again to face me. "Oh, I almost forgot. This came in the post for you. And I'm afraid I opened it before I'd taken note of who it was actually addressed to," she said, appearing chagrined. "You might want to have a look at it straightaway." With that, she handed me the letter and moved hastily inside.

I studied the envelope and was surprised to find it was addressed to "the American travelers."

"Huh," I said, showing Heath and Gil.

"That's weird," said Gilley.

"Open it," Heath encouraged.

I did and pulled out a simple typewritten letter that read:

> *If you want to see your friend Peter alive again, you'll stop dallying at the library and rid the castle of the phantom!*

All three of us sucked in a breath. "What the hell . . . ?" Gilley said, snatching the letter from my hands. "Who wrote this?"

I flipped the envelope over. There was no return address, and both the envelope and the letter were typed. I showed it to him and he snatched that out of my hands as well.

Heath's eyes locked with mine. "What do you think it means?"

I swallowed hard. A terrible feeling was settling into the pit of my stomach. "I'd like to say that someone's just reminding us that Gopher's in trouble, but my gut says there's more at play here."

"He knows Gopher's first name," Gilley said softly. "No one who knows him personally calls him Peter."

"How do you know it's a he?" I asked.

Gilley blinked. "I don't. I just assumed."

I knew what he meant. There was definitely a masculine edge to the language. "And it's addressed to 'the Americans,' which means whoever sent it is likely a local."

"But what's the purpose?" Heath pressed. "I mean, we're working as fast as we can on this. Why send us a letter to taunt us with Gopher's disappearance?"

I pulled the letter back out of Gilley's hands. "I don't think he's taunting us. I think he knows where Gopher is, and he's telling us that we won't get him back until we deal with the phantom."

Gilley appeared skeptical of my theory, but Heath nodded. "That's what my gut said the moment I heard you read it."

"Hold on," Gil said. "Gopher's at the rock. Trapped somewhere in the castle by the phantom, right?"

Again Heath and I locked eyes, and I knew he was thinking the same thing I was. "We don't know that for certain, Gil. We only know that the day Gopher went missing, we were at the rock."

"But where else could he be?" Gilley insisted.

I studied the letter again. "I've no idea. And I'm still open to him being at Dunlow, but the past several times Heath and I have been to the rock, we've tried to find Gopher's spirit and we've been met with bubkes."

"That only means he isn't dead," Gil insisted.

"Not necessarily," I reasoned after thinking on it for a moment. "I mean, we all send off energy, both the living and the dead. And when we went looking for Gopher, we didn't sense his spirit or his ghost, which I took as a really hopeful sign; but now that I think about it, we also didn't pick up any sense of him at all. Not even a murmur. If I'm reaching out to someone's energy, I should be able to detect *something*. Even the smallest trace of his energy should have come to us if we were anywhere within about a quarter mile of him."

"M. J.'s right," Heath said, backing me up. "I mean, I remember when I was a little kid, no one would play hide-and-seek with me because I could *always* tell where my friends were hiding. They gave off a vibe that told me exactly where to find them. It's the same method I use when I'm looking for spirit energy in the ether, although spooks give off a different vibration than living people. I seem to connect to their energy more easily just because I've had so much practice communicating with them."

I nodded enthusiastically. "Exactly," I said. "That's exactly how it feels to me too."

"So, you two are saying that Gopher's not even at the castle?"

I hesitated before answering, thinking that through. At last I told him what I honestly thought. "No, that's not quite what we're saying. What we mean is that when we've gone there to try and feel out Gopher's energy, we haven't been able to. He could be there, or he might not, but from where we were standing, he wasn't within our intuitive range."

"There is a way to find out for sure," Heath said.

My heart sank. I knew what he was going to suggest, and it filled me with dread.

"What's that?" asked Gil.

"Now that the backpack M. J. found has given us plenty of magnetically charged spikes, we could storm the castle and see if we can find Gopher."

Gilley visibly paled. "You mean, you'd go in there and face the phantom head-on?"

"With enough magnets, I don't know that it'll be able to come anywhere near us. What do you think, M. J.?"

Truthfully, I thought that I'd rather join John, Kim, and Meg on that plane home, but what I said was, "If we're both loaded down with enough magnets, then it might keep the phantom at bay, and any other spook, which, in theory, would allow us to only focus on Gopher's energy."

Gilley's face clearly expressed that he wasn't so into the idea. "You people are crazy!"

"What else would you suggest, Gil? I mean, at this point, I think we're out of options."

"You could wait for me to pull more off that recording or find out who this Alex person is!"

"You broke the camera, remember?" I said, a bit frustrated.

Gilley's eyes narrowed. "I saved the recording on my computer, M. J. I mean, what do you take me for, an amateur?"

I was about to make a snarky reply, but Heath interrupted with a question for Gil. "Were you able to pull anything else off the recording?"

Gilley focused all his attention on Heath. "As a matter of fact, I did. I managed to get the words *Amérique du Sud* off the recording."

"America?" I asked. I don't speak a lick of French.

"South America," Heath corrected.

Gilley rocked back on his heels. "Exactly."

I shook my head. "But what does that have to do with anything?"

"I have no idea," said Gilley, "but I know it's important. I mean, why would Bouvet say the word 'South America' when he was talking to his buddy right before the phantom showed up?"

Heath's brow lifted with a sudden realization. "Hey, M. J., didn't Mary say that Jordan found Alex living in Peru right before he convinced her to come here?"

I thought back and remembered the conversation quite clearly. "Yeah, but *how* does that connect to all this?"

No one answered me, but it was clear to each of us that there was in fact a connection.

My attention, however, went back to the letter. Lifting it from Gilley, I said, "I think we need to take this to Constable O'Grady."

Heath cocked his head. "Why?"

"Because on the off chance that Gopher has actually been kidnapped by a living, breathing person, we need to tell the police."

Heath nodded. "Yeah, okay."

"While you guys are informing the authorities, I'll get back to finding this mysterious Alex from Russia but living in Peru."

I studied him for a minute before I asked, "How long do you think that will take?" Gilley opened his mouth to answer and I cut him off by adding, "And please don't lowball it, Gil. Tell me honestly."

He shifted uncomfortably on his feet. "Maybe a few days," he said. "Three at the most."

I shook my head. "That's way too long."

"You guys haven't given me enough useful information to find her!" he nearly shouted. "Do you know how many Alexandra N-A-R-somethings there *are* in the world?"

"Which is why we have to go back to the castle and do a thorough search," I said gently. I eased my arm around his shoulders. Gilley looked like he was about to protest again, but I cut him off by saying, "We'll be very, very careful. I pinkie swear."

Gilley wasn't assured. "But, M. J., if you both get into trouble, who's going to help you? We've lost half our team already! You'd be leaving just me behind to figure all this out!"

"So we won't get into trouble," I vowed. "We'll keep all our magnets exposed, search the castle as quickly as we can, and get out."

Gilley looked down at his feet and pulled out from under my arm to trudge up the steps. "Well, I don't like it," he said moodily. "Not one little bit!"

Chapter 10

After we'd settled on a plan, Heath and I headed to the constable station and found O'Grady right away. "Afternoon to ya!" he said with a warm smile. "Come to tell me you've found your friend, I hope?"

"No," I said wearily. "Unfortunately not. We do have something we want you to look at, however." Pulling the envelope out of my back pocket, I handed it to the constable and waited while he read the letter tucked inside.

"What's this supposed to mean, then?" he asked, lifting his eyes back up to mine.

"We don't really know," I said. "But we think by the tone of that letter that maybe someone knows where Peter is, and they're not going to tell us unless we try to get rid of the phantom."

O'Grady looked thoroughly puzzled. "But why would they do that?" he asked. "After all, if they knew where to find your friend, they should tell you, now, shouldn't they?"

"In a perfect world, yes," said Heath. "But we think

that maybe the person who wrote this might have had something to do with our producer's disappearance."

Quinn sucked in a breath. "You mean, you believe the letter is referring to a kidnapping?"

I nodded reluctantly. "Yes."

O'Grady's reaction surprised me. He actually laughed. "Oh, you Americans!" he said, thoroughly amused. But when he saw our serious expressions, he quickly sobered. "I'm sorry," he apologized. "It's just that here in Dunlee we don't see much in the way of crime, you know. I think we're a far more simple folk than you lot from the U.S. Kidnapping is quite out of our league, you see."

"So, you don't think that someone could have taken him?"

"No, miss, I truly don't."

"Then why would someone write that?" I pressed, pointing back to the letter.

O'Grady read the text again before answering. "What I think you might have here is a bit of mischief from some young lads with nothing better to do than antagonize some poor foreigners," he said sadly. "And I think I know just the ones to reprimand."

I thought back to the three boys Mary had caught stealing from the library. I felt embarrassed for having brought the letter in then, as when I looked at it from that perspective, I could clearly see the prank. "Thank you, sir," I said, motioning for Heath to go. "Sorry to have bothered you with this."

"Think nothing of it," O'Grady said. "And come

round to me pub later and have a pint on me," he said kindly.

Heath and I headed back to the inn and found Gilley typing furiously on his keyboard, attempting to locate the mysterious Alexandra. We left him to his task and Heath and I busied ourselves getting ready by laying out warm clothes and double-checking the supply of magnets. Gilley had graciously lent me the use of his sweatshirt, as it was too tight on Heath and he planned to carry the backpack of spikes anyway.

We also went over our plans at the dining room table, drawing a rough outline of the castle from memory. As Heath was sketching it out on paper, the front door to the B&B opened and Mary from the library stepped into the hall. "Oh, hello!" she said when she saw us. "I've been looking for you two."

"Mary!" called Anya, coming out of the kitchen to greet the newcomer warmly. "I was just putting the finishing touches on some supper for my guests. Would you care to stay for a warm meal?"

Mary blushed. "Oh, thank you, Anya, but I really can't. I must get home to my Charlie. You know how he hates it when his supper's late."

"Oh, very well, then, dear, I won't beg you to stay. But have you come round for a cup of tea with me, then? Any new gossip to share?" Anya's eyes were sparkling with interest.

Mary eyed Heath and me uncomfortably, her blush deepening. "Oh, that's so lovely of you, Anya, to offer me a cup of tea, but I'm afraid I can't stay long and I've actually come round to speak with those two."

Anya's head swiveled curiously to Heath and me. "Oh, of course!" she said warmly. "I'd forgotten you two were at the library earlier. Well, I'll leave you three to it, then. I best get back to the kitchen. That meal's not going to cook itself." And off she padded.

Mary came into the dining room and swept a hand in the direction of a chair at the head of the table. "May I?"

"Of course," Heath and I said together.

Mary sat down across from us. "After you left the library, I remembered something I should have thought to mention, but I believe I was still a wee bit distracted by those naughty lads," she began. "I know someone who has a copy of the blueprints to the castle."

"Who?" I asked anxiously.

"Bartholemew Mulholland. Bertie for short."

My eyebrows shot up in surprise. "There's a *living* Mulholland heir to Dunnyvale?"

"Aye," said Mary. "And Bertie's a lovely chap with a wonderful sense of adventure. He used to write travel books, you see, and his writing took him all over the world before an accident many years ago robbed him of the use of his legs. Hasn't stopped him from enjoying life, though, no. He still gets up every morning and tends to his garden and writes a few articles here and there. I believe you'll find him lovely company."

"And he has a copy of the blueprints?" I said, wanting to be sure.

"Oh, aye! I made it for him myself several years ago.

Bertie loves history and maps and such. He's quite a scholar on Irish folklore and myth too. I'm sure he'll want to help you in whatever way he can."

Heath smiled. "Where can we find him?"

"Oh, Bertie's house you can't miss. It's at the very top of Marney Lane, within walking distance actually. If you turn left at the end of this street and just follow the road up a wee bit, you'll find it. Just look for the blue mailbox with the name Mulholland on it."

We thanked Mary profusely and saw her out. "Should we go now?" I asked Heath the moment the door was closed.

"Supper's ready!" Anya called from the dining room.

I heard Heath's stomach grumble almost at the same moment I heard Gilley's fast footfalls on the stairs.

"After dinner," he promised.

"Okay," I agreed.

We ate a quick but delicious meal and left Gilley in the middle of his second portion. I didn't want to mention it then, but he was looking a little rounder to me, and I wondered if he might be stuffing all the anxiety of this bust down with a few too many calories.

The night was chilly, but otherwise clear, and Heath and I walked along the road without passing a soul. "Everyone must be eating supper," I said.

"Do you think it'll be okay to ring Mulholland's doorbell during the dinner hour?"

I eyed my own watch nervously. "I think it's a mistake to wait too late. Gilley says the low tide will crest around nine p.m. If we hit the causeway by then, we'll have two full hours to search the castle and hustle back home."

"What time is it now?"

"A little after seven."

"If we interrupt his dinner, we can always say we eat early in America."

"We do?"

"No. But he might not know that."

"Good point."

We continued along the road as it wove around to point toward the sea before angling up at a steep slope. From there it wound a bit more in an S curve until we rounded the last bend and there, in front of us, was a huge home sitting atop the peak of a cliff overlooking the channel.

"Whoa," I said, seeing the house and marveling at both it and the view. It was so large compared with all the other quaint little gingerbread houses we'd seen dot the village that both Heath and I stopped midstride.

"Is *that* Mulholland's place?" he asked.

"Has to be," I said, pointing to the blue mailbox.

"I thought his family was broke."

"Guess there's more money in travel books than I thought."

We moved quickly to the door, anxious to see the inside. Heath rang the bell and after a few moments we heard someone call, "Coming!"

We waited a few more moments before the door was opened and I had to drop my gaze a bit. Bertie Mulholland was sitting in a mechanized wheelchair with a plaid blanket thrown over his legs. "Good evening to you," he said with a smile.

He didn't appear the slightest put out by the appearance of two strangers at his door, so Heath and I quickly introduced ourselves before getting right to the point. "We're here because Mary from the library said you might be able to help us," I told him.

Mulholland's smile broadened, and I realized what a handsome older gentleman he was. "Well, I shall certainly do my best to help you in any way I can," he said warmly, motioning for us to come in.

We followed him into the home and I sucked in a breath. The back of the house was made up almost entirely of windows, and the view of the ocean and the dusky pink horizon was spectacular.

Heath whistled appreciatively. "That's some view, there, Mr. Mulholland."

Our host puffed his chest out a bit. "Thank you," he said graciously. "And please, call me Bertie. Everyone else does."

We nodded and continued to follow him down a short ramp to a spacious living room with a crackling fire. "Might I offer you some tea and bikkies?"

"We don't want you to go to any trouble," I said.

"No trouble a'tall," he said with a wave of his hand before wheeling himself down a corridor, which, I assumed, led to the kitchen.

Heath and I took a seat on the overstuffed couch and looked around while we heard the sound of china rattling and cabinet doors opening and closing.

I had a chance to take in the many beautiful artifacts filling every shelf, nook, and cranny. By the looks of it, Bertie favored Asian and African art, but there were things that appeared to be from his homeland too. I noticed on the small desk sitting next to me a beautiful mother-of-pearl antique letter opener in the shape of a cross with an Irish crest at the tip of the handle.

Moving my gaze upward, I took in the many framed antique maps, some showing crude renderings of the continents, and I wondered how old and valuable a few of them must be. Along one wall was a series of star charts, and an antique-looking brass telescope rounded out that corner of the room.

I longed to get up and poke through Bertie's vast and varied collection of antiques, but I figured it was safer to stay put and merely observe from the couch.

"This place is totally cool," Heath whispered from beside me.

I nodded. It really was.

Bertie came back to the living room with a tray balanced on his lap. "I'd just finished the dinner dishes when you rang, and this gives me the perfect excuse for a bit of dessert."

Heath and I both thanked him as he handed us each a steaming cup of light green tea and set a large plate of delicious-looking cookies in the center of the coffee table.

"Now, how is it that Mary has suggested I might be of assistance to you?"

I reached for a cookie to dunk into my tea and let Heath begin the discussion.

"M. J. and I are part of an American television show that investigates haunted locations. We came to Ireland to do an episode on Dunlow Castle, but on the first day of filming, we lost our producer."

Bertie looked taken aback. "Lost him?" he asked, before his face visibly paled. "You don't mean . . ."

I shook my head, knowing he thought the worst. "As far as we know, he hasn't been killed, but we do think the phantom has taken him or has chased him somewhere deep inside the castle."

Bertie's hand moved to his mouth. "Oh, heavens," he said. "I'm relieved to hear that you don't think he's been killed, but that is still very bad news, my dear. Very bad indeed."

The anxious feeling in the pit of my stomach that had formed at the start of this bust intensified. "Yes. I know, sir, which is why we're desperate to try and rescue him."

Heath set his teacup down on its saucer and took a deep breath. "M. J. and I are going back to search the castle tonight at low tide, and we don't plan on leaving Dunlow until we find our friend."

Bertie looked down at his lap, and when he spoke next, his voice was very soft and sad. "I'm sure I cannot talk you out of your expedition, but you would be risking both your lives to enter Dunlow, and I cannot stress enough how dangerous that phantom truly is. I have personally lost two dear friends, not to mention the use of my own legs, to that monster."

I gasped, and reflexively stared down at the limp form of Bertie's legs underneath the blanket in his lap.

"Mary told us you'd been in an accident," I said. "But I thought she was talking about an auto accident or something similar."

Bertie shook his head from side to side. "No," he said. " 'Twas the phantom that made me a cripple."

Heath's hand reached for mine and gave it a gentle squeeze before he asked, "Can you tell us what happened?"

Bertie sighed and took a sip of tea. "It was nearly twenty years ago," he began. "I had opened my home to a man named Gaston Bouvet, a Frenchman who was obsessed with finding the gold one of my ancestors was said to have hidden at Dunlow.

"Gaston was such a charming man, and he quickly became a treasured friend. We talked for hours about the castle and its history, and he relentlessly picked my brain for any hint about the gold bullion said to be hidden there."

"Do you believe the legend?" Heath asked. "I mean, do you believe that Lord Dunnyvale found Spanish gold on that ship and hid it away?"

Bertie smiled sadly. "No."

That surprised me, as I was convinced by now that Dunnyvale had told me the truth about hiding it somewhere in his keep.

Still, Bertie clearly doubted the legend. "My ancestor Lord Ranald Dunnyvale invented that story to help keep his two brutish sons in line."

"You seem so sure," Heath said.

"Aye," Bertie agreed. "I have reason to be. You see, before I lost the use of my legs and when I was quite a bit younger, I traveled extensively in Spain. As Dunlow used to belong to my family, I had a particular interest in the legend, and so I made it a point to research the archival shipping logs for the Spanish vessel that crashed on these very shores."

"Did you find the ship?" I asked.

"Oh, indeed I did," he said proudly. "And along with it, I also discovered the truth, which was most disappointing, but not terribly surprising. The cargo log indicated that the ship was carrying only soldiers, armament, and food supplies. I don't believe there were more than a few dozen gold coins aboard, and all of that was likely in the pockets of the higher-ranking soldiers."

"I'm assuming you told all of this to Bouvet?" Heath said.

"Oh, but of course I did!" Bertie exclaimed. "However, he would not be dissuaded. The thought of discovering real treasure was too much for him to resist. His first venture to Dunlow yielded him several clues to the treasure's location—or so he boasted."

"Where did he think it was?"

Bertie shrugged. "I've no idea. Gaston loved to tell a tale, and I believe that he rather liked the attention his boastful claims ignited. I also believe that he eventually convinced himself that the treasure was real and hidden in a spot only he and his friend Jeffrey knew."

I leaned forward. "Did you also know this Jeffrey?"

Mulholland looked surprised. "Of course I knew him!" he exclaimed. "He was also a dear friend of mine, the poor man. He lost even more than Bouvet, I think."

"Wait—what?" I asked. I wasn't following.

"Jeffrey lost his closest friend when Bouvet fell to his death, and he lost his mind for a time to that dreadful creature. Then, sixteen years later, after he learned that his son had come here and also lost his life, I'm afraid it was too much for poor Jeffrey and he committed suicide. Such a tragedy."

My jaw fell open, but it was a moment before I could say anything because I also noticed how Mulholland's eyes had misted and he turned away from us, clearly upset and attempting to compose himself.

Heath nudged me with his elbow and I sneaked a peek at him. "Jeffrey *Kincaid*?" he whispered in my ear.

I nodded, and mouthed, "I think so."

When Bertie turned back to us, I asked, "Just to clarify, Mr. Mulholland, are you saying that Jeffrey Kincaid was the friend that accompanied Bouvet from France?"

"Aye," he told me, discreetly wiping at his eyes and then taking a sip of tea. "Jeffrey and Gaston were old friends. They met on safari, I believe, in South Africa. Jeffrey was a lovely man, so generous. Always bringing back trinkets for Gaston from all the places his mining business took him. He had mines all over the world, you know. A very wealthy man, and obsessed with treasure of any sort. I believe that is why Gaston asked him to come along. Jeffrey could have given Gaston a true appraisal and the best price for the gold if they found it, but it was not meant to be, I'm afraid."

I stared again at Bertie's legs. "And you went with them that day, didn't you?"

Bertie nodded reluctantly. "That I did," he said sadly. "And what a terrible day it was, although it didn't begin that way. That morning was clear and beautiful and I remember it like yesterday. But I suppose the last day you spend on your feet before you become a cripple is always memorable."

I winced. The poor man.

"We arrived at the castle just after eleven in the morning. Gaston and Jeffrey raced up the stairs, anxious to get to the treasure, but I still held my doubts about it being there, so rather than chase after them, I spent nearly an hour walking all the way round the island, marveling at the beautiful morning. When I was halfway round, I thought I heard someone calling or shouting from the top of the rock. The wind and waves obscured the noise, and so I never assumed something could be amiss. I thought only that Gaston or Jeffrey might be worried about me because I hadn't come up to the castle yet. I now know that was likely when my friend Gaston was sent plunging to his death, but as I was on the far side of the island, I had not a clue that anything so awful had happened.

"I do remember, however, thinking that I should make haste to finish my walk, and when I reached the stairs, I saw that my friends had left a set of pulleys and a length of rope behind. I thought they might need it, so I began the rather difficult task of carrying it up the stairs.

"As you know, it is a very long way up, and just short of the top, I believe, I was panting so hard from the labor of carrying the heavy pulleys and rope that I took a moment to set the equipment down, and take a bit of a rest. That was the moment when my dear friend Jeffrey appeared at the top of the stairs and began racing down as if his very life depended on it!

"He was so distraught, holding his head in his hands and crying out for Gaston. I attempted to catch him as he passed me, but he was clearly out of his mind and he shoved me aside as he ran by, never even looking back. That was my first inkling that something terrible must have happened, and I was still of the mind that my friend Gaston was up at the castle. So I took a step or two up when the most vile feeling crept over me like a great horrible tide and in the next instant . . . *it* appeared."

"The phantom," Heath whispered, his attention totally focused on the old man.

"Aye," said Bertie, his hands shaking slightly as he took another sip of tea. "It took us all by surprise, you see," he continued after a bit. "None of us knew what was happening until that creature was directly on top of us. I only know that I was so stricken with fear that I froze and horrible images began to cloud my thoughts. Scenes from my worst nightmares."

I nodded. I knew exactly what he meant.

"What happened then?" Heath asked softly.

"Well," Bertie said, adjusting the blanket covering his

legs. "I wish I knew. My vision was compromised, you see, but I believe I've been able to put the pieces of what came next back together. I remember being hit by a strong force, and I know that one of my legs became entangled in the rope around my feet, which knocked me off-balance, and I was sent tumbling down those stone stairs, where I lost consciousness. The next thing I knew, I was being carried down by several men on a stretcher, and I've never been able to feel my legs since."

"So the phantom physically attacked you?" Heath asked.

"Aye, I believe it did."

"It barreled into me the same way," I said, feeling especially lucky to be alive and in one piece after hearing Bertie's tale.

Bertie seemed to agree. "You're a very lucky young miss to have survived an encounter with that demon," he said.

"Did you ever talk to Jeffrey after that?" Heath asked. "I mean, did you ever ask him what happened?"

Bertie appeared quite troubled by the question and he took his time answering. "I did," he said softly. "But you must remember the effect the phantom had on his mind. I believe it caused him great mental distress and I don't believe when we talked later that he knew what really happened in that castle."

"What'd he say?" I pressed. I needed to know what Jeffrey Kincaid had seen.

"He said that he and Gaston had had a bit of a quarrel about the gold, and that Gaston had stormed off and

Jeffrey could not find him, although he searched and searched the castle. Then, when he'd heard Gaston's cries for help, he'd gone out of the main door only to encounter a terrible demon who stole his mind and murdered his friend."

I thought back to the crypts where we'd encountered Bouvet's ghost, and the elder Kincaid's account of what had happened suddenly didn't wash with me. "Assuming there really was treasure at the castle, do you think that Bouvet would have told Jeffrey where the gold was hidden?"

Bertie shrugged. "Gaston told me that he'd told only Jeffrey where he thought the gold was hidden, because he trusted his dear friend. He also promised me that once he found the gold, I would get a fair share of it too, even though I doubted its existence. As I said, both Gaston and Jeffrey were extremely generous friends and both of them fully believed the legend of the hidden treasure."

I turned and looked at Heath. Jeffrey's story wasn't adding up. "If Jeffrey knew where the gold was hidden, why didn't he go looking for Bouvet there?"

"Exactly," Heath said, focusing back on Bertie. "Did you suspect that Jeffrey wasn't being honest with you about what might have happened at the castle?"

Bertie's face became guilt-ridden and he looked down at his lap. "I must confess that I did."

I took a quick peek at my watch. The time was nearing eight o'clock, and I nudged Heath. "We have to be off, I'm afraid," I said, getting to my feet. "Thank you so much for sharing that difficult story, Mr. Mulholland, and I'm so sorry, for all that you went through."

Bertie forced a smile. "Oh, don't be sorry, miss. I've still managed to have a wondrous life. And I had time to turn all my adventures to faraway places into a success-ful writing career, so one door might have closed for me, but a window opened wide."

"You have a great attitude at least," I told him.

"Of course I do," he said, and this time his smile was genuine. "I'm Irish after all!"

A mere ten minutes later we had a copy of the blueprints to Dunlow Castle in hand. Bertie had attempted over and over again to convince us not to go back in search of our friend, but Heath and I were resigned. "We'll take plenty of protection," I told him. "This phantom is just like all other spooks in that it hates to be too close to a lot of magnetic energy. And we have magnets aplenty for our return trip."

Still, as we left him, he warned us for the tenth time to be careful. "It's not worth your lives," he'd said. "Just remember to get out at the first sign of trouble, and do your best to keep your wits. The phantom's a devil for playing with your wits."

When Heath and I got back to the B&B, it was nearly eight thirty and Gilley was still tapping away on his com-puter with a cup of chocolate pudding and a few cookies beside him on the nightstand. I filled him in about what Bertie Mulholland had shared, and Gil leaned back against the headboard with a thoughtful expression on his face.

"What?" I asked as I was changing.

"While you guys were gone, I took another listen to that tape from the crypts," he said. "I don't speak French, but I think that Bouvet's ghost was talking about some sort of gift right before he started screaming."

I paused getting into my warm clothes to stare at him. "Gift?"

Gilley nodded. "He says the word *cadeau*, which means gift or present."

"So, what? Kincaid gave him a gift?"

Gilley nodded. "I don't think what you heard was Bouvet opening the lid to one of the crypts. I think, after the count of three, you heard him open his gift from Kincaid. And then he started screaming bloody murder."

All sorts of synapses fired in my brain. "Holy shit," I whispered.

"Mmm-hmm," Gilley said knowingly. "I think your friend Ranald was right. I think Kincaid brought that phantom to the rock because he wanted the gold all to himself, only the plan totally backfired."

I wanted to talk more about all that and bring Heath into the discussion, but a quick glance at the clock on the bedside table made me think twice about it. "I'll fill Heath in on the way to the causeway," I vowed, and shrugged into my long underwear, turtleneck, flannel shirt, thick sweater, and Gilley's sweatshirt. When I was fully clothed, I asked him how I looked.

"Like the Michelin Man."

I scowled and made a point of looking from the pudding in Gilley's hand to his expanding stomach.

"That's a bit of the pot calling the kettle black, don't you think?"

Gilley's jaw fell open and he immediately set down the pudding, only to then pick up a cookie and begin nibbling. "You know I eat when I'm stressed!" he shrieked.

I held up my hands in surrender, already regretting the dig. "Yes, yes," I said. "It was a poor joke. I'm sorry."

But Gilley only harrumphed and got up off the bed to rush into the bathroom to view his profile. "So my jeans are a little tight!" he shouted.

I winced. Again, he can *really* reach those upper octaves. "Honey," I said, gathering up my gloves, tool belt, messenger bag, and flashlight. "You look fine. I was only kidding!"

I heard cabinet doors open. "Is there a scale in this bathroom?"

Oh, boy.

"Seriously! Someone get me a scale!"

I tiptoed out of the room and went in search of Heath. "What's going on?" he asked when I found him at the bottom of the stairs.

"I called Gilley out on his recent weight gain."

Heath winced. "Ouch."

The door to our room flew open and Gilley's head appeared. "I will settle for a tape measure!"

I grabbed Heath's coat and tugged him toward the door. "Time to go!"

We exited before Gilley could start asking for a full-length mirror and jeans that didn't make his butt look big(ger).

Heath drove down to the water and I told him what Gilley had told me. "Then Bertie was right," he said. "Jeffrey wasn't being truthful with him."

"Doesn't look like it."

"But where did Jeffrey get the phantom? And how the heck did he transport it to the castle without being attacked by it?"

I shrugged. "Maybe it came from one of his gold mines," I suggested. "As for how he got it to the castle, maybe it was encased in some sort of relic, you know, like how the knife we found at that hotel in San Francisco had that smoke demon."

Heath looked deeply troubled. "We should have Gilley check to see if the Kincaids had any mining interests in South America. Remember how Bouvet mentioned South America? Maybe he recognized the present as having come from there?"

"That's what I'm thinking too," I agreed, already pulling out my cell to send Gilley a text.

The moment we reached the shore and parked, I received Gilley's reply. Reading the text to Heath, I said, "Gilley's found Kincaid family mining interests in Peru, Chile, and Bolivia."

"It's all starting to fit," Heath said with a shake of his head.

We got out of the van and headed to the base of the causeway. For several long minutes we just stared at the waves rushing in and out. It looked so peaceful and quiet, completely beguiling to the task at hand. "At least it's clear out," Heath said.

I grunted. "That's something at least."

"Do you have the blueprint?"

I pulled it out of my messenger bag along with a flashlight. "How do you want to do this?"

Heath leaned against me and we studied the map.

Castle Dunlow had three levels. The main level had the largest rooms with the main hall, the kitchen, the servants' quarters, the corridor of rooms I'd been trapped in, and a fairly large section at the back of the keep for a church. The two upper levels held many smaller rooms for guests and the living quarters for the Dunnyvale family along with battle stations for the armed guards who lived at Dunlow and protected the keep.

"I think we should start with the upper floors and work our way down," Heath said after he'd taken a good long look at the map.

"Why the upper floors?"

"If Gopher was attacked by the phantom and managed to run for it, he might have tried to climb the stairs and hide out in one of the smaller rooms on the second or third floor. If he was frightened enough, he could have just stayed there, and by now, he's got to be weakened after not having had access to food or water in a few days."

I felt a wave of guilt over the fact that my belly was full and Gopher might be starving somewhere. "That makes sense," I said.

"You ready?"

"Hell no," I told him. "But I'll follow you anyway."

Heath grinned and pulled the straps of the backpack

filled with magnetic spikes over his shoulders. I checked all his straps to make sure they were buckled and secure.

"Whatever you do, don't take your pack off," I told him.

"Don't worry," he said. "That's not happening, even though this thing weighs a ton." We had added all our remaining spikes to Heath's backpack, and I could hear them clinking around in there as he walked.

The two of us trekked onto the causeway and moved quickly and quietly across. When we reached the rock, we paused and surveyed the landscape. Nothing stirred in the cool night air. Without a word we made our way to the stairs, and I felt my heartbeat tick up a notch. I was nervous about encountering the phantom, and inside my gloves my palms started to sweat.

"How you doin'?" Heath panted next to me as we climbed.

"Okay," I told him. "Nervous but okay."

"We should be fine," he assured me. "We already know that the magnets work against the phantom. And we're more than armed. It'll probably allow us to go wherever we want tonight. I bet we even get bored after a few."

I wondered if Heath really believed the line of bull-crap coming out of his mouth, but I chose not to say anything. I figured we were each dealing with our fears in our own way, me by sweating and worrying about facing the phantom, and Heath by telling himself a big ol' lie.

When we got to the top of the rock, we both paused to catch our breath. Heath had had a tougher go of it than me because he'd been carrying a lot more weight. Still, after only a few breaths he tugged me away from the stairs. "I think we'd better steer clear of the edge," he advised. "Let's move in close to the castle."

We approached the dark ominous structure cautiously. From inside I heard a door slam, and wondered if that was the phantom, another spook, or our producer. "Should we call out to Gopher?" I asked.

Heath shook his head. "Let's wait to get inside first."

He led the way and I followed, periodically peeking over his shoulder at the copy of the blueprint he held in his hands. "This way," he said when we reached the large hall.

On tiptoe we crept to the stairs, and I realized I was trembling a little with fear and my teeth were clicking together. Heath paused and regarded me. "M. J.," he said seriously. "You've got to pull it together. This thing enjoys making us afraid, and I think it's actually attracted to that emotion. The less you express it, the more likely it'll stay away from us."

I swallowed hard. "I can't help it," I admitted. "I *am* really scared, Heath."

The corner of his mouth lifted and he pulled me into a tight embrace. I was caught off guard by the move, but realized that I immediately felt better.

After a minute he let me go. "How are you now?"

I nodded. "A little calmer. How'd you know?"

He chucked me softly under the chin. "You're not so hard to figure out, you know."

I grinned. "I'll remember that."

Heath motioned with his head and we started up the spiral stone staircase leading to the upper floors. We arrived on the second story, and had to hunt a little for the next set of stairs that led up to the third floor, but we were soon there and poking our noses into each and every room.

I had my intuition dialed up to high, and was searching the ether for any sign of Gopher—but none lingered and our soft calls to him went unanswered.

What was more, the entire castle felt still and quiet . . . almost too quiet. "Have you noticed that not a single spook has shown itself or made any noise other than the slam of that door?"

"Yeah," Heath said. "And I don't like it."

"Maybe it's all the magnets," I said, lifting one of the sagging sections of Gilley's sweatshirt.

"Maybe," Heath conceded. "But I still think it's weird."

We moved along and inspected every room, closet, nook, and cranny, but couldn't find any sign of our producer.

"Hey," I said, seeing yet another set of spiral stairs. "Look over there."

"That goes up to the parapet," Heath said after considering the map.

"Do you think we should check it out?"

He nodded. "We said we'd search the entire castle."

I followed after him and worked to control my breathing in the confined space of the narrow stairwell. "It's thick in here," I said, feeling a bit of the residual spirit energy still lingering in the air.

"We're dispersing it, though," he said over his shoulder.

A few more steps and we reached the roof toward the back of the castle. It was even windier up there than it had been below, and we could clearly hear the sound of the waves crashing into the rocky shore far below. Although it was dark out, the moon lit the water, offering an amazing view.

"If this weren't such an awful place, I'd love to come back here and see this in the daytime," I said.

But Heath didn't comment as he was looking for Gopher. "Yo!" he called softly. "Goph! You up here?"

There was no reply.

"He's not here," I said, already turning toward the door.

That was when Heath's arm shot out to stop me.

"What?" I asked.

He didn't reply, but merely pointed down and to my left. I leaned forward and peered over the top of the parapet. A monstrous black shadow strode along the ground just inside the keep, maneuvering up to a door at the very back of the castle, before darting back, then pacing back and forth for a moment before inching closer and closer, then suddenly leaping back.

I held my breath and quivered slightly—hell, I even squeaked a little in fear. The phantom abruptly paused its odd sort of pacing, as if it had sensed my reaction in the ether, and Heath quickly wrapped an arm around my shoulders and whispered earnestly, "Push down your fear!"

I gulped and thought about how similar he was to his grandfather. And that brought me a measure of comfort and I was able to calm my pounding heart.

The phantom stood still for a few more moments, and I had the clear impression that it was attempting to feel the night air for any trespassers. How it had missed our arrival I wasn't certain, but after a few tense moments it resumed its strange pacing dance.

"Come on," Heath said softly. "The quicker we search this place, the quicker we can go."

We took advantage of the fact that the phantom was outside and preoccupied with the back door of the keep, and as quickly and quietly as we could, we inspected every room on the second floor. At one point I suggested we split up to get through it faster, but Heath flat out refused. "No freakin' way, M. J."

"It was just a suggestion," I said, a little wounded.

"Do you remember the last time we split up and you went off on your own?"

He had a point there.

We finished with the second story and there was nowhere left but to go back down to the first floor, where the phantom lay . . . lurking.

I could feel the goose bumps form under the many layers of clothing I'd worn, and I stood resolutely at the top of the staircase. "Jesus," I whispered to Heath, who was standing beside me. "I sooooo don't want to go down there."

"Remember to check your fear," he warned softly.

"No matter what happens, you've got to try and stay calm and be brave."

I closed my eyes and took a deep breath. "Better get it over with," I said after exhaling, and I started down.

We descended slowly and carefully, one cautious step at a time. My ears were pricked for any hint of the phantom. Upstairs I heard footsteps and creaking floorboards. "The spooks came back out," I said in a hushed voice.

"They were probably just waiting for our megawatt magnets to leave the area."

"At least the phantom's been keeping a safe distance."

"Let's hope it lasts," he said.

But it didn't.

Just as I was beginning to relax a little, Heath and I rounded the corner of the last group of stairs and came face-to-face with one pissed-off poltergeist.

Chapter 11

"Jesus!" I shouted, and took a step backward, bumping right into Heath. My body knocked him off-balance and he fell back hard onto the stone stairs, howling in pain.

Meanwhile the phantom itself backed up ten yards from us, hissing like a giant angry cobra before growling and spitting in our direction. I was so scared that I clambered past Heath, back up the stairs and shivered, closing my eyes and attempting to push away the images starting to creep into my mind.

Heath continued to arch his back and moan. "Son of a bitch!" he hissed.

And I think that was what snapped my attention away from my own fears—hearing Heath in pain got me to realize that he was actually seriously hurt. Trembling, I inched my way down the stairs to him. He was curled over onto his side, clutching the stair. His flashlight lay next to him and I could see that several of the loose spikes we'd put into his backpack had pierced the canvas and had actually punctured his skin.

"Ohmigod!" I said, hurrying to undo the buckles and get the backpack off him.

"Don't!" he cried, his eyes tightly closed and his face pale. "Wait until it leaves!"

I eyed the phantom nervously. It had moved even farther away from us, but it was pacing again like a caged animal, hissing and growling and spitting in our direction. I wanted to cower in fear and shrink away, but a voice came into my head, loud and clear.

Help him, M. J. Help my grandson to safety.

Sam's presence in my mind gave me courage. As carefully as I could, I eased the zipper on Heath's backpack open and took out a handful of spikes. *"Jesus!"* he gasped when I rattled them.

"Hold on, honey," I whispered urgently. "I need these to get us out of here."

As I removed the spikes, I held them over my head and stood up. The phantom stopped pacing and considered me before it darted forward several feet. I threw several of the spikes right at it and it howled and whirled away. "Stay back!" I shouted. "Stay away from us, you polluted piece of ectoplasm, or I'll dump the entire backpack of spikes on you!"

The phantom moved beyond the spikes I'd thrown, which gave us a little more room to maneuver. "We have to get you out of here!" I told Heath, coming back to crouch at his side.

His jaw was clenched and he was in so much pain he was making a hissing sound through his teeth. "It's blocking the way out!" he groaned, looking just beyond the phantom.

I turned my head with dread, and realized the phantom had gone back to pacing again, right in front of the only way out. "Where's the blueprint?" I asked quickly.

Heath sucked in a breath and moved his hand to his back pocket with a small grunt of pain. I stopped his hand and moved my own into his pocket. With great care I removed the map, unfolded it, and held it under the beam of the flashlight. "There!" I said, pointing to the back of the castle where we'd seen the phantom pacing in front of the door. "There's a door at the back of the church! We can get to the church from here, then out the back, and make a run for the stairs."

"Christ, M. J.!" Heath said, his teeth still clenched. "I don't think I can walk, let alone run!"

I eyed the phantom again and made a decision. "Your backpack has got to come off, sweetheart," I said, my fingers flying over the buckles. He tried to protest, but I glared hard at him and shook my head. "Trust me!"

When the last buckle was undone, I shimmied out of my sweatshirt and tied the sleeves gently around his neck with the bulk of the shirt hanging in front of him so as not to lie against his back.

I then eased the backpack off his shoulders and got one arm through the strap when the phantom suddenly darted forward again. I gasped and reached for a spike to hurtle at the approaching menace. The phantom flinched and backed up to resume its spitting and snarling thing.

I decided then that instead of wearing the backpack, I would hold on to it, and throw spikes at the phantom as needed, because I was fairly certain it planned to follow us. "Let's go," I said, and eased Heath's arm over my shoulders.

He got up with a muffled cry and walked hunched over next to me as we moved away from the stairs.

The phantom sank low to the ground like a crouching tiger, and I did my best to hold my fear at bay. I decided to fight fire with fire and dug into the backpack. "Take that, you flimsy demon!" I yelled, throwing a few spikes at it.

Each time a spike came near the phantom, it darted to the side, spitting and growling and curling up into a ball, but then it would unfold, zip around the spike and continue to stalk us.

We moved as quickly as Heath's injury would allow, which wasn't nearly as fast as I wanted to go, but we finally got to the church and eased inside. In the hallway leading to the church the phantom's snarl became more enraged, but my continual tossing of spikes kept it at bay.

As we moved deeper into the church, the phantom stopped stalking us; instead it remained just beyond the doorway, hissing and growling and making a hell of a racket.

"Why isn't it following us inside?" Heath said through clenched teeth.

"I don't know," I admitted, watching it cautiously. We continued to the back of the small chapel and the phantom appeared to grow more and more agitated the farther away we got, but it made no further move to approach us, even though I was sure the range of our magnets no longer extended to it out in the hallway.

A sudden thought occurred to me as I looked around the church, and I had a theory about why it wasn't approaching. "It's the chapel!" I said. "We're in a holy place of worship, and that thing can't come in here!"

Heath stopped, which forced me to stop too. "If that's the case, can I sit for a second?"

"Oh, God!" I said, easing him over to one of the stone pews. "Of course. Sit here for a minute and let me see your back."

Heath sat down and I slung the backpack over my shoulder, then held the flashlight up and lifted his coat to pull his shirttail out of his jeans. "Easy!" he begged.

I moved as slowly as I dared and pulled up the shirt, exposing his back. I sucked in a breath at the sight.

"Is it bad?"

One of the spikes had punctured a hole right into the bone of his spine, and I was convinced that was the one that was causing the most pain, but much of the middle of his back was bruised and held small wounds as well. From the main wound he was bleeding badly, and I was very worried about him losing too much blood, even though I knew he was lucky the one spike hadn't severed his spinal column. "It's not good," I told him truthfully.

"It hurts like a bitch."

"I'll bet." I lowered his shirt and came around to face him. "We need to get you out of here and we need to do it soon."

"That bad?"

"Like I said, it ain't good."

Heath nodded. "Okay. I'm ready when you are."

I looked over my shoulder and realized that the phantom was gone. "Uh-oh," I whispered.

"What?"

"The phantom's gone." If it wasn't trying to get to us from the hallway, I had little doubt it would make its way to the other side of the castle and attack us as we left.

"Shit," Heath swore.

"Come on," I said, trying to gently lift him off the slab, but he was heavy and started to swoon on his feet.

"M. J.," he said, his voice a bit desperate. "I need to sit for another minute. I'm feeling really dizzy."

I thought about pushing him, but decided against it. If he fainted, then we'd really be up the creek. "Okay," I agreed. "You sit. I'm gonna see if there's anything in here we can take with us to help protect us."

"Here?" he asked. "What's here?"

"I don't know," I told him, my voice sounding a bit desperate. "But that phantom was really put off by the energy in this place, so maybe there's a crucifix or something we can take with us that'll have some of that protective energy."

Heath nodded dully and sat forward hugging his knees. "I'll be okay in a minute," he promised. "I just need to wait for the room to stop spinning."

I looked at him worriedly and sat down to dig through my messenger bag searching for the first aid kit I usually carried but wasn't sure I'd packed this time.

In the lower inside pocket I hit pay dirt. "Thank God!" I said triumphantly, holding up a small bottle of antisep-

tic and a few cotton balls. There were even a small bit of
medical tape and extra bandages that I could use to help
cover Heath's wounds.

"Turn around," I ordered as he eyed me.

Heath took a few deep breaths and swiveled around
to his knees, propping his head and shoulders on the
stone seat.

Carefully I lifted his coat and shirt again and dabbed
at his wounds. He cried out only once when I poured the
antiseptic directly into the main puncture wound, and
I held my hand on his shoulder and told him over and
over how sorry I was. And I truly was sorry. After all,
I'd been the one that'd caused him to fall back on those
stairs.

I felt even more horrible for the pain that I continued to cause him as I treated his wounds. Tears actually
leaked out of his eyes, and his hands were clenched into
fists so tight his knuckles were white, but finally his labored breathing subsided, and he nodded and said he
was okay, but that he was still dizzy.

I then began taking off all my clothes until I got down
to my undershirt. With my teeth I managed to tear off
a strip of the cotton T and used it to apply pressure to
Heath's wound. Once the bleeding slowed, I used smaller
strips and the medical tape to make him a bandage.

When I was finished, he was panting again. "How're
you doing?" I asked, wishing there was something I could
do to take away his pain.

"I'll need another minute," he gasped.

I sat back on my heels and considered our situation. I

still felt terrible for hurting Heath, but I knew I needed to focus on getting us out of there. I quickly put my clothes back on, and slung the pack onto my shoulder. I then went around the chapel, searching for anything that could help.

When I neared the door to the back of the church, I peeked through the window and sure enough I could see the phantom pacing and growling just a short distance away. "You son of a bitch!" I yelled at it.

"Hisssssssssssssss!" it replied.

I turned back and looked at Heath. There was no way I could get him through the castle and back down the stairs. It would take us much longer, and I had little doubt the phantom would eventually find us one way or another.

I swept the beam of my flashlight around the whole church, methodically looking for anything I could carry that would give us a little more breathing room. To my immense relief I finally spotted a crucifix hanging on the wall. I moved quickly toward the crucifix and tripped as I went, stumbling right onto a large marble slab. "Son of a—" I muttered.

"M. J.?" Heath called weakly.

I got up and dusted myself off. "I'm okay," I said, looking down. I realized that I'd stumbled onto a crypt, and the writing indicated that buried there was one Malachi Dunnyvale, beloved son of Ranald and Meara, born 1572, died 1584. I realized that Malachi had died the same year the castle was completed, and wondered if Ranald had added the family crypts later, which would explain why Malachi was buried here instead of with the rest of his family.

Still, there wasn't much time to ponder things and I moved to see if I could retrieve the crucifix.

I had to climb up on the old stone altar to get to it, but my hands finally curled around it and I felt it give way. As I pulled on it, however, it acted like a lever, and the altar I was kneeling on swiveled inward to reveal a stone staircase. "Whoa!" I gasped.

"M. J.!" Heath shouted in alarm.

I realized I'd swung completely out of his view. "I'm here!" I called, hopping down and coming out into the chapel again. "And I believe I just found our way past the phantom!"

Heath and I moved slowly and carefully down the spiral staircase. I had to support a lot of his weight, and the stairwell was narrow, which didn't make it an easy journey, but it was definitely preferable to facing the phantom.

As we descended, I could smell the brine of the ocean and hear the crash of waves echoing up through the stairwell. The air became noticeably chillier and damp.

I knew we would eventually come out somewhere near the shore, but I wasn't sure where.

I was wrong. The staircase ended and Heath and I found ourselves in a very narrow tunnel, and for someone like me, who suffers from bouts of claustrophobia, it was a worst-case scenario. "Aw, crap," I whispered when

I realized the tunnel went on for quite a way. "I don't think I can do that."

My breathing was coming in short little gasps and I knew I was close to hyperventilating.

Ever since I'd been trapped in a narrow underground tunnel with my ex-boyfriend Steven two years before, I found that tight cramped spaces caused me to have panic attacks. The stairwell was bad enough, but this . . . well, this threatened to push me over the edge.

"Breathe slowly, M. J.," Heath said, hugging me slightly around the shoulders.

I closed my eyes and tried to take slower inhalations, but it wasn't working, and very quickly, I became dizzy.

"M. J.!" Heath commanded, squeezing me again. "You have got to calm down, babe."

I nodded, but my breathing and heart rate both increased. I could feel the world spinning and I started to sink. "Can't . . . breathe!" I gasped, feeling my grip on Heath loosen. My knees hit the floor and then I was on all fours, still squeezing my eyes shut and fighting with everything I had to stay conscious.

A moment later, I lost the battle and slipped into the darkness.

The next thing I realized was that someone's hand was warming my forehead. "M. J.?" I heard Heath ask.

My eyelids fluttered.

"Hey, honey," he whispered. "Come on, now. Wake up for me."

I opened my eyes and sat up, blinking at him in a state of disorientation. "What happened?"

"You had a panic attack, and you fainted."

I swallowed hard and my stomach felt queasy. Plus I was really embarrassed. "Sorry."

Heath smiled and squeezed my hand. "What are you sorry for? Being human?"

I shrugged. "The last underground tunnel I was in that was built like this one collapsed and nearly killed me."

Heath's eyebrows shot up. "There's a story I want to hear."

I looked at him in the dim light and took in his hunched-over posture and the pain in his eyes, and realized that I had no choice but to suck it up and get him out of there. "I'll tell you," I said. "But after we get you to a doctor."

Heath smiled again. "Deal."

I got up and focused on the ground in front of me. If I looked up and took in the narrowness of my surroundings, I knew I'd start to panic again. "We're not going to be able to make it through here side by side," I told him. "So you lean on me piggyback-style, okay?"

He agreed and I helped him to his feet; then, when I felt his hands grip my shoulders, I began to move us forward. We could still hear the crash of waves and smell the salty air, but no hint of open sky revealed itself as we moved along, although it was still damp and every once in a while I saw a puddle or two.

We went on like that for quite a while, the tunnel

bending always to the left; then it curved sharply and we came to a slope, traveling upward until finally we were met with an L-shaped corner. Here the tunnel ended in front of us, and we had to make a tight right turn.

When we came around the corner, I was amazed by what I saw.

"Whoa," I said, pointing my light ahead of us to a much wider tunnel that ran straight and true, dripping with moisture.

"Where are we?" Heath asked.

Above us we both heard the crash of a wave, and I realized what I was looking at. "Heath," I said excitedly. "I think we're *under* the causeway!"

I felt his body weight ease forward onto my shoulders as he too peered down the stretch of tunnel in front of us. "No way!"

Another crash of waves echoed right over our heads. "It has to be!" I said. "I mean, think about it. The spiral staircase at the church was at the back of the castle, so we would have come out on the far side of the rock. The narrow tunnel we were just in curved to the left, which means it eventually would have put us on the Irish-coastline side, and this is about the right place for the causeway to be."

"Genius," Heath said admiringly.

"Come on," I told him. "We're almost home."

The tunnel under the causeway was wide enough for Heath and me to walk side by side, which made it easier on Heath as I was able to support his weight. Eventually we reached the end and walked up a flight of stairs to another corridor that bent to the left. We followed that as it sloped upward and eventually ended at a small cramped space with a heavy iron manhole above our heads. I felt my stomach muscles clench when I realized the manhole might be too heavy for me to push aside, but when I pushed up on it, it eased up and over with only a reasonable amount of effort from me. "Thank you, God," I whispered, shoving it the rest of the way, then shimmying out of the hole before helping Heath.

We came out onto a bluff with a small cobblestoned platform surrounded by tall hedges, and I sucked in huge gulps of fresh air and relished the feeling of being in a wide-open space again. "Man! Am I glad to be out of there!"

"Where are we?" Heath wondered as he stood hunched and hurting next to me.

I stepped out from behind the hedges to get a better look at our location and spotted our two vans sitting side by side about fifty yards away. I pointed them out to him, and we could both see that in between the vans and our location was the causeway, confirming that we had indeed traveled under it.

"So, Dunnyvale built an escape route," he said, looking from the causeway to the manhole behind us.

"It makes sense, when you think about it," I told him. "If the castle was ever laid siege to, he could have gotten himself and his family out without the enemy ever being the wiser."

"And now we have a safe and phantom-free route to the castle," Heath said.

I turned to look at him sharply. "Why would we *ever* want to go back there?"

He in turn appeared confused. "To find Gopher."

I shook my head. "Gopher's not there, Heath. We searched the entire top two stories tonight and much of the lower one on our first trip. There's no way he's still in that god-awful place."

"So where is he?" Heath pressed.

I turned to look behind us. "My theory is that he might have followed the same route we did. Or he got clear of the castle and made it to the causeway."

Heath sighed heavily. "Or he's dead and no one's found his body, and you and I are both unable to reach him intuitively."

I frowned. That was a possibility. "Or that," I conceded.

"That theory makes the most sense, really," he told me. "Otherwise, if Gopher had made it out, he would have made contact with us."

I looked back again to the causeway, and tried to reconcile my own gut feelings with the theory that Gopher had been killed. What I realized was that in my heart I didn't feel that was the case. I just knew he was alive. But where was he, and why hadn't he at least called one of us?

I was about to tell Heath what my intuition was saying when I realized that he was clutching his knees with his hands and gritting his teeth. I felt terrible all over again. Here I was trying to figure out our mystery and poor Heath was in a great deal of pain and needed to get to a doctor—pronto.

"Come on," I told him. "Let's see if we can't get you some medical attention."

I called Gilley from the hospital. He reacted to the news that Heath was hurt and in the ER the way I expected him to—by completely freaking out.

It took me about half an hour to calm him down, which was exactly how long it took for Heath to get stitched up. "Lucky us that it was a slow night in the ER," I said as I helped to ease him into the van.

Heath winced when he sat down, but only for a moment. His wounds were mostly superficial, as the spike had poked into the more solid part of one of his vertebrae, so his wound was painful but not serious, and would require little follow-up care.

"Are the pain pills kicking in?" I asked, buckling myself into the driver's side.

He nodded dully. "Oh, yeah."

I drove us back to Anya's and by that time Heath was fast asleep. I had to wake Gilley up to help me get Heath into the house. He was really out of it and barely conscious, so it took us a good ten minutes just to move him from the van to the cushy couch in the living room.

"Should we try and get him upstairs?" Gilley asked.

I shook my head. "I've been pushing him beyond his limits all night. Let's just cover him with a blanket so he can sleep."

After Heath was tucked in, I followed Gil upstairs. "I have news!" he whispered excitedly.

I sighed. I was sick of news. I was sick of this bust.

And I was sick and tired of being sick and tired. "Can it wait until morning?" I pleaded.

Gilley's hopeful expression sagged, but then he laid a hand on my arm and said, "Sure, M. J. Get to bed and I'll fill you in tomorrow."

That night I slept like the dead right up until I dreamed about them. "Hello, lovely lass," said a familiar voice.

"Lord Dunnyvale," I replied mildly, leaning back against the tree and taking a huge whiff of the flower-scented air.

"I see you've finally discovered the key to your success," he told me, stepping out from behind the tree to take a seat next to me.

"You mean the underground tunnel you built as an escape route?"

Ranald smiled winningly at me. "Bit of an engineering marvel that was," he said proudly. "And it's withstood those crashing waves all this time so beautifully. Barely a leak in it."

I had to give him credit on that one. "Yes, it is a marvel, my lord."

Dunnyvale pulled at his goatee. "Aye," he agreed. "But that's not what I was referring to, miss, although you did come across a very large clue last night. You're so close to putting your puzzle pieces together, but you still need Alex. She's the one to put it all in place for you."

I leaned my head back against the tree, trying to rein in my impatience. This man talked in circles and he wasn't helping me nearly as much as he liked to think he was. "Who we need is Gopher," I snapped. So much for reining in that impatience. "And at this point we don't even know if he's dead or alive."

"Oh, he's alive all right, and he's been taken somewhere safe for the time being," Dunnyvale assured me. "Still," he added, "I'm not sure he'll be alive for long without Alex."

I eyed Dunnyvale suspiciously. "You're *sure* he's alive?"

Ranald held up his hand as if he was taking a vow. "I'd swear to it," he assured me.

I sighed. "I don't understand why you won't just tell me where to find him, then."

"Because it's all connected, lass. Don't you see?"

I shook my head. "I don't, Lord Dunnyvale. Please enlighten me."

Ranald's infectious smile returned. "The phantom is connected to where my dearest heart resides, and that is connected to Bouvet's untimely death, which is also connected to Kincaid's, and Alex holds the key to all that and the way to finding your friend. These pieces you've got spinning all round you, lass. The only way to put them together is to bring her back. Bring Alexandra back to Dunlow and slide it all in place."

"You make about as much sense to me as a theoretical physicist explaining quantum physics."

Dunnyvale laughed and got up. Before he left me, he said, "You've a bright mind, M. J. Holliday. You'll get to the root of it. Of that, I've no doubt."

I woke up the moment Dunnyvale stepped out from

under the tree. Frustrated, I got up and dug around for a pen and paper to jot down the dream. A glance at the clock told me it was a little after five a.m. Knowing I'd probably not get back to sleep, I then went downstairs to check on Heath and found him attempting to get a fire going. "Hey," I whispered as I hurried into the room. "Let me do that."

Heath shivered and wrapped his blanket around his shoulders. "It's freezing in here."

I got the fire lit, and we both huddled together on the couch, waiting for its warmth to heat the room. "What's that?" he asked, noticing the paper I'd written my dream on, which I'd placed on the coffee table while I worked on the fire.

I told him all about my dream and how Dunnyvale had been checking in on me periodically.

"What's interesting to me," said Heath, "is that he's essentially telling you that someone *took* Gopher."

"You know, that is a good point," I said, remembering Ranald mentioning that Gopher had been taken somewhere safe. "And it's just like we suspected in that note that was left for us, that sort of hinted that Gopher had been kidnapped."

"What's your gut say?"

I sat with that for a minute. "It says that the letter wasn't some prank by the local kids, and someone really *did* kidnap Gopher."

"But why would anyone take *him* of all people?" Heath wondered. "I mean, yeah, he's got connections to big money at the network, but we know the kidnapper hasn't tried to use them because the network brass doesn't believe that Gopher's missing and they fired us. So what's the objective?"

And then it started to click in my head. "It's exactly like it said in that letter. The kidnapper wants us to deal with the phantom!"

"But why?" Heath pressed. "The phantom is tied to the rock. As far as we know, it can't even move beyond it to the coast, so why force us to deal with it?"

"Because something valuable is on the rock, and you can't get to it without dealing with the phantom," I said, thinking out loud.

"You mean the gold?"

I nodded.

"But Bertie already told us that the treasure's probably just a myth."

"Not everyone believes that, though," I reasoned. "I mean, look at who's already attempted to find it: Bouvet, Kincaid . . . us."

Heath considered that for a bit. "Shit," he said at last. "This could be worse than I thought. I mean, we have no idea how to deal with the phantom. We've barely managed to escape with our lives and our sanity whenever we've gotten up close and personal with it."

I stared into the orange glow of the fire and realized Dunnyvale was probably pushing me to connect these specific dots. "Alex has to be the key," I said. "She has to know how to deal with the phantom."

"Then why didn't she four years ago before her fiancé was killed?"

I shrugged. "That's the sixty-five-thousand-dollar question, my friend. And one we really need to have answered."

A bit later we heard footsteps on the stairs, followed by shuffling around the corner out in the hallway. I cocked my head to listen, knowing it must be Gilley, and wasn't surprised when I heard the icebox open and dishes being rattled. I winked at Heath and got up quietly from the couch to tiptoe into the kitchen, where I found Gilley with his head in the fridge, rummaging around for something to eat. "Anya should be up soon to start breakfast," I said.

"Ahhhhhhhhh!" Gilley squealed, before bumping his head on the top of the icebox.

I laughed hilariously as he backed up and stared at me with wide eyes, clutching a Tupperware container and a plate of custard-filled doughnuts.

"Don't ... *do* ... that!" he said in between deep breaths.

"That'll teach you to raid the fridge at all hours," I told him, still chuckling at the scene.

"I was hungry, okay?" he snapped, setting the Tupperware container down but holding fiercely to the pastries.

"Sweetie," I said gently. "You know how you get when you're on this kind of a food kick. We ride the carbo wave for a while until you can't fit into your pants. Then you starve yourself and make everyone around you miserable because your blood sugar is low."

Gilley glowered at me and pulled back the wrap covering the doughnuts. "I can't help it!" he yelled. "I'm stressed-out!"

"Gil," I warned as he reached for a pastry. "Hand it over."

"No!"

"Gilley," I said more firmly. "I'm serious. Step away from the doughnuts."

But Gil defiantly shoved his hand underneath the wrap and pulled out a doughnut to stuff into his mouth, just to taunt me.

"You stubborn son of a—" I growled, darting forward to grab the dish.

Gilley whirled away from me, stuffing his mouth with more pastry as I chased him around the kitchen. "Mwaaaaah!" he yelled as crumbs flew out of his mouth.

"Gilley Morehouse Gillespie!" I shouted when I tried to grab his shirt and missed. "Gimme that plate!"

But Gil was having none of it. Instead he whirled in a tight circle and sprinted for the door to the hallway. I grabbed for him again and managed to hook my fingers into the waistband of his sweats and pulled hard, but he was carrying way too much momentum; he jerked me forward but tripped in the process and I crashed into him.

Gilley went down with arms flailing, which was unfortunate because he caught all the porcelain containers along the counter holding flour, sugar, dry pasta, and oatmeal flakes. The containers went crashing to the floor, where they broke and their contents exploded. Gilley and I also went down, and I squeezed my eyes shut just before I hit, knowing it was going to hurt.

With a jolt I hit the floor and heard the crashing of

plates, containers, and foodstuff as everything in and on them launched like tiny missiles and gunpowder into the air, landing everywhere ... and I do mean *every*where.

I felt small splats of doughnut, custard filling, pasta, and clumps of sugar hit the top of my hair, shoulders, and back while I sucked in a lungful of flour. Coughing and sputtering, I rolled off Gilley and sat up, blinking furiously as the dust began to settle and I realized just how bad a mess we'd made.

"Jesus, Mary, and Joseph!" wailed a familiar voice.

I cringed and slowly lifted my gaze to see Anya standing in the doorway of the back door with the most horrified look on her face, her robe splattered with bits of custard and flour.

I immediately pointed to Gilley, who was already pointing at me.

"He did it!"

"She did it!"

Anya opened and closed her mouth, unable to speak more than what she'd already exclaimed.

"Holy ... ," I heard Heath say, and I turned my head to see that he'd come in from the sitting room to see what hell had broken loose.

I wiped my hands together and attempted to stand, but the floor was really slippery and it was a struggle. "We'll clean it up," I told our host quickly. "And we'll replace everything we broke."

Anya's lower lip trembled, and she pointed to the broken pieces of the pastry plate. "That was me mum's!" she yelled. "You've broken a family heirloom!"

Aw, crap.

Gilley stood too and I saw out the corner of my eye that he removed a bit of custard off his shirt to pop into his mouth. "Sorry," he muttered, and looked down at the ground. "We're really, really sorry, Anya."

Anya's look of horror turned angry then. "Out!" she ordered, pointing to the hall.

I hung my head in shame. "I'm *so* sorry," I tried, really looking at the mess, which extended to all four corners of the floor, to every wall, and even up to the ceiling. I knew it would take hours to clean. "We'll change and then be back down to mop it all up, Anya. And we'll replace your heirloom with anything you'd like. Something from Harrods dot com or something else really lovely. Whatever the cost, we'll pay it."

"Save your money," she spat. "And pack your things. I won't be hosting the likes of you in my establishment one moment longer!"

I gasped and stared at her. She was kicking us out?

"You're kicking us out?" Gilley whined.

"Aye," she said, her hands finding her hips and her brow set angrily.

"But who's going to cook for—"

"Of course we'll go," I said quickly, grabbing Gilley around the shoulders and placing my hand over his mouth while my eyes told him to shut up. "And we'll replace everything we've broken. And if you'd like us to stay and help to clean this up before we leave, we certainly will."

Anya crossed her arms and sighed. "No," she said. "I

think it best if you lot take your leave and never come back."

I nodded and continued to grip Gilley around the shoulders, tugging him down the hall, where we dripped flour and sugar all over the floor.

"Hey," Heath said gently, moving in behind us. "Maybe you two better strip down before you go upstairs."

"I'm not wearing underwear," Gil said.

I turned away and made a face. "Aw, jeez, Gil! Did you have to share that?"

"Well, I could have kept it to myself, M. J., and just allowed my junk to fall out when I disrobed, but I thought you might like a little warning!"

I eyed Heath, who was still huddled in his blanket. "Can I have that, please?"

He gave it to me and I held it up as a screen for Gilley while he took off his clothes; then I handed it to him so that he could wear it toga-style. "I'll be up in a minute," I told him, before gathering up his clothes and moving out to the lawn, where I gave them a good shake. I also took off my own sweatshirt and beat what I could off it, and wiped down my jeans.

As I was going back inside, I noticed a letter taped to the door. It was addressed to "the Americans" again, and I peeled it off the door and hurried inside.

Heath had a broom and a dustpan and was sweeping up the mess we'd tracked into the hallway. Every time he moved the broom, I saw him wince. "Hey!" I said, stuffing the envelope in my back pocket and hurrying forward to grab the broom from him. "Let me do that."

Heath gave up the broom without argument. "I should go upstairs and pack my things."

I held my arm out to block him from moving in the direction of the stairs. "Uh-uh," I said firmly. "You're going back to the sitting room, and hanging out by the fire until Gil and I get everyone packed, loaded, and in the van." Heath looked like he was about to argue with me, so I added, "And that's an order, buddy."

He frowned but turned and shuffled back to the sitting room.

After I'd swept up the mess, I dashed upstairs, where I found Gilley fresh from the shower. "You took a shower?" I asked, amazed that after what he'd done and how angry he'd made Anya, he would have the nerve to take the time to bathe.

"I was covered in sugar," he complained, rubbing a towel over his wet hair.

I resisted the urge to smack him across the head . . . but just barely . . . and suggested he get busy helping me pack.

It took us twenty minutes, but eventually Gil and I had our things ready to go, plus Heath's and Gopher's. Once the van was loaded and warming up, I came in to get Heath and pay our tab.

"You ready?" I asked him.

He nodded and got up stiffly. "By the way," I asked, "how's your back?"

"Hurts," he admitted.

"Take a pain pill, then," I suggested.

"I can't take it on an empty stomach. I was going to take one at breakfast, but we got sidetracked."

I turned around to glare at Gilley, who finally decided to look guilty. "Sorry," he mumbled.

"Can you help Heath to the van? I have to settle our bill," I said.

"No you don't," said Heath. "I've already signed for it."

Now it was my turn to feel guilty. "We'll settle up our share at the next place we stay," I promised him.

"I'm not worried about it."

Gilley stepped forward and offered his arm. "Here, buddy," he said. "Let's get you to the van and then to someplace where they serve a nice big breakfast."

Once Gil and Heath had moved off to the van, I made a point to find Anya for one last apology. She was on her hands and knees in the kitchen, her own clothes dusty with white powder, a fine sheen across her forehead. I cleared my throat and she regarded me with lips pressed tightly together. "I just wanted to say that we're leaving now."

Anya gave one curt nod.

"And I'm *really* sorry," I added.

"You said that."

I swallowed hard. "I really do intend to replace your dishes."

"There's no need," she said with a sigh and got back to scrubbing the floor.

I felt so bad that tears stung my eyes, and I desperately wanted to make it up to her. "Anya?" I asked.

"Aye," she said without looking up.

"You mother's name was Molly, right?"

Anya's hand stopped making swirling motions on the floor and she sat back on her heels to give me an accusing glare. "Have you been going through me things?"

I shook my head vigorously. "No! It's just that Heath and I have a special talent. When we concentrate really hard, we can make connections to people who have died."

"You're mediums?" she asked, and I noticed a hint of interest in her eyes.

"Yes."

"Are you tellin' me that me mum is talking to you, then?"

"Yes."

"What's she have to say?"

I took a deep breath. "She says that she's glad you finally went to the doctor about that pain in your chest, and not to worry—she doesn't think it's going to be anything bad or something you can't handle. She's also very grateful to you for looking out for your brother, and associated with him I get the name Pat or Patrick. She's saying he's been a handful all these years and you've always put up with it because he's your little brother, and again she's grateful."

Tears appeared in Anya's eyes and her mouth formed a small circle. She didn't speak, and I wondered if I should say more. Finally she asked, "What does me mum say about the plate you broke?"

I bit my lip. I didn't know if she was being funny or

serious, so in my mind I asked her mother what she thought about the broken plate, and hoped the answer wouldn't make me feel worse than I already did. Molly's answer surprised me. "She says you've got two more just like it in the cupboard."

Anya's face brightened into a broad smile. "Aye," she acknowledged with a small laugh. "I do. And the one that broke had a chip in it anyway."

"Again, we're really, *really* sorry, Anya."

This time when she nodded, I felt like she'd finally decided to forgive us. "S'all right," she told me with a wave of her hand. "I'd still prefer you move on to other lodgin's, but it's all right."

"Okay," I said. "Thank you again for all you did for us."

I turned to go and Anya called me back. "Do you know where you'll go?" she asked.

"Not really."

"You might try Sean Tierney's place at the Dunlee Inn. He's always got rooms this time of year."

I thanked her and took my leave.

We found our way to the Dunlee Inn and Anya was right—they did have room for us. As we were trying to be budget conscious now that we didn't have jobs, we took only two rooms. We were given a set of door keys to side-by-side rooms and made our way upstairs.

There was a very awkward moment when we arrived at the rooms, because we hadn't really settled on who would be sleeping with whom. . . . Er . . . I mean, which of the three of us would get his or her own room. Heath finally settled it by suggesting that he bunk with Gilley, which, when I thought about it, was really sweet, because it would give me the power to invite him over if I felt lonely—or not.

Once we'd unloaded our luggage, we made our way back downstairs and out of the inn to find someplace to eat breakfast. Since Gilley was driving, he ended up picking and took us to the first greasy spoon he could find. After we were settled and had ordered our meal, Gilley asked about the previous night.

I filled him in on all of it, and he listened intently, his eyes sparkling with interest, especially when I got to the part about the secret passage under the causeway.

"How many people do you think know about that?" he asked.

I shrugged. "I doubt there are many. That manhole has the entrance pretty well covered."

Gilley popped the last bite of his very big breakfast into his mouth and announced, "I have news to share too!"

I remembered him saying as much to me the night before. "Dish," I said.

"Guess who I found."

My heart skipped a beat and my mind went right to Gopher. "Oh, my God," I said. "And you didn't tell us?"

Gilley smiled broadly. "I wanted it to be a surprise."

I shook my head and glared hard at Gilley. "You're an ass," I spat.

Heath must have been thinking the same thing I was

because he set down his water glass and glared at Gilley too. "So not cool, dude," he growled.

Gilley blinked. "Wait—what?"

"How could you keep that from us?" I demanded. "Do you know what we've *been* through?"

"Uh . . . ," Gilley said.

"So where is he?" Heath asked, looking around suspiciously. "Was he in on your little joke too? I should kick his ass. . . ."

Gilley raised a hand. "Hold on," he said. "*Who* do you think I've found?"

"Gopher," Heath and I said together.

Gilley let out a relieved sigh. "I haven't found Gopher."

It was our turn to blink in surprise. "Then who did you find?" I asked.

"Alex."

"Oh!" I said, feeling the tension leave my shoulders. "Sorry, honey! I was really thinking you'd found Gopher and were torturing us."

"Even I'm not that mean," he told me.

"I know, I know. Again, I'm sorry." And then I wanted to know more. "So where is this mysterious Alex?"

"Belize."

"I thought she was Russian?" Heath said.

"Oh, she is," Gilley assured him. "And sooooo much more."

"I feel a long-winded story coming," I muttered.

Gilley narrowed his eyes at me, but didn't let that

stop him from telling us what he knew. "Alexandra Neverov was born in Novgorod thirty-two years ago. Her father was an archaeologist at the Novgorod Institute of Technology until he and his family defected to the United States in nineteen eighty-five, where he then took up a post at New York University. Alex also went to NYU, graduating with top honors in the same field as her father—archaeology."

I put up my hand. "Hold on, Gil," I said. "*How* do you know all this stuff about her?"

"From her Web page," Gilley said with a smarty-pants smile.

"Ah. Okay, please continue."

"Oh, I'm just getting to the best part! See, according to Alex's Web page, it was about the time that she graduated from NYU that her intuitive abilities began to surface in earnest."

"Her *intuitive* abilities?" Heath repeated.

Gilley nodded his head vigorously. "Yep."

"She's *psychic*?" I clarified.

"Yep."

"Is she also a medium?"

"No," Gilley told me. "Not per se. Her talent is much cooler than that."

I frowned. "Gee, thanks."

Gilley ignored the fact that he'd just insulted both Heath and me and rushed on. "She's a dowser," he said. "And apparently, she's a really good one."

"A dowser," I repeated flatly. "How exactly is walking

around with a rod in the desert looking for water cooler than talking to dead people?"

"Oh, she doesn't hunt for water, M. J. She hunts for *gold*."

My eyebrows shot up and Heath looked equally surprised. "She's a psychic treasure hunter?" he asked. "For real?"

"Yep."

I sat back in my chair and laughed. "Well, now we know how she fits into this puzzle. If she's able to dowse for gold, then that's why Kincaid would have wanted her along to find Dunnyvale's treasure. She probably would have found it too if Kincaid hadn't died. And if they were as close a couple as Mary suggested, I can see why Alex would have left and never come back. Too many bad memories."

Gilley pointed his finger at me. "Bingo. The other point of interest on Alex's Web site is that she claims to have had a good deal of success finding treasure protected by curses, poltergeists, and various angry spooks."

"So she's also a ghostbuster," I said. Gilley nodded and I added, "That explains the backpack filled with spikes that she wore to get past the phantom."

Heath squirmed in his chair trying to find a more comfortable position again. "But how does she figure into this whole mystery with our missing producer?" he asked. "I mean, Dunnyvale keeps telling you we need to find her to bring Gopher back—so what's her connection?"

My good humor faded quickly. "I have no idea."

"And you guys didn't find a single trace of him at the castle?"

I shook my head. "Nope. Heath and I are convinced he made it off the rock, either by way of the causeway or the tunnel that runs underneath it."

"So *where* is he?" Gil pressed. "I mean, if he made it off the rock, why hasn't he tried to contact us?"

With a jolt I remembered the letter taped to the door that I'd shoved into my back pocket earlier. Pulling it out quickly, I told the boys where I'd found it, and tore it open to read it, but the moment my eyes rested on the top line, I sucked in a horrified breath. "Oh, no!" I whispered.

"What?" Gil asked.

I turned the paper around so that he and Heath could see it. "It's Gopher's handwriting."

Gilley snatched the letter out of my hand and held it close to read it.

"Dear Ghoul Getters, I'm being held against my will. I am being ordered to write this letter to beg you to secure my safe return. To achieve this, my captor is insisting that you rid Castle Dunlow of its phantom. You have until Sunday to accomplish this task; otherwise, terrible things will happen to me. And I must warn you that if you go to the police again, I will be killed, and you will never find me. Please, guys, don't let me down. Please, help me."

We fell into a stunned silence and stared at one another with wide eyes. Finally, I broke the silence. "Sunday is in four days," I said, before turning to Gilley. "Honey, find me a phone number for Alex."

"She's in Belize," Gilley reminded me. "In the middle of the jungle. How am I supposed to find you a working phone number for her?"

"I don't know and I don't care, Gil!" I snapped, as the stress over Gopher's confirmed kidnapping got to me. I knew it would be a difficult task for Gil, but he had to try and I didn't want to hear his excuses.

"Why do you need to call her?" Heath asked me, his voice soft and soothing.

I sighed tiredly and folded Gopher's letter, working to rein in my horns. "Because I've got to convince her to come back to Dunlow and help me deal with this phantom. Pronto."

"Help *you*?" Heath pressed. "Don't you mean *us*?"

"No," I said, my hand moving to rest gently right above his wound. "I don't. You're going to sit the rest of this bust out, sweetheart. It's time for the girls' team to go in and kick some phantom ass."

Chapter 12

Gilley found a contact number for Alex, who was actually vacationing at a resort and not in the middle of the jungle excavating some old tomb. I had the much more difficult task of convincing her to come to Ireland.

"We desperately need your help," I explained, after introducing myself and telling her the basic reason for my call. "The person or persons who've taken our friend will not free him until we've gotten rid of the phantom at Castle Dunlow."

The other end of the line was silent for a bit, and I would have thought that we'd been disconnected if I hadn't heard music and lively chatter in the background. "M. J.," she said at last, "you have no idea how abhorrent the idea of returning to Dunlow is to me. I vowed four years ago that I would never return. I meant it then and I mean it now. I'm very sorry, but I cannot help you."

I swallowed hard and closed my eyes. I held in my hand a trump card that just might work, but it was also a terrible way to manipulate this total stranger into agreeing to help us. Still, I didn't see any other option. "What if I were to offer my services and help you in return?" I said. "Or should I say, what if I were to help someone you loved in return?"

"Someone I love?" she asked, the small hint of her Russian accent surfacing and a bit of humor mixed in. "M. J., my parents have no need of a ghostbuster. They live in a brand-new condo in Orlando. No ghosts there."

I squeezed the phone in my hand, regretting what I was about to say and wishing there were another way to convince her. "I'm not talking about your folks," I said carefully. "I'm talking about Jordan."

Through the phone line I heard her gasp. In a hoarse whisper she said, "Jordan is dead."

"Yes," I said. "But his spirit is currently trapped at Dunlow. He's reliving the moments right up until his death over and over again, Alex."

"What are you even talking about?" she demanded, her tone harsh and accusing.

I shifted the phone to my other ear. "The first night we came here was really foggy, but we wanted to cross the causeway and get a look at what we were up against. About halfway across we heard a man desperately calling out the name Alex, but in the dense fog we couldn't pinpoint his location. The next day, as we were climbing up the stairs, we heard the same man crying out again for Alex to please help him. When we looked at the far side of the cliff, we saw the spirit of Jordan Kincaid dangling off the edge of the rock. My partner and I ran up the rest of the stairs and tried to save him, thinking he was a real person, but when we got to him, he slipped away and fell to the rocks below."

I couldn't imagine what my telling all this to Alex was doing to her, but still I continued . . . because I had to. "His spirit is stuck in the ether, Alex, and the phantom is so terrifying that his ghost can't let go. It can only replay what happened to him that awful night over and over and *over* again while he waits for you to come help him. He's begging you to come back and change the outcome."

I listened hard for Alex's reaction, but I couldn't even hear her breathing on the other end. Finally, a small sob came through the line, followed by a sniffle. "Please, tell me you are lying," she cried. "Tell me that you just made that up so that I would agree to come help you!"

I looked down at the ground and wondered if I'd reached a new low. "I'm so sorry, Alex, but it's the truth. I want to help Jordan cross over so that he can finally be released from his nightmare and find some peace, but I can't get through to him while the phantom's on the prowl. If you want me to help the man you were going to marry, the man you loved, then you have to come here and help me deal with the phantom."

I listened to Alex cry softly for a bit, hoping some-day she'd forgive me. At last, she sniffled loudly, took a breath, and said, "Fine. I will book the ticket and be there tomorrow." With that, the line went dead.

Gilley and I met Alex at the airport. She wasn't hard to spot. Tall, leggy, and almost unjustly pretty, Alex probably could even have turned Gilley straight if she'd wanted to. "Wowsa," he said when he first saw her.

"Her Web photo doesn't really do her justice, does it?" I said as we watched her cut through the throng at the baggage claim.

"Uh . . . no."

Alex was roughly five nine, with small hips, broad shoulders, a thin athletic frame, and a heart-shaped face settled perfectly on an elegant neck. Her very long hair was flame red, which accentuated her porcelain white skin and emerald eyes. If I hadn't needed her help so badly, I likely would have turned and left her beautiful self at the airport.

"Wait till Heath gets a load of her," Gilley whispered with an elbow nudge to my side just as she spotted us and began to walk purposefully in our direction.

"Aw, crap," I muttered. I'm not exactly a plain Jane, but this woman was supermodel gorgeous. How could you compete with that?

"Hello," she said when she reached us. "I'm Alex Neverov."

Gilley giggled like a schoolgirl, blushed a deep shade of red, and actually curtsied.

I resisted the urge to roll my eyes and instead extended my hand. "You'll have to excuse him," I said. "I'm M. J. and this is my partner, Gilley."

But Alex was laughing. Taking my hand and giving it a firm pump, she said, "It's nice to meet you."

I motioned for her to follow me to the van, and Gilley

sidled up next to her and said, "Can I take you for your luggage?"

I gave him an exasperated look and Alex giggled again. "Do you mean can you take my luggage for me?"

"Uh . . . yeah," he said, blushing again. "That."

This was going to be a long drive back to the inn.

When we reached our hotel, we found Heath in the bar. He was working his way off the pain meds he'd been prescribed and was substituting it for something a bit milder. Like beer. "Hey, buddy!" Gilley called when we entered with Alex after getting her checked in.

Heath swiveled around carefully and I swear he did the Wile E. Coyote *BAROOGA!* eyes when he saw our Russian friend. Oh, yeah, and he also snorted beer out his nose.

I sighed and sat down at the next table over. This was going to be a long day.

"Sorry about that," Heath said, working furiously to mop up the table with his dainty little cocktail napkin. I didn't have the heart to tell him about the foam resting on his upper lip. "I'm Heath, and you are *way* more gorgeous than your picture!"

"Gee, Heath," I said evenly. "Got beer?" (Huh. Look't that. I had the heart to tell him after all.)

He looked confused until I made a motion across my upper lip. He quickly wiped his sleeve over his face and smiled sheepishly. "Sorry," he said again.

Alex laughed merrily and laid a hand on his shoulder. "It's all right, Heath, and it's very nice to meet you too."

"Can I get you something to drink?" Heath and Gilley said together in a rush.

"Oh!" Alex said, slightly taken aback by all the enthusiasm . . . and nasal spray. "Uh . . . I think I will have a sparkling water with lime if you all will join me for some refreshment."

"Coming right up!" Gilley said, dashing off to the bar.

"I'll get the lime!" Heath said, moving far faster than he had in the last two days to chase after Gilley.

"I'd love a vodka and cranberry," I muttered, glaring hard at their retreating backs.

"Oh, M. J.!" Alex said. "I'm so sorry. I didn't mean for your order to be left out."

"Don't sweat it," I told her. "I'm sure I can flag down a server."

And we actually were treated to some rather immediate table service from three separate waiters, all making goo-goo eyes at Alex. Reluctantly, one of them even took my order.

Gil and Heath returned with one bottle of sparkling water, one chilled glass, and one accompanying lime— each. They set their prizes down on the table in front of Alex like obedient golden retrievers looking for a cookie. "Why, thank you," Alex said politely as she considered the two sets of refreshments in front of her. "I'm quite thirsty, so this won't go to waste."

Heath and Gilley smiled huge, and that was when Heath caught me giving him the evil eye. He quickly lost his smile and moved back into his own chair, where I'm sure he started to consider spending every night in the near future bunking with Gilley.

An awkward and uncomfortable silence followed until my drink was brought. The waiter set down a vodka-grapefruit instead of a vodka-cranberry, but I decided it wasn't worth the effort to send it back.

After he left, Gilley asked, "When did you start drinking greyhounds?"

"When you two failed to ask me if I wanted a drink from the bar," I snapped, still irritated with both of them for making me feel like chopped liver.

Gilley's face softened a bit, and I think he finally started to feel sorry for me. I watched him get up and come around to give me a quick peck on the cheek before he said, "Let me fix it for you, okay, sugar?" He then took my glass and headed to the bar.

"What a charming man," Alex said.

"He has his moments," I told her. Heath slumped farther down in his seat.

"I'm sorry, M. J.," he said. "I should've gotten you something."

"Don't worry about it."

Gilley returned with a vodka-cranberry with two lemons and a bowl of nuts for us to share. And I think that finally broke the ice and relaxed the mood among all of us, because we settled into easy conversation for a bit until Alex brought us around to the topic at hand. "So, tell me about your encounters with the phantom."

We took turns telling her the story of our first, second, third, and fourth encounters. I was the one who filled her in on our last dance with that hateful spook, and how we'd been so fortunate to discover the hidden stairway in the church and the underground tunnel underneath the causeway, which—I also pointed out—had not been outlined on the castle blueprint.

Alex was surprised and I think quite impressed by our discovery. "I so wish we'd known about that four years ago," she said with a hint of sadness.

"Well, we know about it now, and I think we can use it to our advantage," I told her.

Alex nodded and took a sip of her sparkling water. "We're going to need all the advantages we can get when we take on the phantom."

"What can you tell us about it?" Heath asked.

"The phantom?"

"Yes."

Alex inhaled deeply and seemed to gather her thoughts. "It's an incredibly dangerous spirit," she began. "I've been able to trace its origins, in fact."

"Don't tell me," I said. "It came from South America, right?"

Alex's eyebrows rose. "Yes," she said. "How did you know?"

"We met the ghost of Gaston Bouvet. He more or less took us through what happened to him the night he died. A lot of what he said was in French, but we managed to decipher a few words."

Alex leaned forward. "Tell me more about your encounter with him."

"He was in the tunnel with the crypts, and Jeffrey

Kincaid brought him a present, which Bouvet indicated came from South America. When he opened it, the phantom was released."

Alex's face registered a mixture of emotions, from shock to understanding to great sorrow. "I always suspected the rumors were true," she said softly. "That Jordan's father was somehow responsible for the phantom."

"What did Jordan think?" Gilley asked.

Alex shook her head sadly. "He didn't believe it, which was why he came here, actually, to clear his father's name, find the gold, and send the phantom back to hell."

"Did Jeffrey ever tell his son what happened that day with Bouvet at Dunlow?"

"No. Jordan was only twelve when it happened, but he clearly remembered his father leaving for a bit of treasure hunting with his dear friend from France, and returning a week later so distraught that he had to be admitted to a mental hospital for several months.

"According to Jordan, once Jeffrey was released, he was never the same, and he never spoke about what happened that day at Dunlow. I met Jeffrey Kincaid only once, when he came here to take Jordan's body home, and our exchange was heated."

"Why was it heated?" Gilley asked.

Alex looked down at her hands. "Jordan never told his father he was coming here, and in his grief Jeffrey accused me of convincing him to come, even though it was the other way around."

I wanted to learn more about the phantom. "You said

you know of the phantom's origins. What can you tell us about it?"

Alex took another sip of her water. "I've traced its birth all the way back to the Incas," she said. "There is a legend that goes back to the Tupac tribe in Peru that speaks of a time when the Spanish conquistadors invaded their society and corrupted it, taking their gold and disrespecting their people. At that time, some of the most powerful shamans within the great nation gathered together and invoked their ancestors to bring to life a powerful protective spirit. This spirit emerged as a dark phantom, and the shamans invoked it to protect their gold, because they knew the conquistadors valued that above all else. They also gave the phantom spirit the ability to call up the conquistadors' worst nightmares, driving them mad and chasing them from their land, which was hilly and treacherous. Many conquistadors were driven right off the high bluffs that made up the Tupac's terrain.

"The phantom worked wonders to secure the tribe from the conquistadors, but the shamans didn't realize that it might have worked a little too well until they encountered their own issues with the wraith. According to the legend, when the phantom was created, it wreaked havoc, not only on the Spanish invaders, but also on the Incan youth too, whose hearts had not yet learned to hold their courage and steel their minds against a force like the phantom. The shamans decided that their protective spirit was too dangerous to remain on the loose, so they then created a talisman to trap the phantom and hold it until such time as it was needed again."

"That sounds an awful lot like our phantom," Heath said.

"I'm convinced it's the same one of the legends."

"And this talisman sounds like a portal key," I said.

"Like the knife we've got back in Boston?" Gilley asked, referring to another very powerful spook and its portal we'd had to contain in a magnetically lined safe.

"Exactly like that, Gil."

"Portal key," Alex repeated. "That's an interesting description. But I don't believe this talisman is a portal to anywhere. It's simply the phantom's cage."

"So where can we find this talisman?" Heath asked.

Alex shrugged. "I don't know," she admitted. "But that's what Jordan and I were here four years ago trying to locate. Jordan came to South America, in fact, to find me and convince me to aid him in researching the phantom. When we thought we knew where it came from, and how to control it, we set out for Ireland to see if we could find the talisman and the treasure. But none of it went according to plan."

"Alex," Gilley said, "I know this question might make you uncomfortable, but can you tell us what happened that night on the rock when Jordan was killed?"

Our guest shivered slightly and looked down at the tabletop. "It was an awful night," she said. "The worst of my life, really."

I put my hand on her arm and squeezed. I'd seen what'd happened from Jordan's perspective, and I could only imagine what she'd gone through. "I'm so sorry to drag you back here," I told her. "But we're desperate to help our friend."

Alex took a deep breath and forced a small sad smile. "Yes," she said. "I know. And if I help you, you'll help Jordan, right?"

I held up my hand and vowed, "I promise I will not leave Dunlow until I've helped Jordan Kincaid cross over to the other side."

Alex nodded, blinking back tears, and she took another big breath. "We'd been at it for several days," she said. "And we'd already encountered so many setbacks. Our friend Antonio had been ambushed by the phantom for several hours in one of the smaller rooms of the castle, and he was tortured for all of that time until we were finally able to break through to him and get him out.

"He'd been so traumatized that we had to admit him to the hospital, and Jordan and I almost quit because of it. My greatest regret in the world is that we didn't."

Alex's voice had dropped to barely above a whisper, and the three of us were leaning in close to listen to her.

"Jordan wanted to carry on," she said. "He was convinced that the phantom was far too destructive to allow it to remain free. More than anything, he wanted to find the talisman and contain the phantom. And I believe he wanted that even more than the gold.

"We made plans to make one more thorough search of the castle, but that night I had the most amazing dream, and I woke up thinking that I might know exactly where Dunnyvale's treasure was."

"In the crypts," I said, remembering her backpack next to Dunnyvale's tomb.

Alex smiled. "Yes," she said. "How did you know?" I told her that I'd found her pack filled with spikes and she nodded. "I was so stupid to venture there alone," she admitted. "I should have woken Jordan up to go with me, or waited until the morning, but he'd had such little sleep in the four days we were there, and he was resting so peacefully that I thought I could just check to see if my hunch was correct before disturbing him.

"I was sure I could do it on my own, so I wrote him a note telling him where I'd gone in case he woke up, and I took most of the magnetic spikes and left him sleeping in our camp. After I'd made my way to the crypts, I began to use my dowsing abilities to look for the gold I was convinced was there. It took me some time, but eventually I thought I had discovered the location. Just as I was about to get to work to recover it, I heard Jordan's scream. I grabbed several spikes and ran to help him." Alex's eyes had filled with moisture, and her voice began to shake with emotion. "But by the time I reached the cliffside, it was too late."

"I'm so sorry," I said, reaching out to squeeze her arm again.

She nodded and wiped at her eyes. "Thank you," she said after a moment.

I then pulled out the letter that Jordan had written to Alex, and handed it to her. "We found this at your campsite."

Alex regarded it, recognizing the handwriting immediately. "It's from Jordan," she gasped. "To me."

We waited while she read it, pausing at parts I suspected were the sections where Jordan explained how
much he loved her, and what he planned to do to break
through the phantom and get to the gold. The letter itself
moved her deeply, because she began to openly weep.
Finally, she swallowed hard and wiped at her cheeks.
"He was such a fool to go off alone like that," she said.
"Why didn't he wait for me to get back?"

"Because he'd had the same dream you did," I said,
understanding blossoming in my own mind.

Alex cocked her head. "What?"

"That night you dreamed of Ranald Dunnyvale, right
before you went to the crypts—am I right?"

Alex's eyes grew wide with surprise. "Yes," she said.

"So did Jordan."

"But why didn't he come to me?" she insisted. "If we
dreamed the same thing, why didn't he come find me
in the crypts instead of venturing into the castle with
barely any protection from the phantom?"

I shrugged. "I don't know," I admitted.

We sat in silence for a bit before Gilley came up with
another question for our guest. "Alex, how do you know
that the talisman is even on the island? I mean, Bouvet could have unwittingly unleashed the phantom and
taken the talisman over the side with him. For all we
know, it's been washed out to sea."

"I know the talisman is still at that rock because the

shaman legend states that the phantom is bound to return to it. While it's true that the talisman is the phantom's cage or prison, it is also its home, and it is bound by powerful magic to return there. If the talisman had been thrown over the side of the cliffs, then the phantom would have moved to the base of the rock or into the water in search of it, and it most certainly would have entered the talisman again."

"In other words, the phantom can't go beyond a certain distance of the talisman?" I said, wanting to be sure I understood.

"Exactly. Given that the phantom cannot move down the stairs, I'd say that the talisman is somewhere hidden in the center of the castle."

"You noticed it wouldn't come down the stairs too, huh?"

"Yes," she said. "It seems strangely bound to the first story of the castle."

"What rooms did you manage to search when you went looking for the talisman?" I asked next.

"Most of the ones on the first story except for a section of the west end of the castle with several small parlors and the church at the back. The phantom seemed to guard those two areas fiercely."

"Both of them had escape routes," I commented. When Alex appeared confused, I added, "One of those rooms down that corridor in the west section had a trapdoor similar to the one we found in the church, only that door led to the crypts."

"It did?" she asked, surprised.

I nodded.

"Maybe the talisman is within the crypts?" Gilley suggested. "And because of Alex's backpack filled with spikes, it couldn't get to it."

But Alex shook her head. "I don't think so. If the talisman were still at the crypts, then the phantom would be able to move down the outside stairs at least to the door leading to it from the stairs. I believe, given the radius of the phantom's range, that it is somewhere in the heart of the castle on the first floor."

"How big do you think this talisman is?" I asked.

"Oh, it can be as small as a coaster. In the tradition of other Incan talismans, I'd say it's a round disk made of stone inscribed with Incan words of power. In the center there will likely be a hole with some sort of stopper made of gold or precious metal. It's when the metal is pulled from the hole that the phantom is released."

"Like a genie from the bottle," Heath murmured.

"Exactly," Alex agreed. "Only this genie's a mean son of a bitch. And my dowsing abilities have never been at their best when I'm distracted. Finding that talisman is going to be like looking for a needle in a haystack, but I'm hoping I can focus my sixth sense on the gold in the stopper and locate it."

"Well, at least now we have a general description of what we're looking for," I reasoned. "And if we go in together, I can let you focus on finding that talisman, while I work to give you a nice wide berth from the phantom."

"How're you going to do that, exactly?" Gilley asked, his forehead creased with concern and his hand reaching for the nuts.

"The phantom likes to chase things," I said more calmly than I felt. "I plan to give it something to chase."

The table erupted in a chorus of objections, but my mind was made up and I wasn't going to back down. "Listen to me!" I said loudly, getting them all to quiet down. "It's the only way to make sure that Alex can focus her intuition on finding the gold in the talisman."

"It's suicide," Heath spat. "And I'm not letting you do it."

I raised an eyebrow. "Really? And how exactly are you going to stop me, Heath?"

"I'm going with you."

"Right," I snapped. "And how fast do you think you can run with that wound on your back? Don't be ridiculous!"

Heath winced as if I'd physically hurt him. "Gee, M. J.," Gilley said. "Cut the guy some slack. He's just worried about you."

I blew out a sigh and considered what I'd said. "You know what, Gil? You're right. Heath, I'm really sorry. That was totally out of line."

"It's okay," Heath muttered, but I knew he was still a little wounded.

Alex tried to ease the sudden tension by saying, "I think it will be okay." We all looked at her. "I think M. J. knows her limits, and if the phantom starts getting too close, she can head to the church or the stairs. Those are our safety zones."

I reached down and took out the copy of the blue-print to the castle. Unfolding it, I spread it onto the table and began mapping out a plan of attack. "Alex, you and I will go in through the underground causeway tunnel and come up here," I said, pointing to the church. "That way, we can avoid having the phantom know that we're coming. We'll just suddenly appear in his territory. From there we can work in a circular fashion outward from the church. I'll use my spikes to push the phantom to the far-thest corners while you work the middle, slowly moving toward the outside stairs. While I'm distracting it over on the west side of the castle, you can head upstairs and search the upper floors." When everyone eyed me as if I'd suggested the wrong thing, I added, "I think it's important to be thorough. We suspect that the talisman is on the first floor, but Alex already said she'd looked for it almost everywhere but for a few spots, and I didn't see anything like the talisman she describes in the church, so we have to assume that it's possible that this disk is upstairs."

Alex nodded. "I'm with you," she said.

"How fast can you dowse?" I asked, wondering if she needed to go slowly and carefully.

"Fast," she assured me. "Just like water in the tradi-tional dowsing field, gold has a particularly unique energy associated with it. When I focus on searching for it, I can find it fairly quickly if it's anywhere within about a ten-foot radius. In other words, I could probably search the en-tire second and third floors in fifteen to twenty minutes."

"Okay, then," I said. "Let's agree to have you search in short bursts, because I might not be able to take more than twenty minutes of the phantom at one time. You'll start with the upper stories, clear those or bring back the talisman, and we'll regroup again in the church for a short break and to reassess if necessary."

"Good," she said. "When do we start?"

I looked at my watch. It was a little after four and I didn't want to wait another day because we were already pushing our limits with the deadline Gopher's kidnappers had set. "Why don't we head to the manhole right after an early dinner?"

"Perfect," she agreed.

I tried not to notice that Gilley and Heath looked less than enthused.

We were fed, geared up, and well protected with plenty of magnets by quarter to six. Alex brought along a padded belt filled with magnetized metal balls. "Where can I get one of those?" I asked when she told me about it.

She smiled. "I know a guy. I'll have him make you one and ship it to you."

"That's way better than carrying around a bunch of metal spikes," I said.

"The drawback for you is that as long as you're wearing a belt like this, no ghost will come near you."

"Ah, yeah," I said, remembering that my primary job was ghostbusting, not phantom chasing.

As for me, I wore a whole belt filled with capped grenades, and just four spikes taped to my upper back and chest. I hoped that would be enough exposed magnetic energy to keep the phantom at least ten yards away from me at all times. He was a powerful spook, however, and the grenades were there in case I was underestimating him.

The point was to make myself a more appealing target than Alex. Heath, however, still wasn't into the idea. "I think you need more," he said as he helped to tape me up.

"Four is plenty," I assured him.

"Five is better."

"If I need a fifth, I can uncap a grenade."

"It could overpower you before you get to it. How about wearing Gilley's sweatshirt?"

I shook my head. "Too many magnets. He could go for Alex if he thought I was too hard to get to."

"I really hate that you're using yourself as bait, M. J."

I leaned in and gave him a light kiss. "I know," I whispered. "But it's the only way to get Gopher back."

"It'd be safer to figure out who took Gopher in the first place."

I stepped back and eyed him curiously. "You know, Heath, I think you might be on to something. While Alex and I are at the castle, have Gilley work on that, okay?"

Heath put both his hands on the side of my face and kissed me long and sweet. "Do me one favor," he said when I was good and dizzy.

"Wha . . . what's that?"

"Be careful, and come back in one piece."

I grinned. "I'll do my level best."

Alex and I arrived at the manhole cover leading to the underground tunnel at six on the dot. I was furious and frustrated by one minute past. "*Who* would throw a lock on this thing?" I yelled as I stomped around the outside, inspecting the bolts holding a latch and newly attached padlock barring our entrance.

Alex squatted next to me. "It looks like some official from the town did it," she said, shining her flashlight over the seal.

"But why?" I demanded. "Why would they lock us out?"

Alex stood and surveyed the area, her eyes roving to the nearby houses with windows all facing the ocean. "It's likely that someone saw you come out of the tunnel and reported it to the authorities. My guess is that it was then talked about up the chain of command, and once the town council got wind of the entrance you and Heath discovered and where it led, they probably didn't want the liability of a bunch of tourists trekking through a four-hundred-year-old tunnel under the causeway, so they made sure to seal it off."

"Bastards!" I growled. "That was our safe way in!"

Alex sighed and pivoted to the causeway, where the tide was still covering the stones. "We'll have to wait for the tide to recede," she said.

I folded my arms and grimaced. "Low tide's well after nine, so we won't be able to get across until close to nine thirty."

Alex sank low and sat down on the patchy grass nearby. "Then we wait."

While we waited for the tide to lower, Alex and I had a chance to talk a bit more. "So, are you and Heath an item?" she asked.

I felt heat sear my cheeks. "Um . . . ," I said. "I guess. I mean, there's a definite attraction, but I just got out of a relationship and I'm not sure diving right into another one is the way to go."

"He obviously cares about you."

I smiled. "Yeah," I said softly. "I know."

"And he's totally hot," she added with a laugh and a nudge.

"Honey, you don't know the half of it."

"So dive in, M. J."

I was growing a little uncomfortable, and I decided to turn the conversation back on her. "What about you?" I asked. "Are you attached?"

Alex's good humor seemed to seep right out of her, and her eyes moved back to the sea. She took her time answering me. "You know, I don't know that I'm ready. Jordan really was the love of my life, and I've mourned him so much these past few years, but I haven't gotten to that place yet where I can let go of my feelings for him and allow someone else in."

I let that sit with me for a bit before I asked, "What did Jordan mean in the letter when he said that he was sick of hiding his love for you from the world?"

Alex smiled, but it was filled with melancholy. "I'm a psychic dowser, M. J. And Jordan had had a string of somewhat infamous missteps in his youth. Part of his mission to Dunlow was to prove that he had grown up a little. He really wanted to win back the approval of his father, who could be very harsh on him. So, Jordan had been working to clean up his act for over a year when

we met. But his reputation followed him, and in the beginning of our relationship, he wanted to keep the two
of us private because if the press got wind that Jordan
Kincaid was going around with a woman who claimed to
be psychic . . . well . . ."

Alex's voice trailed off and I thought I really understood what she was getting at. It seemed that intuitives
like us always faced the uphill battle of legitimacy, and
the press never cut us any slack. It was as if the media as
a whole was afraid to portray us as normal people with
a natural extrasensory ability—lest its own members be
criticized by the public—so reporters and media person-
nel worked very hard to always present us in the worst,
most skeptical light possible. The double standard drove
me crazy.

From that perspective, I could see how Jordan would
really want to keep his relationship with Alex on the
down-low.

And yet, he'd proposed to her, which meant that he
was getting ready to bring it all out into the open, and I
had to give him credit for that.

Finally, the tide receded enough for us to begin the
trek across the causeway. There was still a bit of water
on the stones as we went along, but we were both anxious to get to the castle and get on with it.

When we arrived at Dunlow, I squinted at the top
of the rock, which was bathed in silver light by the low
moon. I couldn't see the phantom, but I could sense it,
and that sent a shiver up my spine.

At the base of the stairs I went first, and kept my

senses on high alert. After fifteen minutes of climbing, we were close to the top when we heard it. The moment it came to my ears, I closed my eyes and thought, *Oh, no!*

"Alex!" cried a voice, faint and distant. "Alex, help me!"

Behind me I heard a gasp.

I took a breath and turned around to face my new friend just as the voice cried out again.

Alex's face was a mixture of emotions, from hope to horror to abject pain. *"No!"* she cried at last.

I stepped down quickly and held her by the arms. "It's not real!" I told her firmly. "Alex, it's just an echo!"

"Help me!" Jordan's ghost begged. *"Allllex!"*

Alex pushed away from me and began racing up the stairs, crying out for Jordan as she went. I went tearing after her because I knew what she'd find at the top. "Wait!" I yelled. "Alex, *stop*!"

But she wasn't listening. She was too intent on getting to Jordan and she was just out of my reach. She was ten stairs from the top when I made a desperate last bid attempt to catch her. I lunged forward, gripping her by the ankles and pulling her down onto the stair with a hard thud.

"Uh!" she cried, smacking the stone.

"Shit!" I swore as I fell too. I hit the stairs on my side and it knocked the wind right out of me. For a minute, all I could do was clutch my rib cage and gasp for air that stubbornly refused to enter my lungs. The edge of my vision danced with stars and began to close in, and in the back of my mind I prayed that I wouldn't black out.

"Breathe!" said someone right next to me. "M. J., just breathe."

I looked up to see a bright light blurring my vision further, but I was able to take one small breath.

"That's it," the voice coaxed.

It sounded so familiar, that voice telling me to breathe when I couldn't. Where had I heard it before?

"Alex! Help me!"

I looked up the stairs in the direction of the voice. Alex's crumpled form lay across the stairs.

"Pay no attention to Jordan," the voice said. "You'll see to him later. For now you need to take another breath."

I inhaled and a little more air crept into my lungs. I closed my eyes and exhaled, then took another breath, this time deeper, and before long I was breathing somewhat normally.

When I opened my eyes, I realized that Samuel Whitefeather was crouched next to me. "Thanks," I wheezed when I felt I could talk.

"Allllex!"

I cringed as the sound reverberated off the rocks.

"He's in a great deal of pain," said Sam.

"I can't believe he showed up tonight of all nights." I looked up to see Alex still lying in a crumpled heap on the stairs. "Ohmigod!" I gasped, and clawed my way up to her, only to find a big bump on her forehead and her eyes closed.

Very gently I moved the hair out of her face and checked to make sure she was breathing and had a pulse. To my immense relief she was very much alive. "Alex?" I said as I eased her over onto her back. "Alex, honey? Can you hear me?"

She didn't respond.

"The girl needs to get somewhere safe," Sam advised. "The phantom is coming, and he will be able to creep into her dreams even at this distance."

I stared at the top of the steps, and sure enough the hair on my arms began to stand up on end. "I don't know if I can move her!" I said.

"You can," Samuel assured me. "Bring her down just a ways to the door. It's only ten steps and you're there."

I looked behind me and Samuel faded away into nothing, but beyond him I could see the step that was a bit longer than the others, and I knew that marked the entrance to the tunnel leading to the crypts.

Next to me Alex shivered and jerked, and I knew the phantom was very close. Praying that I wouldn't hurt her further, I wrapped her arms around my neck and half shimmied, half pulled her onto my back piggyback-style.

She was tall, but thin, and didn't weigh a lot more than me. Still, I had a hell of a time getting her down those ten steps.

Behind me I heard a growl and a hiss, but I refused to turn around. I could feel the phantom radiating its evil energy, and my thoughts started to fill with scary images. But then Samuel appeared again by my side. "Steel your mind, M. J. Call upon your courage. The phantom cannot break a courageous mind."

I thought about what Samuel said as I moved the remaining few steps to the crypt tunnel. Easing Alex to the ground as gently as I could, I took a moment to steady my breathing, then opened the door and lifted her under the arms to pull her inside.

After moving her, I fished around in my messenger bag for an extra flashlight and anything I might be able to use for a pillow. I came up with the flashlight, but no pillow. With little else to offer I yanked off my own sweatshirt, ripping off the tape that held the spikes and tossing them aside. I then wadded the shirt into a ball to place under her head before inspecting the bump on her head.

"Ouch," I muttered, seeing the egg-sized lump forming just above her left eye.

Alex moaned and her eyelids fluttered.

"Can you hear me?" I whispered. Alex's arm jerked reflexively. "Hey, Alex," I said. "Honey, can you hear me?"

She moaned again, but this time she also spoke. "Yeah. I can hear you."

I felt a wave of relief flood through me. "I'm *so* sorry about tripping you."

Alex's hand went to her head and she winced. "Why'd you do that, anyway?"

"I had to stop you," I told her. "You were headed for dangerous territory and I just had to stop you from running after Jordan."

Alex opened her eyes and I saw the pain registered there. I didn't think it was caused solely by her injury.

"Again, I'm really, really sorry," I said, feeling terrible and not just for tripping her.

"We need to help him, M. J."

I nodded. "It's on my list," I promised. "I won't leave Ireland until I get Jordan across to the other side."

Alex seemed somewhat satisfied and she tried to sit up. "Whoa," she said, putting both hands to her head and lying back down.

"Does it hurt?"

"Yes. And I'm superdizzy."

"I think you might have a concussion."

She inhaled deeply and kept her eyes closed. "That's not good."

I looked anxiously out the door, where a little light from the moon was seeping in. I had no idea how I was going to get her down those stairs and across the causeway. "I should go for help."

Alex's hand reached out and took hold of my arm, her grip like a vise. "Do *not* leave me on this rock with that *thing*!"

I pulled her hand off my arm and held it tight. "Listen," I said, trying not to sound panicked. "I have to get you some help, and there's no way I can carry you down the rest of the stairs by myself."

"But the phantom!" she cried.

"I'll leave all the magnets with you," I told her. "There's no way it'll come anywhere close to this place with all of that magnetic energy."

From outside we both heard a very faint cry from Jordan's ghost pleading for Alex to help him. The timing couldn't have been worse. Alex began to cry, and I knew I couldn't leave her with both the phantom lurking nearby and the ghost of her fiancé. One or the other would send her insane.

But I couldn't just stay without trying to help her. "I don't know what to do," I admitted.

Find the talisman, said a voice in my head.

Alex made another feeble attempt to sit up, but she failed and her tears of misery and frustration came in earnest. "Give me a minute," she said. "Just give me a minute, and I'll walk out of here myself."

M. J., said the voice, and I knew it was Samuel. *If you want to help Alex and Jordan, find the talisman.*

I closed my eyes and whispered, "I don't even know where to *start* looking for it, Samuel!"

"What?" Alex asked.

I opened my eyes and stared down at her. "Heath's deceased grandfather likes to talk to me sometimes," I told her. "I think he's become my unofficial spirit guide."

"What's he saying?"

"He says that if I want to help you, I have to find the talisman."

Between the two of you, you can figure out exactly where to look, Samuel assured me.

"Maybe Heath's grandfather can tell us where it is?" Alex asked.

"He says that between the two of us we should be able to figure it out."

"What's that supposed to mean?"

The answer is in your dreams, Samuel suggested.

And that made me pause.

"What?" she asked.

Turning to her, I said, "When you went looking for the gold, why did you think it was in here?"

Alex squinted up at me. "It was my dream," she said. "And it made sense. Dunnyvale told me that his gold was buried where his true heart lay. He also told me that I could find the talisman there."

I smiled, because I knew where she'd thought to look: in the crypt of his first wife. "Meara's tomb."

Alex gave a small nod and it looked like it pained her. "Yes."

"Did you lift the lid to see?"

"I never got a chance. I had a hard time finding it and kept going back to Ranald's tomb, and that's when I heard Jordan calling for me."

We both listened as outside—as if Jordan's ghost had heard her—he mournfully called for her to help him.

"Please," she begged, her voice a ragged sob. "Help me move away from that door. I can't take listening to him anymore."

I crouched low next to her and told her to keep her eyes closed to help with the dizziness, and then I half lifted, half dragged her well down the long tunnel, settling her in the middle of all the crypts.

"We have to find that talisman," I said, shining my light up at the inscriptions above the doorways.

Alex lay with her arm slung over her eyes. "If you give me a minute, I'll try and stand up and help you look."

I eyed her skeptically. She'd need longer than a minute, of that I was certain. "Maybe I'll just poke around for a bit," I suggested before getting up and walking down a little farther, checking each name until I finally found Meara's tomb. It was small and narrow, barely more than a cubby, and her bones were laid to rest in what looked like a child's coffin. "I found Meara's tomb," I called from the doorway.

Alex tilted her head to the side and looked back at me. Confusion lit her features. "There's no gold in there," she said.

"You're sure?"

"Yes. I can't sense anything but rock and bone in there."

"You're dowsing?" I was shocked that she was able to use her abilities even in her condition.

"It comes naturally," she said. "But yes, even through my throbbing headache I can feel that there's no gold in there. The tomb opposite you has some, though. I remember being drawn to it the last time I was in here."

I looked at Ranald's stone sarcophagus straight across from Meara's tomb and wondered if he hadn't had someone bury his gold with him. Remembering the crowbar I'd found next to Alex's pack, I went into the tomb and found it still lying on the floor. Picking it up, I wedged it into the crevice between the lid and the coffin and heaved.

The stone moved more easily than I would have expected, and I managed to shift it to the side just far enough to shine my light in and look around.

There in the bottom of the sarcophagus lay a skeleton clothed in tattered but elegant textiles, and on his chest was a large gold chain with a beautiful gold coin medallion. I knew without even seeing it up close that it was in fact a piece of Spanish bullion, but that was all the gold this tomb held.

Stepping back out into the tunnel, I asked Alex, "When you came up here four years ago, was this the only tomb where you felt there was gold?"

"Yes."

I stepped back out into the hallway and eyed the names of Ranald Dunnyvale's descendants. And then, like a chest full of gold bullion, it hit me, and I knew *exactly* where to find the gold and the talisman. I also knew what had kept the phantom from going back into its home all these years.

Hurrying back to Alex, I squatted down and wrestled with the dangerous mission I was about to undertake. It wasn't much different from the one I'd proposed earlier, but there was even more at stake now, because Alex was injured and she was counting on me. "I have to go," I told her.

Her arm came away from her eyes and she reached out to clutch my shirt. "Please, don't leave me, M. J.!"

"Alex," I said firmly, peeling her fingers from my clothes and anxious to be on my way. "I promise I won't be far, and I swear to God I'll be back as soon as I can, but I need you to be brave and wait here for me. You're wearing your belt and I'll give you a few of my canisters to keep you safe, but I have to go." I pulled off two of the grenades around my waist and stood up.

"Where are you going?"

I pointed my flashlight at the end of the tunnel, where the spiral stairs led up to that small room on the first floor. Already moving away, I said, "I'm going to church."

Chapter 13

I climbed those stairs quickly, but the closer I got to the top, the more nervous I became. I kept thinking about the power of the phantom when it had attacked me in the room above.

And that made the hairs on my arms and the back of my neck stand up on end. I could feel the menacing energy of the phantom lurking somewhere in the castle. I wondered if it would be waiting for me when I pushed through the door.

At the top of the staircase I realized I was panting hard and my heart was beating fast. I was in no shape to walk through that door and face the phantom. I also realized that I'd left six of my spikes down the stairs with Alex, because the ones I'd taped to my sweatshirt were probably right now still on the floor where I left them. "Damn it!" I swore, fear and anxiety building inside of me.

I was about to turn around to go back and retrieve them when a calm Irish voice whispered, "Easy, lass. You're almost to the prize now."

I jumped a foot. "Will you not sneak up on me, please?"

He laughed, the bastard. "Apologies," he said. "I didn't know you were so jumpy."

I was about to tell him that I had to go back for my spikes when I thought of another plan, one that just might work. "Lord Dunnyvale, would you please accompany me to the church inside your keep? I could really use your knowledge of the castle as a guide."

"You're looking to sneak past the phantom?"

"Yes. Or get as close to the church as possible before it attacks me."

"Leave it to me," he said.

"Thank you." I hesitated and then asked, "Would you also do me a favor and take a peek inside the room behind this panel to see if the phantom's already in there?"

"A moment," he said. While I waited, I focused on breathing in the good air, and exhaling out the bad. There was quite a bit of wheezing involved.

"The way is clear, my lady," Ranald announced.

"Thank God," I muttered. I pressed on the panel and it swiveled to the side, exposing the creepy room beyond. Tiptoeing inside, I moved to the door, which was closed, and pressed my ear to it. I heard nothing on the other side. Taking a deep breath, I reached for the handle, but Ranald stopped me by whispering, "A moment!" I froze, and felt my heart rate increase. "Steel yourself!" Ranald commanded.

I swallowed hard and inhaled deeply. I thought of all the times I'd faced off against dangerous and angry poltergeists and won. If I'd done it before, I could do it again, right?

Still, as much as I attempted to calm myself, goose bumps along my arms told me that the phantom was approaching. My mind recalled the scariest horror movie I could remember seeing when I was about twelve. Images from that movie began to play across my mind's eye.

"Calm," Ranald ordered. "Or you'll lose the battle before you've even begun the fight."

"Samuel," I whispered. "Help me!"

I'm here, M. J., I heard in my head. *And I won't leave you.* A wave of calm energy washed over me, and I was immensely grateful. And that was also when I felt something like a pause in the ether out beyond the room I was standing in—the approaching menacing energy stopped for a moment, then began to slowly fade away.

"That's a lass," said Ranald. "It's moving on from the hallway."

"We need a distraction," I told the ghost, knowing I'd never get more than five feet down that hallway without alerting the phantom. "How many grounded spirits live here, Lord Dunnyvale?"

There was a pause, then, "Oh, I'd say at least three dozen."

"Perfect. Will they all listen to you?"

"Of course," he said confidently. "I'm the lord of the keep, after all."

"Great. How afraid are they of the phantom?"

"Oh, they're quite terrified."

"But they'll listen to you? Follow an order if you give it?"

"Aye."

"Then I need you to order them to engage the phantom."

"All of them?" he asked me.

"Yes. Every last grounded spirit that you can enlist to taunt, tease, distract, or otherwise be a menace to the phantom, just long enough for me to get to that church. That's all I need."

Dunnyvale was silent for a moment, considering my request. Finally, he asked, "Do you know how to find your way there from here?"

"No clue whatsoever."

He chuckled. "I'll tell you the most direct path, lass, and spare you from having to travel through the middle of my keep. You'll take the corridor just beyond that door, turn left, follow that hall all the way to the end and through the door outside to the back of the castle. Run along the side for a bit until you see the rear door to the church."

"Straight, left, straight, through the door, outside, back of the church," I repeated. "Got it."

"Excellent," he said. "Now wait until you hear the commotion before you leave this room. If the phantom enters while I'm gathering the others, dart back down those stairs and you'll be safe enough."

I nodded, but I absolutely knew that if I went back

down those stairs, I'd never find the courage to come up them again. I had to get to that talisman by going either around the phantom or straight through it.

Ranald left me and I paced the floor in the meantime, steeling my nerves, thinking happy thoughts, and tamping down my anxiety.

Finally, I heard at least a dozen doors slam all throughout the castle. Then I heard a parade of footsteps, catcalls, more doors slamming, and the sound of running horses followed by battle cries. The commotion was amazing, and I had to hand it to Ranald.

I wasted no more time and moved quickly to the door. Taking one deep breath before opening it, I stepped out into the hallway and jogged along to the end. "Left," I whispered to myself, and darted around the corner. Behind me loud footsteps pounded down a stairwell, followed by a cascade of pots banging together, merry music being played, more doors being slammed, and laughter, deep and boisterous.

I hustled to the end of the next corridor and found the door to the outside as a shriek sounded in my ear. I jumped and felt my heart thump against my chest. "Sorry!" some disembodied voice said next to me before the sound of footsteps ran away.

I took a very deep breath and did my level best to chill out.

But it was too late. The phantom probably had been distracted by all the ghosts running amok in the castle, but the moment it felt my fear, it knew I was in the area.

It came at me fast and furious; I could feel it like a

large wave, bearing down on me. "Son of a—" I swore, and bolted through the door to the outside. I ran for all I was worth along the wall, desperate to keep out of the phantom's reach.

Behind me I heard a snarl and a growl. It was closing in.

My mind flooded with images, and I began to struggle just to see where I was going. "Dunnyvale!" I shouted. *"Help me!"*

A chorus of noise erupted all around me. My nostrils filled with the smell of horses, smoked meat, and musk; loud voices called to each other, and then, like a miracle, fully embodied spirits began to appear all around, running alongside me stride for stride. To my right a young boy of about eleven grinned broadly when I looked at him. To my left was a portly man-at-arms, and three soldiers flanked my back. And just ahead, Ranald himself appeared, handsome, tall, and even a little dashing. "To the church!" he cried.

More spirits surrounded me until I was running in the middle of the largest crowd of spooks I'd ever witnessed. My senses were abuzz with all the energy and I felt a surge of courage course through my veins. The phantom was still behind us, but it was held back by the brave ghosts buffering me and seeing me to safety.

Ahead, Ranald led the way before he disappeared around a corner, and I dug deep for more speed. When I rounded the edge of the stone wall, I saw the door open and inviting just fifty yards ahead.

But the snarling and growling behind me increased

and the phantom saw that I was close to reaching the safe haven. I could feel it pushing at the back of the large crowd of spirits surrounding me, and one by one my brave ghosts began to fall away.

I heard cries and shrieks and painful shouts. Ranald's expression changed from victorious to one of shock and horror in a heartbeat. "Run, lass!" he shouted at me.

I was panting so hard that I could barely take in a breath. And then, an unexpected and horribly nightmarish image burst into my mind with such suddenness that it caused me to trip. I went sprawling to the ground, and the spirits around me scattered. Somewhere nearby I heard Dunnyvale shout, "To all who have sworn fealty to me, I order you to attack! Attack the phantom!"

At first, nothing happened except that the phantom came racing toward me and I was powerless against it. I put my arm up to shield my head, waiting for the full weight of that terrible thing to hit me, when out of nowhere the ghost of Ranald leaped over my head and landed between me and the phantom.

"Attack!" he shouted again, waving a silver sword. Immediately a group of guards surrounded him and together they pushed the phantom back.

I lay sprawled on the ground, completely speechless for several moments, when I heard Ranald yell, "Malachi! Help her to the church!"

In the blink of an eye the young lad who'd been running beside me earlier appeared. He said nothing but offered me a shy smile.

I scrambled to my feet and he took off. I chased after him and we reached the sanctuary at last. Dashing through the door, I took several more strides until I finally collapsed right next to the stone tomb.

It took me several minutes to collect myself. Outside the battle raged on for a bit before fading away into silence.

When I felt able to, I got up and hedged toward the door. I looked outside but saw nothing. No ghost or phantom was about. Still, my sixth sense indicated that the phantom was nearby, waiting and watching for any attempt of my escape.

My heart sagged a little at the prospect, because there was no way I could use the hidden stairwell in the church again; the manhole was sealed tight. My only choice was to find the talisman.

I waited until I'd caught my breath to pull the crowbar from my messenger bag, and still, it was a moment before I could work up the nerve to squat down next to the young boy's tomb and wedge the tool into the crevice. "Lord Dunnyvale," I said to the empty church. "If you're around, I want you to know how sorry I am for disturbing your son's final resting place."

There was no reply, which left me a bit sad, but I was a woman on a mission, and after working the crowbar into the crevice and giving it a few good heaves, I was finally able to push the top of the tomb aside several inches.

Shining my flashlight inside, I gasped when I took hold of the contents.

There, lying peacefully on a huge mound of gold bullion, lay the remains of Malachi Dunnyvale, the true love of his father's heart.

I couldn't help it; I sat back on my heels and shed a tear or two for the heartbreak that not even gold could heal.

With a final sniffle, I leaned in again and squinted into the stone coffin. There, lying against the opposite side from me, as if it had been slipped carefully inside, was the stone Incan disk, its gold stopper removed. "Gotcha," I said, and worked my hand and arm in to retrieve it. Taking it out to inspect it, I marveled at how simple it was, and how powerful. My intuitive sense felt the waves of energy emanating off it, but its design was so simple that it could have passed for just another flat stone.

About the size of a saucer, it was round, just like Alex described, with a hole drilled into the middle. I was guessing that was where the gold stopper had once been, only what'd happened to it was anyone's guess. Still, the hole wasn't much bigger than the coins inside the coffin, and I wondered if one would fit.

Reaching back into Malachi's tomb, I pulled out one gold coin and hovered it over the top of the hole in the disk. It would certainly work in a pinch, I thought.

Outside the interior door of the church there was a sudden loud hissing sound, and I jumped. Looking in the direction of the noise, I saw that the phantom had decided to make its reappearance, and it was closer than I'd ever seen it to the sanctuary, right on the edge of the doorway, and to say that it appeared furious is to understate its mood dramatically.

I stared at it in stunned disbelief for a moment, shocked by the nearness of it, and that was when it lunged forward into the church, where it curled into a small ball as if it was in great pain. I got up and edged away from the tomb, so scared I could barely breathe. There weren't any nightmarish images filling my mind, and I assumed the church was buffering the power of the phantom's control over me, but watching the raging demon was enough of a nightmare to scare me down to my toes.

The phantom continued to curl in on itself, then unfurl an spin around wildly, like a small and deadly tornado. In an instant I realized that I'd likely done the worst thing possible by retrieving the disk. I also realized I had no idea how to get the genie back inside its bottle.

At that moment there was a loud noise right behind me. Startled, I looked over my shoulder to see Heath and Gilley emerging from the secret passage. Heath was panting hard and hunched over in pain, and Gilley was carrying a set of bolt cutters.

"M. J.!" Gilley cried when he saw me. "You're not dead!"

The phantom shrieked, unfolded itself from its ball, and lunged forward again, coming to within ten feet of me.

"*Ahhhhhhhhhhhhhhhhhhhhhhhhhhhhhh!!!!*" Gilley screamed, before fleeing back down the steps.

Heath remained where he was and shouted to get my attention. "M. J.! Come over here! We can get down the stairs where it can't follow us!"

But I knew that as long as I held the disk, the phantom would follow me. I set the disk down on the ground and slid it over the floor in the direction of the phantom. The ball of dark shadow and growling fury tumbled this way and that, darting toward the disk only to curl up in a ball again, as if fighting off unseen attackers.

With a feeling of dread I realized that it wouldn't be able to enter the disk within the confines of the church. The protective energy of the place was simply overwhelming it.

I looked at Heath and bit my lower lip. He was urgently waving at me to come to him, but I knew what I had to do.

Calling upon every ounce of courage I possessed, I darted forward to the disk, snatched it up off the ground, and bolted for the back door.

Behind me Heath yelled, *"Don't!"* but I ignored him and ran as if my life depended on it, which—let's face it—it did.

Behind me I heard the fury of the phantom increase to a deafening crescendo of noise, and if I hadn't been so focused on my mission, I might have been scared witless.

Once I was free of the church, I dug in for ten long strides, took the gold coin out of the hole, bent low, and dropped the disk in the grass before getting the hell out of there. I made it another yard when something hit me like a freight train, and I went tumbling head over heels in the grass, and my mind filled with a dizzying array of noise, horrible images, and a dread so deep I could not breathe. Worse still, my body was being pummeled by unseen fists, and even curling into a tight ball did not relieve me of the attacks to my stomach, sides, and back.

The torture was so intense that I knew my mind would snap if it continued, and just when I thought I couldn't take one more second of it, I heard a whoosh and *BANG!*

The end of the attack was so immediate that it took me quite a few seconds to realize it had stopped, and as I lay there panting and wheezing, I listened intently to the eerie silence that followed. I rolled to my knees, battered and sore and picked my head up, chancing a glance up and then all around, but saw nothing out of the ordinary. No trace of the phantom remained.

With some difficulty I got to my feet and walked over to the talisman lying peacefully in the grass. With a grunt I bent double, literally trembling with relief.

"M. J.!" Heath shouted again. I looked up and saw him leaving the doorway of the church, attempting to run to me.

I held up my hand, knowing he had to be in great pain from the wound in his back, and managed to say, "I'm fine! Stay there and I'll come to you."

Heath slowed and pulled out two spikes from his back pocket. He held them warily and looked around, as if he thought at any moment the phantom would attack.

But I knew better. Placing the coin I still clutched in my hand in the center, I carefully lifted the talisman, and carried it with me over to Heath. "You can put those away," I told him, referring to the spikes.

"Where'd it go?" he asked, still eyeing the surrounding terrain suspiciously.

"In here," I said, lifting the disk so that he could see.

"You found the talisman?"

I nodded.

"Can it get out of there?"

"Not as long as the gold's in place," I told him.

Heath let out a heavy sigh of relief. "Thank you, God."

"Come on," I told him. "Now that the genie's back in its bottle, we've got to get Alex to a doctor, and then we've got a kidnapper and a thief to catch."

Chapter 14

I figured we had about eight hours of darkness left to work with, and I just hoped it was enough time to do what we had to do to save Gopher.

Gilley and I managed to help Alex down the church's spiral staircase and back through the underground tunnel. When we emerged from the manhole, I noticed with satisfaction that the night had turned cloudy, and it was nice and dark on the beach. I'd told everyone to turn off their flashlights right before moving through the manhole exit, and also ordered my friends to be quiet lest our talking reach suspicious ears.

As quickly as we dared, given Alex's woozy condition, we got to the van, loaded her inside, and drove directly to the hospital. Once she was taken down the hall for a CT scan, Gil and I sneaked over to a nurses' station, and while I created a distraction, Gilley did a search of the hospital's records using one of their computers.

When I saw him nod triumphantly and hold up a

paper he'd printed, he and I made a hasty exit, leaving Heath to look after Alex.

Once Gilley and I were back in the van, we drove to the inn, and for the next few hours Gil did his covert hacking into old records and files till we had what we needed. We then drove an hour and a half to an all-night hardware store, where we got our supplies, and just before dawn, when Heath called to say that Alex had only a minor concussion, Gilley and I hustled our butts back to the castle, once again using the underground tunnel, but making sure to park our van much farther down the beach and well out of sight of the causeway.

Convincing my partner that the phantom was securely locked inside the disk had been a challenge, and as I carried it through the tunnel and up the stairs to the church, he kept glancing fearfully at it.

"You're *sure* it can't get out?" he asked for the hundredth time.

I sighed. "If you ask me again, I'll remove the gold stopper and let it out just to get you to keep quiet."

"You're not very nice when you're sleep deprived," he muttered.

I pointedly ignored him and kept climbing the stairs.

"M. J.?"

I gritted my teeth. "Yeah?"

"Got any food on you?"

"If you promise not to ask me any more questions, I'll give you the Snickers bar in my bag when we get to the church."

That worked like a charm. Gilley said not one word

more. Of course, we had only about twelve more steps to the top, but I was taking my victories where I could.

Once we were there, and Gilley was happily munching on his snack, I moved to the tomb where Malachi was buried and got out my supplies, lining them up on the ground by the tomb.

Gilley came over to stare sadly down at me, his eyes roving to the interior of the sarcophagus with envy. "Do we really have to leave *all* the gold?" he whimpered.

I smiled up at him and sighed. "It's not our treasure, Gilley. It's Ranald's, and now that I know him, I'm finding it kind of hard to take what isn't rightfully mine. Plus, I think enough of it has already been stolen, and we need to prevent the rest of it from disappearing."

"But, M. J.," Gilley pressed, "wouldn't Dunnyvale want you to have even a little bit of it after all you've done to rid the castle of the phantom?"

I wanted to say yes, but I kept thinking back to how Ranald had buried his firstborn son. He'd laid him down on a bed of gold, and I thought it incredibly symbolic—as if the loss of Malachi was too much for Ranald to bear, so he'd buried his treasure with his treasure. It was a final gesture of love to his son. And Ranald had kept only one gold coin from the cache of bullion, which he'd worn around his neck as a symbol of his devotion to his firstborn. To me, that made the gold more than just something to plunder. That made it sacred and untouchable.

"It's not ours," I said firmly. "It belongs with Malachi."

Gilley whimpered a bit more until I gave him another

Snickers bar, and then, fully hopped up on sugar, he helped me move the lid back into place. Once Malachi and the gold were firmly covered again, I began to seal the crevice between the lid and the coffin with liquid cement.

"That'll need about an hour to dry," I said, wiping my brow when I was done.

Gil had polished off the second Snickers bar by then and was rummaging through my messenger bag looking for more. Pulling up my last remaining candy bar, he shouted, "Aha! I knew you were holding out on me!"

I put my hands on my hips and marched over to him, snatching the candy bar out of his greedy little hands. "Dude!" I snapped. "Get a grip! You're getting fat!"

Gilley gasped, reeling backward as if I'd slapped him. "Mean!" he accused, pointing his chocolate smeared finger at me. "I can't believe you just used the *f* word to describe *me*!"

I stuffed the candy bar into my jacket pocket. "Had to be said, buddy. You've put on at least ten pounds since we got here."

Gilley's lower lip trembled. "You know I eat when I'm anxious!" he accused. "I can't help it! It's a nervous condition."

"I'm telling you this for your own good, Gilley Gillespie. It's time for you to get a grip and some exercise."

Gilley sniffled but didn't say anything in reply. Instead he stomped over to a corner and sat there, pouting while I got busy setting up the camera equipment and monitors.

After a while, I guess he forgave me, because he came over and pushed me out of the way when I struggled to secure our one and only remaining camera to a stone cornice. "Let me do that," he said. "Or we'll be here forever."

After setting up the camera, Gil and I moved to the hallway just beyond the church's interior door. There, we set up the computer monitor and made sure we were getting a good clear feed from the camera. After that, we sat back and waited.

The minutes ticked by and I kept glancing at my watch, waiting for the breakfast hour to come and word to spread. "You're sure this'll work?" Gilley asked after a bit.

"No," I admitted. "But as long as Heath is able to get the word out at the inn that we've sent the phantom packing, and that we've gone to bring back some *special* equipment for our investigation, I'm pretty sure it'll trigger a reaction from the people who took Gopher. They'll know that what we've really done is locate the gold and we're going to try and move it out of the castle as soon as possible."

"Who do you think the other kidnapper is?" Gilley asked me.

We were fairly certain we'd discovered the mastermind behind this whole thing; it was his accomplice that still had yet to be identified. "I've no idea," I told him, glancing again at my watch. "But I'm pretty sure we're about to find out."

My intuition was right on the money. Not five minutes later we heard the familiar slide of the panel at the back of the church. Gilley and I immediately focused our attention on the monitor, and I sighed when I realized who'd just walked into the church, because, although I'd suspected the intruder as the accomplice, I'd really wanted it to be someone else.

"Crap," I whispered. "This is going to be tricky."

"What do we do?" Gilley asked softly.

I didn't reply right away, but waited and watched until I was sure of the intruder's intentions. "We'll have to get him to confess on camera," I told Gilley softly. "Otherwise, it's our word against his."

"I don't like that plan," Gilley muttered.

Ignoring his comment, I said, "Stay here and monitor the situation. If I get into trouble, create a distraction or something and we'll run for it."

Gilley opened his mouth to protest, but I was already moving away. I eased around the corner, keeping flat against the wall. A peek into the church showed me that our guest had already gotten to work, and was busy pounding a crowbar similar to the one I'd used into the crevice now sealed with liquid cement.

I smiled, then took a breath and stepped quietly into the room. "Need some help, Constable?" I asked casually.

The man driving in the wedge jumped and his hammer slipped and hit his hand. He let out a yelp of pain and whirled around to glare furiously at me. "What're you doin' here?" he demanded.

I leaned against the stone wall and folded my arms across my chest. "I've been waiting for you, Quinn."

He eyed me suspiciously, and I noticed that he also moved the hammer and crowbar behind him. "How'd you know I'd come, then?"

I casually inspected the fingernails on my right hand. "It was a fairly easy deduction," I told him. "I mean, through a pretty thorough records check we figured out that your buddy Bertie was actually the one that brought the talisman back from South America and gave it to Bouvet twenty years ago. His story, which implicated that it was Jeffrey Kincaid who was responsible for the phantom, didn't really hold water after we'd finished looking at the evidence. Kincaid was a fairly convincing suspect for Bertie, though—I'll give him that—what with Jeffrey's mental collapse and living so far away in South Africa, and not here to defend himself. I'm pretty sure Jordan's father had no idea the talisman even existed, until his son decided to go looking into the affair. And then, when both father and son died, well, that just made Mulholland's story all that more believable.

"And then we managed a rather covert look into the hospital records and saw that Bertie Mulholland was admitted to the hospital the day *after* Bouvet fell from the cliffs. The same day *you* claimed to have ventured here to have a look at the phantom, and I'm guessing you not only had a good look at the phantom, Quinn, but you also found Bertie lying helpless with a broken back somewhere here at Dunlow."

Constable O'Grady's face registered the guilt I'm sure he felt for his part in the lie all those years ago. "You see," I continued, feeling my way along the truth, "what I'm thinking is that Bertie really did find the gold twenty years ago, and to make sure he got Bouvet out of the way, he gave him a little present in the form of a small round disk with a gold stopper, which Gaston obviously uncorked, unleashing the phantom.

"Then while the phantom was off chasing Bouvet right off the edge of the cliffs, and sending Kincaid insane, Mulholland came here and discovered the gold. While everyone else was preoccupied with recovering Bouvet's body and getting Kincaid to the hospital, Bertie managed to hide the talisman in Malachi's tomb so that the phantom could guard his gold. He thought he could come back here later with some rope, pulleys, winches, et cetera, to slide the lid aside to get at all the gold and take it before anyone was the wiser.

"The problem was, he couldn't get all of his equipment through the narrow tunnel under the causeway that led up here. He had to use the outside entrance, and the phantom proved to be far more dangerous than even he had estimated.

"I believe he made it as far as the castle before encountering the phantom. It probably chased him to the outside stairs, where he got tangled in his rope, tripped and fell, and ended up breaking his back. That's where you found him, Quinn—am I right? You found him badly hurt right on those stairs."

Quinn glared hard at me. "I only wanted to help the poor man," he said.

"Oh, I'm sure you did. But Bertie must have been in a terrible state, terrified really and in quite a bit of pain. I'm assuming, to keep you quiet, he offered you some of the gold he'd already taken from in there." For emphasis I pointed to Malachi's tomb. "And that's how you had the money to buy your pub—am I right, Quinn? We looked up the township records. You opened your pub the day you turned eighteen. Where would an eighteen-year-old son of a bricklayer get forty thousand pounds to put down on a pub?"

The constable took a shaky breath and sat down on the stone slab. "Aye," he said grudgingly. "It's true."

"I'm also guessing that Bertie's tried to convince you all these years to come back to this church and take the rest of the gold, but you were too afraid of the phantom."

Quinn shuddered and then he eyed the secret passage leading out of the church. I knew he was thinking of running for it, so I said quickly, "The one question I have for you, though, is, who was it that actually kidnapped Gopher? Was that you? Or did Mulholland manage that from his wheelchair?"

The constable's eyes darted back to me. "I had no part in that!"

"Ah," I said. "Then Mulholland somehow managed that on his own. Still, I'm guessing you were the one that stole the original blueprint from the library, right? And I can see why. It had to have shown the inside stairwell to the church, and Mulholland couldn't have anyone know about that. But why you didn't use it when he hired you to do his dirty work still puzzles me."

O'Grady's jaw bunched. "I tried," he said. "Right after that young man Kincaid fell to his death. I came here and tried to retrieve the talisman, but the phantom, it started to come inside the church. So I left it alone and told Mulholland I'd have none of it until the phantom was dealt with. He's the one who sent word to your producer friend. He told Peter about the treasure and the haunted castle, and he even told him about the phantom."

I now knew how Mulholland had lured Gopher to his home, which was where I was now convinced Gopher was being held captive. Still, I wanted to be sure. "Where is Peter, Quinn?"

O'Grady scowled and stared at the floor without answering me.

"How many children did you say you had?" I asked, reminding him of exactly how much he had to lose.

The constable's eyes came back to meet mine. "Seven. I've seven hungry mouths to feed, Miss Holliday."

"Then I think it's time for you to help me get Gopher back—don't you agree?"

Quinn stared at the tomb again. "I could take care of all of them with a bit of this gold."

"Yes, you could," I told him, smiling like I had a big secret. "Of course, once you pried that lid up—and trust me when I tell you that you'd need a forklift now that we've resealed it—you'd discover the tomb empty of all the gold."

Quinn stood and glared at me. "You've already taken it? All of it?"

"Yep," I said. "We had all night, after all. It was a lot of work, but we've managed to clear Dunlow of its infamous treasure."

O'Grady threw the crowbar and hammer onto the floor. "You'll never prove I had a hand in any of it," he said. "It's your word against mine."

My smile grew even bigger. "Say, Quinn?"

"Aye?"

"Could you turn a little to your left? I don't think our video camera is capturing your good side." For emphasis I pointed to the cornice where we'd attached the camera. "The feed is traveling right across the Internet as we speak. I figure you'll be a YouTube sensation in about three hours."

O'Grady's shoulders slumped and he sat back down on the tomb, covering his face with his hands. "What's going to happen to me children?" he wailed.

In that moment I took pity on him, and truth be told, I knew I needed his help to get Gopher back. "I don't know that anyone really has to know about your part in this," I said. "I'd be willing to have the feed erased, especially if you decide to help us."

The constable's head lifted and he looked hopefully at me. "What do you want me to do?"

"Help me get Peter Gophner back."

Quinn looked again at the camera with its little red recording light glowing in the dim church, and I knew he was considering all he had to lose. "All right," he agreed wearily. "I'll do what you ask. But I want to warn you, miss: Bertie Mulholland is a dangerous and deceptive man. He might be in a wheelchair, but it wouldn't be wise to underestimate him."

"Noted," I said. "Now, let's work on a plan. . . ."

Gilley and I approached Mulholland's large house warily. We'd already spent a little time scouting the perimeter and making sure that the camera I carried in my messenger bag was sending a good signal to Quinn and Heath in the van.

I was taking a big chance with the constable, but I hoped that the footage I already had of his confession at the castle was enough to get him to cooperate fully. I'd made sure to let him know that if I even sensed a double cross from him, I'd make sure it ended up on YouTube and in the e-mail of every member of the town council and he'd be taken from his wife and children.

"Are you sure this'll work?" Gil asked me for the hundredth time as we walked up the drive.

"Just let me do all the talking," I told him.

Gilley's stomach rumbled. "You got any food on you?"

I gave him an exasperated look and walked up the ramp to Mulholland's front door. Ringing the bell, I stepped back and waited.

No one came to the door and Gilley whispered, "I don't think he's home."

I eyed the van at the end of the drive. "Oh, he's home all right."

Ringing the doorbell again, I stepped back and leaned against the side of the house, looking like I wasn't about to go anywhere. A moment or two later I heard, "A moment!" from inside.

The door was opened and Bertie sat in his chair looking rather flushed. "Good morning to you, Miss Holliday!"

"Hello, Bertie," I said, smiling all friendly-like. Turning to Gilley, I said, "This is my associate Gilley Gillespie."

Bertie extended his hand. "Lovely to meet you."

Gilley shook his hand and smiled cordially. "And you, sir."

Bertie then turned his attention back to me. "I hope you're here with good news?"

"Oh, we are," I gushed.

For a moment, Bertie appeared a little taken aback. "You've found your friend, then?"

I laughed like he'd just said the funniest thing. "Oh, no," I said. Turning to Gilley, I added, "Isn't that funny? It's been such an exciting twenty-four hours that I totally forgot about Gopher!"

"Gopher who?" Gilley mocked with a chuckle. And the two of us laughed and laughed.

I took note of the fact that Bertie appeared confused and perhaps even a little irritated. Collecting himself, he backed his chair up and said, "Won't you please come in, then, and share your good news?"

Gilley and I waltzed into Bertie's home and followed him down the ramp to the sitting room. Taking a seat, I made sure to gaze appreciatively at all the artwork and knickknacks again. "I swear, this house gets lovelier every time I see it!" I said.

Bertie placed his chair opposite us at the coffee table, his smile a bit strained and his eyes impatient. "Thank you," he said. "Now, you were saying something about good news?"

"Oh!" I giggled. "Yes, that!"

Gilley laughed wickedly next to me, and Bertie's confusion deepened.

I decided to get to the point. "We're leaving this morning," I told him.

"Leaving?" he gasped, then caught himself. "So soon?"

I nodded and beamed him a happy smile. Gilley snickered and held his hand up to his mouth as if he were struggling to hold back a fit of laughter. "We've come across a bit of good fortune," I said. "And we really must be on our way."

Bertie blinked in surprise. "Good fortune?"

I nodded again, and added a wink as if he were in on the joke.

Understanding seemed to blossom in his eyes . . . along with something far more cunning. "But what about your friend? The producer you were looking for?"

I flicked my wrist impatiently. "Oh, *phhhht*!" I said. "Screw him. Gopher was always a pain in the ass, and if he wants to wander off and not call, well, then he deserves to get cut out—I mean left behind."

Gilley giggled.

Bertie fidgeted nervously. "I see," he said. "But I thought you were terribly worried about him."

I sighed. "Yeah, well, it's funny how good fortune can take your worries away. Right, Gil?"

Gilley laughed and nudged me. "Good one," he said.

Bertie's eyes darted back and forth between us. "Where will you go?" he asked.

I looked at Gil as if that was the first time I'd considered the question. "Someplace tropical?"

"Definitely. I could totally use a vacation. Especially after all that heavy lifting last night. Man, I could go for a massage!"

"Heavy lifting?" Bertie asked anxiously.

I ignored his question and stood up. "Yes, well, we really do have to go," I said. "We just wanted to stop by and thank you for all your help."

"My help?"

"Yes," I said with another happy smile. "We couldn't have done it without you, Bertie."

"Done what exactly?"

"Accomplished our mission," I said, motioning to Gilley that it was time to leave.

As we began to move to the door, I stopped abruptly and said, "Oh! I almost forgot!" Whirling back around to face Bertie, I said, "We're so appreciative of your help that we got you something."

Gilley nodded enthusiastically. "A present."

"Yes, a present, and it's well deserved." I then reached

into the side pocket of the messenger bag and slid the talisman out carefully. Making sure to hold it in range of the camera, I said, "Here, Bertie. This is for you."

Mulholland wheeled backward from us. "Get that away from me!" he snapped.

I continued to hold the disk out to him. "Oh," I said innocently. "You recognize this?"

Bertie realized his mistake and tried to catch himself. "No," he said. "Of course not."

I looked at Gilley as if I were truly puzzled. "Huh," I said. "You know, that's *so* interesting, because I would have thought for sure you'd remember it."

"Maybe he thinks we're being rude by regifting it to him."

I nodded. "Yeah, that must be it. I mean, how often do you give someone a gift, and then twenty years later it's given back to you by someone completely different?"

"I've no idea what you're going on about!" Mulholland snapped, still eyeing the talisman warily.

I sat down on a chair, cradling the talisman in my lap. "Oh, Bertie, I'm afraid you do." When he remained silent, I explained, "You see, you already told us everything we needed to know to point the finger at you. You were the one that told us you'd ventured to Spain to research the ship from the Spanish Armada that crashed on these shores. And in that research, Bertie, I think you came across a story about a group of Spanish conquistadors who were driven out of Peru by a mysterious phantom who could be drawn from an Incan stone if its stopper of gold was removed.

"And then I believe you traveled to Peru in search of this talisman, and I believe you found it."

"Loved your book on Machu Picchu," Gilley said with a sly smile. "Didn't sell many copies, though, did it?"

Bertie glared hard at Gilley.

But I picked up on the thread. "No, it didn't sell many copies. In fact, there's not nearly as much money in travel books as you'd have people believe, right, Bertie?"

Again he remained silent, which wasn't helping our cause, so I continued to goad him.

"Wonder how you got the money to pay for this gorgeous house?" I said. "And all these expensive artifacts . . ."

"Things like that don't come cheap," Gilley remarked. "Especially not that antiquey-looking telescope."

I made a show of eyeing the telescope. "Oh, that is too cool! I'll bet it still works, too, huh, Bertie?"

"I'll bet he can see all the way down to the beach with that thing," Gilley added.

"And to the secret passage just to the right of the causeway," I agreed.

"Which is how he knew that we'd found the church exit," Gil said.

"Even though he'd conveniently left it off the copy of the blueprint he made for us."

"Again, I've no idea what you two are rambling on about," Bertie snapped, all pretense of the kindly older gentleman gone.

I let go of the act and got deadly serious with him. "Struggling to keep up with us, Bertie?" I snarled. "Well, then. Let me spell it out for you. We know you were the one that gave Bouvet this talisman and encouraged him to uncork the stopper.

"The phantom went after him with a vengeance, didn't it? And he never stood a chance. And then you worked out where the gold was, from the letter that Josephine had written to her friend about her husband's deathbed confession. I figure that either Bouvet did actually tell you what she'd said, or you lifted the letter off him one night while he was asleep here in your home.

"Bouvet had it wrong, though, didn't he? Being a romantic, the Frenchman would have naturally assumed the treasure was buried in the tomb of the first wife. But it wasn't, Bertie, was it? No, you found it exactly where we did. In the tomb of his firstborn son.

"And I'm figuring that you discovered it shortly after Bouvet was pushed over the cliffs and the phantom began hunting for poor Jeffrey. You then stuffed your pockets with all the gold you could carry, which is how you eventually managed to pay for this place, and went back to Dunlow the day after Gaston was killed to retrieve the rest of the gold."

"But the phantom caught you," Gilley supplied. "And it chased you to the stairs, where you tripped over the rope you'd brought along with you."

Mulholland's face registered the truth.

"It never attacked you *on* the stairs, Bertie," I said to him. "Because it couldn't. It was bound by the talisman, hidden in a tomb it couldn't get to. And you tortured it for twenty years by keeping it from its house. No wonder it went after Jordan and that poor coast guard officer with a vengeance."

"They never stood a chance," Gil said with a *tsk*.

"And after the money started running out, you came up with a new plan, didn't you, Bertie? You knew that if Jordan would risk his life to find the gold, others might follow, and you couldn't let that happen, because someday, someone might get lucky. So you tried to buy the castle back from the government, but they wanted more than you could pay."

"We found your bid online," Gil told him. "You had until the end of next week to come up with the money."

I smiled sweetly at Mulholland. "And as long as there's a bid in for the purchase of the property, you could have laid claim to any treasure on it as long as the sale eventually happened. You must have thought after reading about our success in Scotland that we were the perfect team to tackle the phantom."

"And we were," Gilley reminded me.

"And we were," I agreed. "But we weren't moving fast enough, were we, Bertie? You were running out of time, and you needed some assurance that we would stay until the phantom had been taken care of. So that night when Gopher found his way back across the causeway, and he was so traumatized by what had happened to him, you lured him here, and somehow managed to imprison him. And you sent us letters letting us know that we had to get rid of the phantom, or else. But I figure that you were thinking that if we did get the phantom back in its disk, and started taking the gold for ourselves, then you'd ransom Gopher for all of it. It was win-win any way you looked at it, right, Bertie?"

Bertie's lips were pressed tightly together. "You Americans," he snarled. "Always making up such tall tales."

Gilley and I exchanged a mock look of surprise. "Tall tales?" I said.

"Really," Gilley sneered. "As if we're capable of having any imagination at all. Clearly, M. J., the man is completely underestimating your intuitive abilities."

"I think what Mr. Mulholland needs is a little demonstration," I said, getting up and turning on my sixth sense. Closing my eyes for a moment, I focused and was rewarded with a feeling of Gopher's presence at the back of the house in a cold, damp space.

Opening my eyes, I regarded Bertie and asked, "Which way to the garage, sir?"

"Get out of my house!" he shouted.

"Not without Gopher," I replied evenly. I then began to move in the direction I had felt the subtle waves of Gopher's energy coming from. "The door to the garage is down that hall, isn't it?" I asked, moving to pass Mulholland.

As I went by him, however, I heard a gasp and Gilley cry, "M. J., watch out!"

Something very hard whacked me across the back, and I stumbled forward to crash into one of the bookcases. The disk I'd been carrying flew out of my hands to land with a hard thud on the floor near Mulholland's wheelchair, and I saw then that he held a walking stick gripped in his hands.

I was in complete shock that he'd hit me, and at first didn't notice that the gold coin I'd placed in the center of the disk was rolling around on the floor. At least, I didn't take note of it until the hole in the middle of the disk began to ooze inky black smoke.

"*Ahhhhhh!*" Mulholland screamed as he tried to back away from the disk at his feet.

Gilley also whirled away from the talisman as its terrible genie poured out of the bottle.

My head had hit the bookcase hard and it began to throb, and for a moment I had a difficult time putting the scene together—that is, until the phantom formed fully in the middle of the room, angry at having been disturbed.

I froze and couldn't even take a breath as it turned to consider first me, then Gilley, and finally Mulholland.

Gilley was wearing his sweatshirt, and I'd come to the house with Alex's magnetic belt secured around my waist. We were taking no chances with the disk while we carried it.

But Mulholland was defenseless, and the phantom seemed to know it. "*Help me!*" he screamed.

I crawled over to the gold coin, but I was a little late, because in the next instant the phantom launched itself at Mulholland.

Bertie was pushed back several feet by the force of the energy hitting him, and his terrified screams cut me to the quick. Grabbing the gold coin, I staggered to my feet and stumbled over to the disk. "Here!" I shouted at the phantom, holding the gold coin right above the hole in the center of the talisman. "I've got your gold stopper right here!"

The dark mass attacking Mulholland seemed to pause, and I had the distinct feeling it was now considering me as I waved the gold coin above the hole. "Back inside!" I ordered. "NOW!"

But the phantom didn't seem to want to take orders from me, and it continued to attack Mulholland.

With desperation I looked around for anything I could use to threaten the phantom and encourage it to get back inside the disk. "M. J.!" Gilley screamed while Mulholland's anguished cries went on and on. "Do something!"

The edges of my mind began to cloud with horrible images, and I knew that the phantom's effect was taking hold now of both Gilley and me. It was proving difficult to see, but in that moment my eyes lit on something on the desk right next to me.

I lunged for the mother-of-pearl letter opener and moved to stand over the disk. Holding the cross aloft, I yelled, "Phantom! Get back in this disk or I swear to God I'm going to drive this symbol of divine light right into the heart of your talisman!"

The ether seemed to crackle with energy and I knew that I'd caught the phantom's attention. It snarled and spat at me as it left Mulholland to inch forward threateningly. Inside my head I reached out to Samuel Whitefeather. *Please, Sam! Give me one last huge dose of courage!*

To the side of the phantom there was a bright flash of light, and the phantom backed away from me. In the next instant warmth and courage flowed strongly through my veins, and I honestly felt like I could climb a mountain and kick some serious spectral ass along the way. I puffed out my chest, tilted my chin up, and yelled, "Get in that disk now, you filthy spook!"

The phantom hesitated, and I had the distinct feeling it was attempting to take over my thoughts, but the impenetrable wall of courage Sam had helped me create wouldn't allow it to control me.

I snarled at the beastly thing and lifted the cross even higher. "What do you want to bet that if I drive this cross into the heart of your disk, it'll destroy both of you?" I shouted. And then I began to bring the cross down. A nanosecond later, just before my weapon would have made contact with the heart of the disk, there was a tremendous *BOOM* as the phantom dived into its talisman and I was knocked right off my feet to fly backward through the air and slam into the bookcase for a second time.

I dropped to the floor, and it was a full minute before I could collect myself. When I felt I could breathe again, I sat up and looked around. The phantom was nowhere to be seen, and Gilley was moaning against the far wall. Mulholland lay limp and pale and gasping for air in his chair, but otherwise, the room was still.

Until a series of loud thumps sounded at the back of the house, and Gopher's muffled cries echoed softly from down the long hallway.

Trembling from head to toe, I reached again for the gold coin still lying on the floor and placed it in the center of the disk before struggling to get up. Moving as quickly as my legs would allow, I staggered down a long corridor and found the door to the garage. The door was latched and a padlock at waist level told me Gopher was on the other side.

I found the key on the table next to a bottle of sleeping pills and a stun gun, and it only took me three tries to get the key into the keyhole. In the other room I heard the commotion as Heath and Constable O'Grady burst into the front hall.

When I opened the garage door to find Gopher chained to a bed in the dark, looking pale, very thin, and much worse for wear, all he said was "Whatever happened in there, I hope to hell you got it on film!"

Chapter 15

"Is he really across?" Alex said as we stood side by side on the edge of the cliffs at Dunlow Castle.

I smiled. I'd seen Jordan so clearly in my mind's eye, stepping into the bright ball of light that would carry him to the other side. "Yes."

"And Bouvet too?"

"And Bouvet too. And the coast guard officer. They have all made it and they never again have to relive those terrible moments."

Alex wound her arm through mine. "Thank you," she said hoarsely.

"My pleasure."

"M. J.!" I heard someone yell.

I turned around and saw Heath jogging toward me. You'd never know he had a serious back injury. When he reached us, he pointed to the castle and said, "We got some great footage in there."

I laughed. "Spooks putting on a good show?"

Heath chuckled. "Yeah, it's ghouls, ghouls, ghouls in

there! Your friendship with Lord Dunnyvale has really come in handy. Carrack and Keevan are even putting on a joust for us! Gopher says we definitely have enough terrific footage to take our show to A&E or the Travel Channel."

After the crap that our old network bosses had pulled, Gopher wanted nothing to do with them ever again, and he was currently in strong negotiations with two competing networks.

"Awesome," I said. "At least I think that's awesome."

"And as soon as Gopher finishes giving his deposition to the court in the kidnapping case against Mulholland, we can move on to the next shoot."

I shook my head. "I can't believe they're still going to prosecute him," I said. "I mean, it's almost sad."

But Heath shrugged. He had little sympathy for Bertie Mulholland, even after the stroke he'd suffered during the phantom's attack that had left him unable to speak and barely able to move. "I guess people are pretty mad about what Bertie did."

"At least O'Grady's kept his part of the bargain," I said. The former constable had made sure to provide as much evidence as was needed to bring Mulholland to justice. He'd also resigned his post as town constable.

The wind began to pick up and I shivered. "We should go," I said.

Heath smiled at me oddly just then and said, "Hold on. You've got something in your hair again."

Reaching up, his fingers brushed the side of my face and I felt a tingle of electricity shoot through me. We hadn't been able to get physical with each other since his back injury, which was driving both of us a bit crazy, as we had definitely decided to take Alex's advice and dive in already.

Heath pulled his hand away and held a small white feather, which made me smile, and I was flooded with warmth. "Your grandfather," I said with a laugh, taking the feather and tucking it into my coat pocket for safe-keeping. "At this rate I'll have a enough for a full head-dress in no time."

As the three of us walked back to the castle, Gilley came out and hurried up to me. "You got anything to eat?" he asked, his eyebrows bouncing.

"I thought you weren't eating," I told him with a smile.

"I'm eating," he said. "I'm just eating less."

I laughed again. "Yeah," I told him, digging around in my messenger bag. "I've got a granola bar in here some-where."

Something clinked against my fingers and I paused at the unfamiliar object, wondering what I'd put in there that could make that kind of noise. Handing Gilley the granola bar, I reached back in and pulled out a long gold chain with one beautiful Spanish gold coin attached.

"Whoa!" Gilley gasped.

"Where'd that come from?" Heath asked.

"M. J.!" Alex exclaimed. "You took that from Ranald's tomb?"

I shook my head vehemently. I'd no idea how it'd ended up in the bottom of my bag. "I didn't!"

"It's a present," said a very distinct disembodied voice, and we all stopped to look around in shock. "A gift for setting my castle to rights and something to remember me by, my lovely Miss Holliday."

And as we all gazed at one another in stunned silence, strong, confident footfalls could be heard walking away toward the keep.

I've always believed in ghosts. Actually, I had no choice in the matter. My childhood had been full of encounters with disembodied voices, strange blue flashes, flickering shadows at the edge of my peripheral vision, and odd-looking orbs appearing right over my head.

And then, of course, my mother died and her ghost came to see me.

I was eleven going on twelve when her cancer finally won the war it'd raged so savagely against her. I knew the instant that she had passed, even though every adult in my world had tried to shield me from the knowledge that it was coming. I remember playing with my new best friend, Gilley Gillespie, on the back porch of his house in beautiful Valdosta, Georgia, like it was yesterday.

Even back then his mother had indulged his rather effeminate tastes. Gil had one of the best collections of Barbie and Ken dolls you've ever seen, and we played with those dolls almost constantly.

In fact, on that bright and sunny early-fall morning, that was exactly what we'd been doing. While Gilley was setting up Ken on a blind date with G.I. Joe, I'd been happily working Barbie into a new pair of gold disco pants and just like that, I knew my mother was gone.

I remember dropping the Barbie and getting to my feet, the shock from the certainty of Mamma's passing crushing something fragile inside of me. I couldn't breathe, couldn't move, and couldn't really even think.

My vision had clouded, and stars had begun to dance in front of my eyes, and I felt myself sway on wobbly knees. I could sense that, somewhere nearby, Gilley had noticed my strange posture and he was calling my name, but I was unable to reply or even acknowledge him. I felt like I was dying, and I didn't know how I would ever be able to live in a world without my mother. My only thought was to pray that she'd somehow find a way to stay with me.

And then, as if by some miracle, my silent prayer had been answered and my mother appeared, standing in the doorway right in front of me.

"Breathe, Mary Jane," she said softly, coming quickly to my side. "It's okay, dumplin'. Just breathe."

I'd managed to take a very ragged breath then, and with it, my vision had cleared. I'd blinked and she hadn't vanished, and that crushing feeling inside me had lessened a bit. Maybe I'd gotten it wrong. Maybe she hadn't died after all.

"I have to go away for a spell, puddin'," she said, that Southern lilt in her voice so sweet and caring.

"Mamma?" I said as she knelt down in front of me and placed her warm hands on the sides of my cheeks.

"I'm so sorry I couldn't stay with you, Mary Jane," she whispered tenderly, bending in to kiss my forehead. And then she looked me right in the eyes and added, "I know what you can see, and I know what you can hear. I also know that your daddy and your nanny, Miss Tallulah, don't want to believe that you're special like that and not just imaginin' things. But you are special, dumplin'. I've known it from the day you were born. And during this whole time I been fightin' the cancer, I've known in my heart that if I lost my fight, that you'd still be able to hear me when I come round to visit with you. I'll never really leave you, puddin'," she assured me as I started to cry. "Anytime you need me, you just call out to your mamma and I'll come, so don't be scared and don't be sad. You hear?"

I nodded with a loud sniffle, trying hard to be brave for her, and she let go of me and stood up. I noticed then how beautiful she looked. How radiant and gloriously healthy she seemed. Such a far cry from the bone-thin, pale woman who'd occupied her bed for the last year.

A little gasp from behind me told me that Gilley could see her too. She looked at him then, and she said, "Now, Gilley Gillespie, you don't be afraid neither. I need you to stay close to my Mary Jane. You hear? You be a good friend to her, 'cause I believe she'll be needin' a real good friend for a spell."

"Yes, ma'am," Gil squeaked obediently.

And then my mother looked one last time at me with such tenderness and love that I nearly shattered inside. She blew me a kiss, mouthed, "I love you," and then she vanished into thin air.

Gilley and I had never once spoken about that morning, and I carried the memory of it like a safely guarded secret. It was such a bittersweet memory that to tell anyone about it might forever taint it in some way, which was why I told no one, and I pushed it to the back of my thoughts to keep it safe and pure.

So, I couldn't imagine why, after all these years, I'd be dreaming about it on the eve of leaving Ireland for Dunkirk to film the next segment of our reality TV show, *Ghoul Getters,* but here I was all grown-up now, having a dream about visiting that same porch back in Valdosta, which was once again scattered with Barbies, Ken dolls, and tiny clothes, and there was my mother, standing in the doorway, looking every bit as lovely as I had remembered.

"Hello, Mary Jane," she said softly, almost shyly.

I blinked—just like when I was eleven. "Mamma?"

My mother stepped forward, her smile filling up the room and my heart. "I been watchin' you," she said with a twinkle in her eye. "My, what a lovely lady you've turned into!"

I opened my mouth to speak, but the emotion of seeing my mother was too much and the words just wouldn't come.

Mamma was kind enough to ignore that and simply stepped closer. Taking my hand she said, "I am so proud of you, Mary Jane. You just light me up with how smart you are and how courageous you've become. Why, I remember when you were afraid of your own shadow!"

I swallowed hard and attempted a smile. In recent years I'd played on my natural psychic-medium talents and become a credible ghostbuster. While working on the *Ghoul Getters* show, I'd faced and fought back against some of the most fearsome poltergeists you could ever imagine.

"Lord, Mary Jane!" my mother exclaimed knowingly. "I've watched you tackle murderous spirits, and vengeful witches, and now, even a phantom!"

My chest filled with the pride and love from my mother. But just then my mother's beaming face turned serious, and she seemed to hesitate—as if she were about to choose her next words carefully. "There is a mission about to be offered to you that I know you'll accept, honey child. One that involves the most horrendous evil imaginable."

I blinked again. Was she talking about the ghosts in the haunted village in Dunkirk? The next place on the *Ghoul Getters* agenda? "I've already read the literature," I tried to assure her. "This time I'm going in prepared, and honestly, Mamma, I don't think it's anything we can't handle."

My mother squeezed my hand, however, and sighed heavily. "Nothing can prepare you for this, Mary Jane. But I know better than to try to talk you out of it. Sam has come to me, you know."

I shook my head, utterly confused. Was she talking about the deceased grandfather of my fellow ghostbuster and current boyfriend, Heath? "You mean, Sam Whitefeather?"

My mother nodded. "He's tellin' me he's your new spirit guide."

I smiled. Sam had made himself noticeable to me shortly after I'd met his grandson and since then he'd worked hard to keep me from getting too beat up on our ghost hunts.

"He needs your help," my mother continued. "He wants my blessin' before he asks you to help his people. I've seen how Sam's been lookin' out for you, and how he's even saved your life a time or two. For that I'm truly grateful, but I just don't know that I can give my blessin' on this."

"Mamma," I said, trying to sort through this cryptic bundle of information and decipher why my mother looked so uncharacteristically worried. "I don't understand. Are you telling me Sam won't be coming with us to Dunkirk or something?"

My mother didn't answer me. Instead she stroked my hair, stared deep into my eyes, as if she was considering telling me more, and then abruptly looked over her shoulder. I followed her gaze and saw that Sam Whitefeather was now standing in the doorway. He seemed to be waiting for something like an invitation or permission to enter the room.

"May I, Maddie?" he asked, bowing formally to my mother.

Without answering him, my mother turned back to me and cupped my face in those familiar warm hands. "Stay safe, Mary Jane," she whispered, leaning in to kiss me on the forehead. "And under no circumstances are you to even *think* about joining me for a very, *very* long time. You hear?"

I nodded, still wondering what this was all about, but my mother got up then and moved away from me. "Mamma, wait!" I called after her, but she simply walked over to Sam, placed a gentle hand on his arm and said, "Protect her as much as possible or you'll have me to answer to, Samuel Whitefeather."

And then she was gone.

It was another moment before I could tear my eyes away from the place where she'd been standing to look directly into Sam Whitefeather's grim-looking face. "What's this all about?" I managed to ask.

Sam studied me for several moments, as if he were privately weighing whether to fill me in. "My grandson is about to receive a call. His uncle has been murdered."

I gasped. "Oh, no!"

Sam's shoulders sagged a little. "I didn't know until it was too late, M. J. Whoever released the demon used dark magic to obscure it from us, and by then, my son was dead."

My hand flew to my mouth. "Oh, Sam! I'm so, so sorry!" Vaguely I remembered Heath talking at length about his three uncles, and I wondered which one of them had been murdered. I knew his favorite uncle was Saul, who'd been like a second father to Heath, and I held my breath, hoping that it wasn't him.

"He's stuck," Sam said sadly, referring to the murdered man. "I've tried with our ancestors to reach out to him, but he's been through a terrible trauma, and he's trapped now by his own fear."

I opened my mouth to tell him that Heath and I would certainly do what we could to help the poor man's soul cross over, but Sam held up his hand. "I know you're going to volunteer to do what you can," he said to me, "but I want you to know what you're getting into by volunteering."

"What am I getting into, Sam?"

My spirit guide sighed, as if the weight of the world now rested on his shoulders. "There is a terrible evil afoot amongst my people. It will kill again. And it will keep killing until every last descendant from my tribe is wiped from your world."

"Sounds serious."

"It is."

"How do we stop it?"

"You must find the one that controls it, and you must kill them."

I sucked in a breath. *What* had he just asked me to do? "You're joking!" And when Sam's serious expres-